Critical Murder

Peter Hodgson

PNEUMA SPRINGS PUBLISHING UK

First Published in 2009 by:
Pneuma Springs Publishing

Pneuma Springs Publishing
A Subsidiary of Pneuma Springs Ltd.
7 Groveherst Road, Dartford Kent, DA1 5JD.
E: admin@pneumasprings.co.uk
W: www.pneumasprings.co.uk

A catalogue record for this book is available from the British Library.

Critical Murder

In memory of dad - love lives forever

One

It should have been a day off for Fletcher Mack. He had risen early that morning, showered himself briskly before attacking a healthy low-fat breakfast washed down by a cup of newly-advertised tea that didn't taste like tea at all.

His wife, Susan, was still in bed when he quietly left the house. The June sun was sitting on the immense Scarp Hill, beaming down onto the historic Cumbrian town named Carron Green. He'd hardly reached the end of the road when his mobile vibrated against his chest. Can't have a moment's peace, he thought, snatching the phone from his shirt pocket. The Control Room icon was flashing. That meant business. A Wednesday off on a lovely summer's day and somebody wanted him. Just his luck. He pressed the keypad harder than usual and read the message: Can't reach Pez. Where is he? Urgent. Tell him to contact Mushroom – Franks.

Mack strolled back to his home and stopped on the driveway, surprised to see his wife waiting on the doorstep.

'I'm going to have a great day,' he said, waving the phone at her. 'PC Franks wants to know where Pez is.'

Mack went back inside the house and crashed onto the settee.

'What's the matter, Fletcher? Has something happened?' she asked.

Mack shrugged. 'Nothing ever happens round here, not unless you're on a day's leave.' He settled back and thought about ringing Pez's home number. It wasn't a good idea. If Laura Perry answered he didn't want to catch her off-guard.

'Going for a walk were you?' Susan asked, drifting off into the kitchen. He didn't answer. 'Fancy a cuppa before you dash off somewhere?'

'No! Thank you,' came the reply. He switched the TV on and caught a re-run of the morning news showing Iran's uranium conversion plants being blown up by American fighter planes. To him, this latest action was just an extension of the problems that had arisen between America and Iraq following the destruction of the World Trade Centre. He switched the TV off. His phone vibrated again. He immediately recognised the hoarse voice of Chris Harvey telling him to get his arse into gear.

'Hang on a minute, Harv. Tell me what's going on.'

'There's been a murder at the forest. It's a bad business. I mean, this is bloody terrible.' Sometimes Harv exaggerated. This time he sounded really serious.

'Someone's trying to locate Pez –'

'I know that. I think I know where he is, too. Meet you at the market in five.'

'Make it ten.'

'OK. Ten it is.'

Market Place stood more or less in the middle of town. You couldn't reach it by car. The roads had changed over the years: more one-way systems and prohibited parking; but at least one could walk the streets at leisure, breathe the cleaner air and, better still, detect the assorted odours when market days were in full flow.

The old town, built predominantly of grey limestone quarried from a nearby fell, attracted visitors from far afield. There were many curiosities to experience, such as the Old Dairy House which was the only building that had a roof made from sandstone flags instead of slate. Some of the alleys, weaving their way amidst the town's construction, contained paved flagstones showing patterns made by currents flowing across a river bed some 300 million years ago. A short distance to the east stood the 13th century remains of Carron Castle where, on a clear day, one could view the entire town and the shimmering River Melt slicing through it. Coral, snails and brachiopods could be seen on the parapets of its three bridges. The old town presented a geological feast for those who were interested.

Harv and Mack's pace became slower as they entered Market Place. Harv was momentarily drawn to the pheasant and wild duck temptingly arranged for the buyers. He licked his lips and stroked his short beard in consideration. His colleague had moved on by several paces. Harv caught up to him at the entrance to Bakers Alley.

'You don't have to tell me,' Mack said. 'Hadrian's Bar again, isn't it?'

Harv nodded in reply.

They found Pez in the guts of the place. The ceiling, caked with sticky brown cigarette smoke, almost matched the colour of the massive oak timbers. Pez loved the dark atmosphere of this illegal smoking den. He looked out of place dressed in dark-blue suit with white shirt supporting a loosened red tie. His spiky black hair accentuated the pallor of his long face. His lips broke into a smile when he saw them.

'Sorry to bother you, Pez,' Mack said, pulling out a chair. Harv remained standing and wafted smoke away from his face.

'I thought it was you as soon as I saw two shiny bald heads bobbing amongst the morning revellers,' Pez droned. He angrily stubbed his cigarette.

'I'm not entirely bald,' Harv said, stroking the side of his head. 'Not yet.'

Mack was looking around the place. 'You won't pull any talent in here,' he said. 'You must be desperate.'

Pez didn't take kindly to that remark and it showed in his eyes. The last few months had been tough for him. His marriage was rocky. His wife, Laura, hadn't showed any interest in him socially or otherwise.

'Spencer's trying to get hold of you,' Harv came in. 'You know how persistent he can be. A quick response would be most appreciated, especially at a time like this.'

Pez lit another cigarette and purposely blew a cloud above Mack's head. He was glad they'd come along to rescue him from lethargy and boredom. If a big case was on the horizon he wanted it; but right now he wasn't in the best frame of mind to give his absolute undivided attention as certain family problems were a cause for concern.

Mack looked him straight in the eye. 'Why do you keep coming to this dive? There's lots of better places: The Eagle, George and Dragon _'

'Because this is the only place you can have a fag without some do-gooder complaining about it. And I'll tell you something else . . .' Pez inhaled deeply and stood up. 'You know what? They sell alcohol here as well, so it's really what a pub should be. Don't you agree?'

Mack rose slowly and patted his shoulder. 'Well said, Pez. Well said.'

Pez finished his drink and sucked his cigarette to a stump, then the trio made their way up the wooden steps and out into the glaring sunlight.

'You haven't asked.'

Pez knew what dead-keen Harv meant. 'I was going to ask, you know. Destination?'

'Glenmar Forest,' Harv replied flatly. He answered his phone and spoke to the chief superintendent. 'Yes, sir . . . We'll be there as soon as possible. Pez is with me and Mack's coming along too.'

'That must have been Spencer,' Mack surmised, leading the way through the bustling market crowd. 'What's happened at the forest?'

'Come on, Harv, spill the beans.'

'From what I can gather, it's a murder.'

'Who says?'

'Don't know, Pez.'

'Well, how do they know it's not suicide? There's millions of secluded spots to commit suicide.'

Harv turned to Pez and said, 'I've never heard of a bloke cutting off his own head.'

Pez had never even read about a case involving decapitation. This *was* something extraordinary. He felt an adrenaline rush and his brain suddenly kicked into another gear. He pulled out his ciggy packet before entering Harv's car. Harv shook his head indicating no smoking in his vehicle.

It would take about half-an-hour to reach Glenmar Forest. The busy streets gradually melted away into jagged stone-lined roads which became narrower and narrower. Twenty minutes later the majestic outline of the forest came into view. The road ahead, rising and dipping along the splendid hills, eventually became steep with barely enough space for oncoming cars to pass. It led into thick luxurious woodland consisting of towering douglas firs, larches and Norway spruces. After several minutes of hard-on-the-brake driving Pez spotted blue lights flashing amidst the trees. The wheels crunched over the gritty, orange-coloured surface of the parking area as Harv swung right and brought the car to a sudden halt. Pez and Harv got out first and breathed refreshing tree-scented air. Mack followed them to the police tape securing the scene.

'Inspector Perry, DCs Harvey and Mack,' Pez said to the officer assigned the job of recording arrival and departure times of all those attending the crime scene. Grey-haired, fragile-looking Detective Chief Superintendent Lesley Spencer – who preferred to be called 'Spencer' at all times – was waiting for them. The 56-year-old veteran had only supervised a couple of homicides during his thirty years' experience in the force. He was just as baffled as anyone else as to why someone should need to remove a victim's head.

He flicked a Rennie from its packet and gave Pez and his colleagues the thumbs-up to approach. 'You took your time, Pez,' he said before crunching the antacid tablet. 'You are bored, and you have been for these past few months.'

'More than a few months.'

Pez was hoping and praying to be assigned the case. Their boss led them to the headless body lying on a tree-canopied grass border of the parking area. Stumpy Harrison Draper, the ageing police surgeon, was examining the corpse carefully. He stood up and gave a brief nod of recognition to Pez, who made a mental note of the victim's blue T-shirt and jeans. The fact he was casually dressed meant something to him. Harv and Mack moved in for a closer look and grimaced at the bloody stump of the crimson neck.

Spencer could hardly bring himself to look again. 'My job's finished here,' he said, his mouth close to Pez's ear. 'It's all yours from here on.'

Pez was elated and Harv could tell. He detected a very low, 'Yes.'

'Come across this sort of thing before?' Pez to Draper.

'Never.'

'Footprints,' Mack said. 'Why are people trampling all over the place?'

'Ground's a bit too hard for footies,' Pez answered, turning to him.

'He's mid-to-late thirties,' Draper continued. 'He died from two stab wounds to the abdomen. Internal bleeding killed him. I had to turn the body over. He was face down, so to speak, considering his head is absent.'

Pez knelt beside the body and ran his fingers across the jean pockets. He glanced at the stationary vehicles. 'Have all these cars been accounted for?' he asked. Draper didn't know. Mack left them for a while and returned with the info. 'All but one,' he said.

'I think I know which one,' Pez said thoughtfully. 'Bring me some gloves.'

Mack brought them. Pez snapped one into place, fumbled inside the jean pocket and removed a set of car keys. 'Try these in that Citroën C6.'

The keys worked. An officer ran a registration check. Harv and Mack threw a glance at each other, acknowledging Pez's sharpness. He also noticed indentations in the fallen tree trunk close by. 'This is where the decap took place. Right?'

'That's right, inspector,' Draper said. He took them to a protected area a few yards away and pointed out the clotted blood clinging to the grass. 'He was attacked here before being dragged to the fallen tree.'

'His head placed over it to afford a solid surface for the chopping,' Harv added.

The surgeon nodded and went up to Harv. 'The head has been photographed, of course, and placed inside a refrigerated pod. If you wish to see it, it's in the back of the Exhibits van.'

Both Harv and Mack shook their heads.

'Anything about the features we should know about?' Pez asked.

'No. He's got dark, receding hair, slightly tanned skin . . . Difficult to determine exact time of death: twelve hours ago, at an educated guess.'

'I'd like a precise time as soon as,' Pez requested. 'It goes dark at ten. The murder could have happened before ten.'

The scene was set. There hadn't been much crime lately, except in certain parts of Carron Green where a bunch of yobs had taken to throwing piss-filled balloons at passing cars, and driving mini-motor bikes in the town centre at night. At least Pez could now escape having to check reports, statements and cost-cutting proposals.

He circled the body, seemingly concentrating his gaze on the man's footwear. The first break then came. Pez was given a piece of paper. 'OK. Here we have it. If this poor bastard is the owner of that car his name is Jack Samson. He lives at 22 Zetland Avenue in Mermaid's Bridge.'

'Not far from here,' Mack responded. 'So, what's on the agenda?'

'You and Harv work on Samson: where, when, how. Put a unit together to trace everyone who's been here the last few days, and instruct the search team to go over this place as if they're looking for a grain of sand.'

10

Harv considered and said, 'We'll have to check Glenmar Lodge, too. There's always visitors up here especially this time of year.'

'Good thinking, Harv.'

Pez stared at the body. Harv came to his side. 'What's with the beheading, Pez? Any ideas?'

'*Beheading* . . . Interesting choice of words. You know, decapitation still goes on out in Saudi.'

'Really?'

'Oh, yes . . . Fanatical sects and lone psychopaths also go in for this kind of thing: an indignity that heaps desecration on death.'

'Could be a gang,' Draper said, quietly to himself.

'Or some weirdo who gets kicks out of this shit,' Mack added. 'But do such people exist?'

'Pay-per-view nutcases,' Pez muttered, and louder, 'fantasy decapitation websites. I've heard about them. Death by decapitation is the ultimate erotic buzz for some. "Christine's Head on a Platter" and "Double Decap Delight" are sick films featuring nude girls and burly, leather-masked executioners.'

'You seem to know a lot about it,' Harv said, a slight tension in his voice.

'Not really. We could be looking at a revenge crime, a bloody execution even. In nations under Sharia law, like Iran and Saudi, the accused are routinely decapitated for drugs use and sexual offences.'

'A mystery, no doubt,' Draper said. 'I'm almost finished here.'

Pez wasn't. He looked closely at the footwear again. 'His trainers aren't on properly,' he pointed out. 'And the laces are loose.'

'What about it?' Draper asked.

Pez snapped another glove on and removed the trainers and socks. 'There's writing on the soles of his feet! . . . His right foot has the letters, A, L, something, something, H, something . . . And his left has, A, K, something, A, R . . . Make sure the photographer records this.'

Draper nodded. Pez turned and headed for the car.

'A clue?' Harv said, trailing behind.

'Probably bullshit,' Mack said, catching up to Harv. 'What say, Pez?'

'Haven't the foggiest idea. Let's wait and see.

Two

The day after the discovery of the body Harv was sent to Jack Samson's modest terraced house in Mermaid's Bridge. As soon as the front door opened he was hit by the unmistakable odour of dogs. Two Yorkshire Terriers were yapping somewhere in the background, and a sturdy German Shepherd wasn't pleased to see him standing there. Eileen Samson half-dragged the powerful animal into the kitchen and managed to quieten it down. Harv made his introduction and followed her into the lounge.

'Inspector Perry's been here. He said someone else might come round,' she said, pointing him to the sofa.

Eileen Samson took a seat by the filthy living-room window. She was a few years younger than her dead husband, though it was hard to believe her age owing to the wisps of grey amongst the black hair. Her nose was big and looked even bigger above her small lips. Not attractive. She had no dress sense either. Harv noticed her skinny legs, hardly covered by a cheap green skirt which clashed against a bright-red blouse hanging from her shoulders.

'This is a terrible and tragic business, I know,' Harv began. 'Unfortunately, there are many questions to ask and I might have to come back again, you understand?'

'I understand.'

Harv took notepad and pen from his jacket. 'I take it you're alone now, Mrs Samson?'

'I've only got the dogs.'

'No children?'

'Jack never wanted any. I have two older sisters. One lives in Southern Ireland, the other on the South coast, near Brighton. They're both married.'

'See much of them?'

'Years since I saw them. Christmas and birthdays are the only times we write to each other . . . Sometimes I forget birthdays. I've never been much good at remembering dates.'

'I see.' He had a feeling – a kind of copper's intuition – that all had not been well with this marriage.

'That's our wedding photograph,' she said, pointing at a shelf in the corner of the room. 'We first met in Carron Green. There's a little shop near the market: Eat Chocolate, Drink Chocolate, Learn Chocolate. Do you know which one I mean?'

'Afraid not.'

'Well, I bumped into him one day as I was coming out of it. We talked for a while. He asked me if I'd go for a drink with him, so I did.'

'He liked a drink, did he?'

She thought for a while, eyes half-shut. Her lips tightened. She gave a long sigh and said, 'He drank every now and then, up until about six months ago; then things started to change.'

'In what way?'

'It's hard to say what caused the change.'

She fell silent. Her reply wasn't helpful. He remembered Pez telling him to squeeze as much info out of her as possible and to make note of any unusual detail concerning Jack Samson's life: anything that appeared out-of-sync with the general pattern of his interests or activities.

'You say there was a change. Can you be more specific?'

'Normally he'd go out once a week or once a fortnight, but he started going out more and more.'

'Was everything all right between the two of you?'

'Of course,' she answered defensively.

'Where did he go?'

'To the pub, I suspect.'

'Which one?'

'There's a couple of pubs here in the village, but he used the car. He must have gone into Carron Green. I could smell drink on him when he returned.'

'Was the drinking a big problem?'

13

'No, it wasn't.'

'He didn't become violent and knock you about?'

She looked him straight in the eye. 'Certainly not! Jack never hit me. We had rows occasionally . . .'

'What about?'

'Do I have to answer these questions?' she asked, turning her head towards the window. 'My husband is dead, detective constable. That's bad enough without accusing him of being violent.'

'I'm sorry, Mrs Samson. Homicide cases are never easy to deal with. We have to see the full picture.'

'I suppose you do,' she said, rising from her chair. 'I'm going to make a brew, if you don't mind. Do you take sugar?'

'No, thanks . . . Oh, any chance I could use the toilet?'

'Up the stairs and first door on the right.'

The staircase was shabby and creaked with every step. The walls had been covered with an off-white paint, peeling with age. When he reached the top, Harv noticed a painting on the wall depicting Carron Green's *High Street* in the late 1800s: spectacular brushwork, unbelievable attention to detail. He recognised the style of local artist William Stringer who died from pneumonia at the age of twenty-eight. During his short life he captured the magic and charm of Carron Green as only he could.

Back in the living room he waited for her. She soon appeared, carrying two huge mugs of hot tea. Harv thanked her and took a sip. He wished he hadn't accepted the offer.

'Is it all right?' she asked, with a nervous smile.

Harv noticed a holiday-snap on the mantle. 'It's fine . . . Did you go on holiday much?' he said, hoping to make her feel at ease.

'We hadn't been away for years. Jack had a break a couple of months back. He went to Greece.'

Something amiss here, Harv thought. Time to dig.

'Holiday in Greece – without you?'

'Yes. He went with one of his friends from work. It was only for a week. I didn't go with him because I don't like it too hot.'

'A male friend?'

'Oh, yes. I checked all that out, and I've seen the photos too. I think the rest did him good.'

'He'd been working hard, I suppose?'

'Yes. His friend was Eric Prescott, one of his drinking partners. He lives here in the village,' she said helpfully, and then gave the address.

Harv added it to the notes he'd made whilst going to the loo. He sipped some more of the disgusting tea and said, 'Let's talk about work.'

'Well, I'm a cleaner at the primary school here. Jack worked at Seven Moons. He was there for ten years. Do you know the place?'

'I've heard of it: the nuclear plant on the coast. I know a few people who used to work up there.'

'It's kept a lot of folk in jobs for many years,' she added. 'Jack was a process worker.'

'What's a process worker?'

'To be honest, I'm not really sure. He never talked about his work much. I guess it would have been something manual. He wasn't one for office work, not Jack.'

'Did he speak of anyone who didn't like him?'

'Never. He was happy enough, and very popular.'

Judging by the location and state of the house, Harv reckoned Jack Samson wasn't a high earner. She confirmed this.

'We have to establish a motive for the murder,' he went on. 'Was he into the drug scene?'

She shook her head. 'Jack hated anything like that. His life revolved around the dogs. He loved walking them. He'd often take them to the forest.'

'What else did he like doing?'

'He enjoyed watching action and thriller films, and he was fond of paintings. He bought one every now and then.'

'Like the one at the top of the stairs?'

She nodded. 'I can't think why someone should want to kill him, and in such a horrible way.'

'Is there anyone you can think of who might have held a grudge?'

'No.'

'There must have been someone who disliked him.'

Eileen Samson searched her mind and came up with one person. 'He has a sister called Hazel. She lives in Carron Green. They weren't fond of each other. It was something to do with their mother's will, but that was years ago.'

'Were they in recent contact?'

'They never saw each other. Jack thought she was a trouble maker. She's involved with all this Greenpeace anti-nuclear stuff.'

Interesting. Maybe significant, Harv thought. 'Do you know her address?'

'No. Her married name is "Bamber," if that's any use.'

He scribbled down the name. 'Did your husband receive any strange phone calls that gave him cause for concern?'

'Can't say I noticed any,' she replied, pulling a face.

'Did he have any visitors, anybody you didn't recognize?'

'None at all.' She held her cup in both hands, drank a little whilst pondering over his questions. 'Why do you ask about visitors and phone calls?'

'The way in which the murder was committed is suggestive. There's a possibility it could have been an execution-style killing.'

'I don't understand. Wasn't it just some maniac?'

Harv considered. 'Possibly . . . What was the reason for his visit to Glenmar?'

'He must have gone for a walk. He didn't take the dogs. I found that a bit strange.'

'What time did he leave the house?'

'About half past eight in the evening.'

Harv pretended to drink more tea before rising quickly from the sofa.

'Are you leaving already?' she asked, wanting him to stay longer.

'Yes. Sorry to trouble you at such a time as this. I'll let myself out.'

She nodded slowly and gazed out of the window. When he was outside, Harv found the fresh air to be a relief after enduring the stale dog-stink of the Samson house. He looked up and down the road, saw nothing except a few twitching curtains. Nothing much to work on, he thought; and yet something wasn't quite right: the holiday to Greece, the sudden change in his drinking habits. And there was the 'anti-nuclear' sister who he disliked. Could she have had something to do with his death?

Jack Samson had probably gone out to meet somebody. As yet, Harv could think of no clear reason as to why such a heinous crime was committed.

Looking down from Castle Hill, and towards the northern part of Carron Green, one could see a building which resembled a huge mushroom. The town's police headquarters was the most modern addition. It certainly didn't make the town look any quainter. The original building, that once accommodated the local force, was boarded up and protected by high fences to keep the public away. The new building, known not surprisingly as the Mushroom to both police and residents, had gradually 'grown' over a period of months. Some people hadn't even noticed the construction taking place, and were rather startled when the upper part was finally finished. The upper part – the head of the 'mushroom' –had the appearance of a UFO when illuminated by offices at night.

Pez occupied one of those offices. At ten past eight in the evening he decided to call it a day. He had a throbbing headache and felt tired. The weather was hot and sticky and his lack of sleep wasn't helped by all those headless-corpse images crashing through his head. He left the office, slung his jacket over his shoulder and strolled along the curved corridor. He stared at the floor, wondering what kind of mood his wife would be in when he arrived home. It suddenly occurred to him that Spencer might still be at work. He tapped on the door and quietly entered the office. Spencer was there all right. He smiled faintly and pushed some pieces of paper around his desk.

'Working late, Spencer?'

'No way,' he replied with a double head-shake. 'I've had enough. An early night is the best thing for me.'

'You're not the only officer in CID whose sleep patterns are disturbed.'

'I can well believe that. Sit yourself down.'

'I'm off home. Don't want to spend another minute hanging around this place . . . By the way, have you read the statements given by the hikers?'

'I have.'

'Jack Samson was alive at nine-thirty. The hikers saw him in Glenmar car-park Number One.'

'So, your theory was correct: he *was* waiting for somebody, and that person's identity remains a mystery.'

'Not for long, I hope. The local paper's running the story, and the TV news media. Information is still being collated, mainly from visitors to the forest. We wait, and with a bit of luck . . .'

Spencer gave a big nod. 'The wheels are turning, my lad . . . Go on home. Get some rest.'

Pez went on his way, took the lift instead of the stairs. Ten minutes later he drove into his driveway on the New Bradshaw Estate. When he reached the front door it opened. Miranda, his 6-year-old daughter, looked up and grinned at him. 'Have you brought anything for me daddy?' she asked, her eyes following his hands as he hung his jacket.

'Not today, sweetheart. Daddy's been too busy,' he replied, wrapping his arms around her. He lifted her up, kissed her cheek. The lovely peach fragrance of her long blonde hair told him she'd had a bath, and yet she wasn't dressed for bed. She ran into the living room to watch TV. Pez heard a noise from upstairs. 'Laura, are you going out again?' he asked loudly.

'That's right, Pez,' she answered, coming down the stairs.

Somehow, Laura Perry's features didn't look as pointed since she'd had her strawberry-blonde hair cut short. It made her face look fatter. He didn't like that. Not that it mattered much anyway. The marriage was failing. The Perrys had spent too much time apart, and now Laura had no time for him at all.

'Where the hell are you going?' he asked, trying to grab her arm as she brushed past.

'I'm going to Diana's house. Miranda is coming with me. You can find your own tea . . . Miranda!'

Their little daughter ran into the hall. Pez bent down and kissed her forehead. Before he had chance to say anything Laura whisked her away and slammed the door behind them. Pez swore under his breath. It wasn't *his* fault he was home late, wasn't his fault he had a serious investigation to keep him busy. He moved swiftly into the living room and caught a glimpse of them through the window. He watched until they had disappeared, and he wondered if anything could be done to relight the fire of a love that had already died.

Three

Fletcher Mack had a vague memory of Crown Point Nuclear Plant. He was fifteen when the head of the school's science department took his students on a day trip to the coast; and how beneficial it was to be able to supplement the 'Nuclear Power' section of their syllabus with a visit to an actual uranium conversion plant. It was thirty years ago when he last visited the place. Amazing how time flies, he thought.

Mack could remember miles of steam pipes traversing the entire site, and dozens of silver cylindrical tanks that were several times higher than a house. He also remembered why it became known as the Seven Moons atomic plant. At night it was illuminated by dozens of high-powered arc lights perched high above the many segregated work-units and roads, put in place for security rather than safety reasons. The site was built on a landscape-rise close to the sea at a stretch called Salter Bay. On misty nights, when driving west towards the coast, only seven lights would be visible from a particular stretch of the road: seven glowing 'moons' in the sky above this major industrial nuclear plant.

The journey from Carron Green to Salter Bay could take as long as an hour and twenty minutes. Mack had set off at the right time: late enough in the morning to allow the nuclear employees to reach their destination. When driving through Oak Valley he caught a glimpse of Seven Moons, imposing and stark against the sky's dense white clouds. The journey took seventy minutes. He came off the accelerator and turned into the parking area to the left of the site's main entrance. He observed the ten-feet high notice board flashing the words, 'Safety Recall – 10 a.m., Security Status – Orange Alert.' A twelve-foot high fence ran the perimeter of Seven Moons, encompassing an area big enough to accommodate Mermaid's Bridge itself.

Mack heard a shrill voice. He stamped on the brake pedal and stopped a short distance from a young, uniformed policeman who was employed by the Civil Nuclear Constabulary. 'You ought to watch were you're going,' he said, his eyes searching the interior of the vehicle.

'Sorry, officer,' Mack said, and blew a nervous puff of air.

'What's your business?'

'I am Detective Constable Fletcher Mack. I have an appointment with Victor Brooks.'

'An appointment? This isn't a doctor's surgery you know. Identification please.'

Mack flashed his ID and was asked to show it again. The officer stepped back, told him to report to the police lodge and indicated a space for him to park. He then went about his business, commanding a driver to bring his Dangerous Goods Vehicle to a halt.

The lodge stood next to the main check point. Two officers were stationed there, ready to examine all relevant paperwork provided by goods drivers. Their main task was to check identity-passes of all employees entering the site daily. Nobody was allowed in without a valid pass or appropriate and up-to-date documentation. CCTV cameras monitored all main-gate movement.

Mack was impressed. When he reached the lodge he pushed the bullet-proof glass door open and stepped inside. Four civilians, seated in comfy chairs, were waiting to be escorted to the administration building to be interviewed for forthcoming job vacancies. Two officers were talking amiably from behind a counter. A buzz of activity sounded from the computer operators working behind them. Mack showed his ID again, holding it in front of their faces longer than was necessary. He explained the purpose of his visit and was promptly taken down a brightly-lit corridor to Brooks' office. He knocked twice and entered. The inspector was in uniform. Victor Brooks was in his late fifties, sturdily built, with a square-jaw and heavily-lined features. His ginger hair was thick and cut very short. He leaned forward and offered his hand. Mack couldn't believe the size of it – seven inches across, at least.

The office comprised a table with computer strategically positioned, a couple of filing cabinets and two telephones: one red, one blue. An aerial photograph of the entire Crown Point site covered one of the walls.

Brooks leaned back in his swivel chair and cupped his hands. 'I've spoken to your inspector,' he began. 'He told me about your investigation into the murder of Jack Samson.'

'We know very little about him. Our inquiries are on-going . . . Did you know the man?'

'Detective Constable Mack, I hardly know anybody who works here apart from my own staff. It's a very big place. Our work doesn't often bring us into close personal contact with the employees.'

'I see,' Mack said, looking at the aerial photo which confirmed what Brooks said.

'That photograph was taken from our very own helicopter,' he said, glancing at it with some pride. 'Did you know the air space above Seven Moons is restricted?'

'No, I didn't . . . So, you call it Seven Moons as well?'

'Everybody does; but don't let me keep you from your business.'

'Your job is, *security*?'

'Basically, yes.'

'And who is your boss?'

'Ultimately, the government. We are here to protect the civil nuclear industry against terrorist and proliferation threats. The government, through its regulator the DTI's Office for Civil Nuclear Security, is absolutely committed to maintaining an effective and robust regulatory regime.'

'Do you believe there is a real danger from terrorist threats?'

Brooks straightened himself, tightened his lips, then replied, 'All nuclear establishments must be protected. Only a few months ago a bomb was exploded in North London's Perbury – a dirty bomb containing some form of toxic chemical.'

'Could the toxic chemical have been stolen from here?'

Brooks gave an intense look. 'You've already witnessed some of our security procedures. It would be practically impossible for that to happen.'

'*Practically*?'

'It would be impossible,' came the stern reply. Brooks wasn't giving anything away. 'Apart from Perbury, the only dirty bomb-related incident occurred when Chechen rebels planted radioactive caesium and dynamite in a Moscow park. The authorities located it before it was dispersed. You see, radioactive materials can be stolen – but not from here. Our security is much tighter since the events of September eleven.'

'The World Trade Centre attacks had nothing to do with the UK's nuclear policies.'

'Not true. Consider this: the American airlines flight that struck the North Tower of the World Trade Centre could just as easily been aimed at the Indian Point nuclear power plant, forty miles north of Times Square.'

'I wasn't aware of that,' Mack replied, shaking his head.

'You can understand the government's concern. If terrorists manage to obtain nuclear material, imagine what could happen.'

'Point taken. Obviously, Britain is high on the list for a terrorist attack.'

'You're right. A few years ago a risk assessment study by the World Markets Research Centre revealed that the UK ranked tenth in the world for its vulnerability to a terrorist attack. All that has changed.'

'And our close political relationship with the United States makes us even more vulnerable, I suppose.'

'It does . . . We are drifting a little, detective constable. What can *you* tell me about Jack Samson?'

'He was stabbed to death at Glenmar Forest, and his head was removed. A chopping action was used to do this, rather than one clean sweep of a blade. What bothers us is the fact that he worked here.'

'Do you think there's some significance?'

'Could be. We have to consider the possibility of it being a terrorist-style execution.'

Brooks laughed, a deep laugh that emanated from his throat. 'A terrorist execution in a Cumbrian forest?'

'You may think it's a ridiculous theory. However, I'm here to find out as much as I can about Samson.'

Brooks reached for the cabinet, retrieved a pale-pink folder and opened it. 'Samson started work here ten years ago. He was a process worker in one of the canning plants.'

'Canning plants?'

'Don't ask me what goes on here. As far as I can tell, he worked in a fuel components unit that involves cleaning and checking –' He moved the folder closer to his face. '– fuel element rods. I assume those rods are made into fuel element assemblies which go into nuclear reactors.'

It all sounded very interesting to Mack. 'Is it difficult work for someone to do?'

'I couldn't say. I *can* tell you that Samson's record is clean. He had very little time off due to illness and, let me see, he attended the usual training courses: radiation, safety workshops and criticality.'

'What does *criticality* mean?'

'I think you need to attend some of these courses yourself,' he responded, pleasantly enough.

'Would that be possible?'

'Not really. I suggest you speak to your superiors and see if they'll let you come back for a guided tour.'

Mack smiled. 'I'd like that very much.'

'I'll do whatever it takes to help you solve this murder,' he said, his voice falling into a deep tone. 'There's an additional paragraph here, at the bottom of the page. Samson was transferred from his regular job and sent to another building. This occurred a couple of months ago.'

'Any reason?'

'No reason given. It says here that he went to work in ASD.'

'That being?'

'I think it stands for, Analytical Services Department. Seems odd to me.'

'Odd?'

'ASD personnel are well qualified.'

'Maybe he wanted a change. Any academic qualifications?'

Brooks turned back a page. 'Only four poor-grade GCSEs. I suppose he could have worked there as a laboratory cleaner. Who knows? There's little else I can tell you.'

Mack took it all in. Brooks leaned back, folded his arms, said nothing.

Mack thanked him, and left with a feeling he'd wasted his morning.

On the Friday morning, three days after the murder, Harv found himself back in Mermaid's Bridge and only a few blocks away from where Samson lived.

A weary-looking Eric Prescott was pulling weeds out of his dry garden. His house had a typically council-house look about it: run down, drab, badly in need of a coat of paint on the door and window frames. Prescott knew someone was watching him. He tugged at a particularly stubborn weed before standing up. Harv stroked his well-trimmed, greying beard whilst waiting for him to say something. He was slightly amused by Prescott's small round glasses and Hitler moustache.

'Yeah, what do you want?' he asked, rubbing his hands on his scruffy jeans. 'I'm not interested in double glazing, insurance, Telewest TV and God botherers.'

'But you *are* interested in who might have killed your friend,' Harv said, straight-faced.

'You're a copper, eh?'

Harv nodded. 'Your wife said you might be at home this morning. You are Eric Prescott?'

'That's me. You'd better come inside.'

Prescott led him to the living room. It was in a worse state than Samson's. Harv could feel the springs of the minging settee biting into his backside as he lowered his heavy frame onto it.

'Not at work today?'

'I rang in and told my boss I needed a day off. I work at Crossland's Car Maintenance and Repairs in Carron Green.'

'Don't blame you – it's a lovely day . . . Wife gone out?'

'Yes. Are you an inspector, or what?'

'Sorry. I'm Detective Constable Harvey . . . How long did you know Jack Samson?'

'Several years. We were drinking partners.'

'Did you get on well?'

'Oh, yeah. Never an argument between us.'

'Are you sure about that?'

A direct question from Harv. Prescott stared straight at him, annoyance on his face. 'Of course I'm bloody sure.'

'Tell me about him. What was he like?'

'He was a good guy, an ordinary sort of guy. He liked to have a laugh.'

'Any problems with his wife?'

'I don't think so.'

'Do you know his sister, Hazel Bamber?'

'No.'

'Did he ever talk about her?'

'Never mentioned her. Jack didn't speak much about other people.'

'Did he give you the impression that something was bothering him?'

Prescott shook his head. 'I don't think anything bothered him.'

'So, Jack was a guy with no problems and he never got into trouble.'

'The only trouble he had was a few months ago when he sold his car.'

'Tell me what you know.'

'He sold his car to a bloke who's a bit of a nutter. His name's Billy Wright. He goes in our local pub, the Wheatsheaf.'

'What happened between the two of them?'

'Wright wasn't happy with the car. It was running rough. Jack said to him, "Tough shit." They nearly came to blows.'

Harv scribbled a note. 'You could have checked the car before he sold it.'

'Wasn't my job. Anyway, he never asked me to.'

Harv stood up, ready to leave.

'That's it, then? You finished already?' Prescott asked.

'For now, yes.'

Harv went outside. Prescott was close behind him.

'Something's just occurred to me. How come you went to Greece with him?'

'He offered to pay, see; and *no*, we didn't take any women with us.'

'Your wife didn't bother, then?'

'Why should she?'

'I might need to question her at a later stage.'

'Fine by me.'

Harv dug into his pocket for his notepad. 'When did you go on holiday?'

Prescott had to think for a while. 'We went on the eighth of April. Came back on the sixteenth.'

'Pull any skirt while you were there?'

Prescott stared at him stonily. 'No, we didn't. I'm not like that; neither was Jack.'

'Aren't you a good lad? What were you doing on Tuesday evening?'

'I was in all night watching television. My wife was with me.'

'You've nothing to worry about then. Thanks for your time.'

Harv made a note of the holiday dates and left. Another dead-end inquiry, he thought. Except for the Billy Wright lead.

Four

Nick Sinclair was one of the youngest Deputy Assistant Commissioners that New Scotland Yard's anti-terrorist branch had ever seen. His white hair and rosy cheeks made his age hard to judge. His colleagues often wondered if he'd applied rouge to his face and mascara on his eyelashes.

He turned away from the window of SO13's headquarters and sat at the table opposite the man who had welcomed and enhanced his promotion. The Metropolitan Police Commissioner, Sir Douglas Henderson, wore his immaculate uniform with great pride. Henderson, who wasn't easily perturbed by problematic inquiries, could taste the sourness of an investigation that seemed to be grinding to a halt. Britain had suffered one of its biggest acts of terrorism for years. To some, it was no big deal, nothing compared to Lockerbie or the unbelievable devastation wreaked on the World Trade Centre. And yet there were some who cheered at the spectacle of destruction. One man's terrorist is another man's freedom fighter. That's the way it was, the way of the world today. The threat of the terrorist in Britain could not be underestimated.

Three members of a relatively new unit were sitting quietly at the same table as their mighty superiors. SATA was a name to be proud of, especially if you were part of it. SATA meant, Special Anti-Terrorist Agent. It could have been SATO, the 'O' denoting 'Officer,' but somebody high in the echelons of SO13 reckoned 'Agent' had more of an FBI ring to it.

Ian McIver's dark eyes had been darting around the room for the last five minutes, occasionally fixing on the two men who were under his command. Daniel Meyers was one of them. Powerfully-built Meyers had piercing blue eyes and thick platinum-blond hair which was only manageable by using his favourite lemon-scented gel. His stare could be intimidating. At thirty-four – nearly twenty years younger than McIver – he had already experienced fighter-plane

27

bombing raids in Northern Iraq. Before that, he spent two years working alongside members of a Critical Response Team in New York. The CRT were one of the best-equipped SWAT teams in the world, extremely adept at resolving high risk incidents involving the threat of a gun or knife, and extremely lethal – if required – when confronting potential terrorists. Meyers himself had shown just how effective he could be in a threatening situation. He was as good as they come: dependable, trained to perfection, ruthless when necessary.

Jason Bryce was the same age as Meyers. Although he was strikingly handsome, his short greying hair and glasses made him look older. His voice was soft and betrayed a durability that was difficult to match. Bryce reached chief inspector rank during his employ with the Met. His mundane job changed dramatically when he opted for something more challenging, more life threatening. His stint with the army's Bomb Disposal Unit brought him in line with his expectations. Bryce came close to being blown to bits daily whilst working undercover in Northern Ireland. More importantly, he managed to infiltrate a terrorist group operating in Germany. Bryce had turned double-agent, as it were, and amassed sensitive information that reached Interpol and MI5. Thanks to the terrorists, he became familiar with Improvised Explosive Devices that used chemicals such as ammonium nitrate, and the more potent Semtex, RDX and TNT. Unusual job-moves like this were allowed for the preparation of potential SAT agents.

McIver was their 'daddy.' He called the tune. He was responsible for strategy, knew what moves to make and when. Right now, it all seemed to be going wrong for the ex-SAS man who became an anti-terrorist officer.

Henderson broke the silence by conveying his thoughts out loud. 'Going back several years, the politician's role was to look into the future for the worst that might happen.' He waited for some kind of response. McIver wondered were he was coming from. Meyers was hot and loosened his tie, even though the air conditioning was working to full effect.

'What are you driving at?' Bryce asked.

'Imagine the worst and act ahead of time to prevent it,' Henderson replied. 'In doing this the Prime Minister was embracing an idea developed by the green movement.'

'Do any of you know what it was called?' Sinclair asked, sitting smugly. He waited. No response. 'It was called the precautionary principle.'

'You are correct, Nick.'

'Thank you, sir,' Sinclair said, and gestured for his boss to continue.

'Once over, fear of a phantom enemy was all the politicians had to maintain their power. In the USA, and in our country, individuals are detained in high-security prisons not for crimes they committed, but for what politicians believe they might commit in the future.'

Meyers started drumming his fingers on the highly-polished table. He knew what was coming next.

'Nothing for years,' Henderson said robotically, 'and now we have this dirty bomb attack on our hands. He looked at Sinclair for a comment.

'The intelligence at our disposal points to a terrorist cell. They call themselves, the Amama.'

'Indeed. And what does the British public expect to hear about this tragic incident that ended the lives of innocent people? . . . They expect results, gentlemen. The families of the victims expect justice.'

'They'll have their justice,' McIver came in.

'And soon,' Meyers added, straightening himself.

'Well said. So, what's the current state of play?' ice-cool Sinclair asked.

'We are currently assessing information received concerning friends of the Toxic Terrorist,' answered McIver very positively.

'Toxic Terrorist?' The Commissioner vaguely remembered the name. 'Refresh my memory, McIver.'

'A few years ago a suspected member of the al-Qaeda was arrested by Special Branch officer, Mark Kenyon. Kenyon was stabbed to death and two other officers were seriously injured.'

'I remember the incident now.'

Sinclair took over. 'Information received suggests that a branch of the Amama is operational in our city. They could be experimenting with deadly poisons like cyanide.'

Henderson pursed his lips and said, 'Their objective, so it seems, would be the advancement of an extremist Islamic cause.'

'God damn those bastards!' Meyers said, with venom. He shot up and moved rapidly to the window.

Everybody seemed unperturbed by his sudden outbreak, except Henderson who was annoyed. He fought back the urge to put him in check. 'Perhaps this terrorist cell is responsible for the explosion in Perbury.'

'Exactly what we are hoping to find out,' McIver said. He looked towards the twelve-feet high window and scowled. 'Sit down, Danny . . . Just sit yourself down.'

Daniel Meyers obeyed him.

'If you feel frustrated gentlemen, I can empathise with you,' Henderson said very clearly. 'I may be able to cheer you up. SATA has acquired a new agent. Your investigation could be a little easier.'

Sinclair rose from his chair and slipped out of the room. The remaining agents were reluctant to say anything to each other in the presence of the Commissioner.

McIver looked down, somewhat dejected. His reservations were about to be confirmed. When Sinclair returned he wasn't alone. McIver and his men stared at the 33-year-old female as she clicked the door shut. Her black high-heel shoes and tight-fitting skirt accentuated her shapely, tanned legs. She wore a pale-blue shirt that hugged an obvious pair of solid breasts and did little to conceal the shape of her Rolls Royce wheel-nut nipples. She had large green eyes and full lips, making her a deliciously attractive woman. She smiled, and with a quick head-jerk flicked back her shoulder-length, shiny auburn hair.

The Commissioner waved her to a chair. 'This is Tara Drake, gentlemen. Your new member.'

Mixed feelings permeated the Perbury team. McIver nodded and forced a smile. Bryce removed and cleaned his glasses. Meyers' mind was already running riot. He wondered how long it would take to get her into his bed . . . or hers.

The general aura was one of, *Wow!*

McIver gave a side-glance to Sinclair. He lifted his head slightly in brief contemplation, licked his thin lips and said, 'Miss Drake has been transferred from Southern Division where she worked with the Intelligence Services.'

Not married, then, Meyers thought. Even better. Henderson raised his hand, and after a few polite words Sinclair continued. He apologised for not introducing the team members to her. Once that was over, the newcomer spoke about her activities. Her voice was quite deep and sharp. Meyers was impressed by her composure and confidence.

'During the last twelve months I've been training for SATA,' she went on. 'Before my involvement with the Intelligence Services I was a detective sergeant working on the periphery of SO13's fight against terrorism. Much of my work was implementing security arrangements at Heathrow Airport and the government's communications centre. More recently, as part of my training, I devised a terrorist exercise which took place in Harrogate. I helped the emergency services by showing them how a decontamination unit would be used to deal with the after-effects of a dirty bomb attack.

'I am trained in ballistics and combat initiatives. I've also experienced in-the-field manoeuvres. I have a degree in biochemistry –'

'Thank you, Miss Drake,' Sinclair interrupted.

'– and I speak four languages.'

'Why have you decided to work with us?' Jason Bryce asked, sounding a tad annoyed.

'It wasn't Miss Drake's decision,' Henderson said.

'Do you think Miss Drake is suitable for this kind of investigation?' McIver asked.

Tara Drake suddenly felt a pang of disdain. 'I'm sure you wouldn't be disappointed, Mr McIver.'

Bryce frowned, but the Commissioner looked at her with a reassuring smile and said, 'Out of two hundred female officers in the Metropolitan service, only ten successfully completed their training for SATA. This young lady was one of them . . . Your attention, please. ' He pressed a button on the control panel next to him. A huge white screen descended slowly, blocking the light from the window. The room darkened. He moved to the side, allowing the projector on the table to fire its images onto the screen. Sinclair quietly moved to another position. The SATA operatives had seen the footage many times. The images were firmly embedded in their minds.

'Watch carefully, Miss Drake,' Henderson said. 'This CCTV footage has been enhanced.'

Everyone concentrated on the screen. One of the main highways in Perbury, North London, had turned into a seething mass of people.

Their nationalities and creeds were varied. The majority were British-born citizens. About forty percent were Muslims. One Muslim father was visible in the foreground, carrying his 4-year-old son on his shoulders. Drake read the writing on some of the banners: Global Women's Strike, Justice for the Innocents, No War on Iran, No Justice – No Peace.

'This took place because of the American invasion into Iran,' Henderson said. 'The invasion parallels the reasons for the bombing of Iraq – the possibility they may create weapons of mass destruction.'

He altered the speed-setting to make it slower, and aimed his laser pen at the screen. The red dot highlighted a disturbance in the crowd. Something low was moving amongst the protesters. Suddenly, its route ended. An explosion occurred, apparently without any warning. Drake's eyes narrowed. White smoke bellowed into the atmosphere. Chaos and confusion reigned. People surrounding the centre of the explosion tried desperately to retreat from the broken bodies, from the spray of blood, from detached limbs flying through the air. Young men and women were trampled underfoot in the ensuing panic. Shop owners were forced to lock their doors to prevent a toxic white mist from entering.

The images were disturbing, even without sound.

McIver shook his head in disbelief.

'Most people have seen that incident on the news,' Henderson continued. 'What they have not seen is this.'

Other cameras in the area had recorded a running dog. Drake was intrigued. 'Isn't that a German Shepherd, Commissioner?'

'Correct. German Shepherds and Rottweilers are used for crowd control. This particular animal has been trained for a different task.' He paused the film. 'Observe those straps attached to its body . . . They were used to secure a toxic uranic compound – probably stored in plastic bags – that could only have come from a nuclear plant. The large collar around its neck is actually made from plastic explosive. The detonator is situated on the other side of the dog and is not visible on any of the footage . . . This represents the first dirty bomb attack in mainland Britain.'

The four SAT agents were relaxing in the communal room. Meyers was making his way from the bar carrying two glasses of whisky and lemonade. His colleagues were happily playing snooker whilst quietly discussing their new partner.

Drake knew he would make a fuss over her. He sat beside her, moved up close and passed the drink. She caught a whiff of his lemon gel which clashed with an obscure aftershave.

'I don't know what we're going to do with you, Tara,' he said smiling. He rested his arm on the sofa behind her, hoping to let it slide onto her shoulders.

'How do you mean, Mr Meyers?'

He laughed out loud and shook his head. 'You can call me, "Danny."'

'Let's talk about what happened at Perbury. That's what we are here for, isn't it? . . . The whole thing strikes me as being, well, odd.'

'For what reason?'

'A terrorist unleashes a dirty bomb which killed not only British citizens but men of the Muslim faith – not to mention the mixed nationality casualties.'

'Question being: who could have done it?'

'Not just *who*, but why are they not targeting a specific creed?'

Meyers allowed his arm to fall onto her shoulders. Drake sipped her drink and waited for him to speak.

'I'm very happy you've joined us . . . Very happy . . . You know the dance, Tara. Your place or mine?'

She looked at him and smiled endearingly. My God, he thought, she's up for it; but Drake slammed the drink on the table and grabbed his bollocks. His high-pitched scream halted the snooker game.

'Just because you're a big, good-looking Special Agent doesn't mean you can take liberties,' she spat.

Meyers' eyes were twice their normal size. He shook his head, the pain unbearable. She squeezed his manhood harder still.

'I'm dedicated, ambitious, want to make something of myself,' she said, through clenched teeth.

She released her grip and shot up. Meyers threw back his head, gasping and moaning from the intense aching.

'Yes, Meyers, I do know the dance. Right now it's not the kind of dance I'm willing to participate in, so go find a king-size cucumber and fuck yourself with it!'

She marched out of the room, tossing her hair back with a defiant head jerk.

Idiot Meyers, Bryce thought.

McIver laughed and gave the thumbs-down sign.

Five

Pez caught a glimpse of himself as he sauntered into the Mushroom's main entrance. He stepped back a few paces, looked at his reflection and ran his fingers through his hair. Hardly a day went by when he didn't pay some attention to his looks. The age-lines were creeping in, bestowing upon him a haggard look. Premature ageing, he guessed, due to the nature of the job. That was his excuse, anyway. In a vain sort of way he wanted to appear attractive to other women. He was painfully aware that his younger wife wasn't giving him the attention he craved. She had changed over the years. Not surprisingly, he had changed too. He was beginning to realize that Miranda was the reason why the marriage hadn't already ended.

Why bother fixing my hair, he thought. None of the female officers fancied him anyway; even if someone did, what good would it do? Pez laughed to himself. He turned to the desk-sergeant who waved him to come closer and said, 'Pez, aren't you supposed to be with forensics?'

'Don't know. Am I?'

'That's what I've heard. Sweaty Yeti wants to see you.'

'I'm busy.'

'He says it's urgent.'

'I'll kill him if he's wasting my time,' he snapped.

Pez exited the lift at the second floor. A few steps took him to a reinforced steel door. He ran his swipe-card over the code-reader and the doors opened automatically. Paunchy, long-haired, BO-ridden Jacob Riley – 'Sweaty Yeti' to his work colleagues – was waiting for him. 'Follow me,' he said, with a smile that revealed a set of crooked yellow teeth.

'This had better be good . . . By the way, you need a hair cut.'

'I'll think about it.'

'Yeah, yeah.'

He followed him into a small room known as, Image Analysis. Riley fell into a chair and activated the computer. He turned his head quickly when he heard Pez lighting a cigarette.

'Don't let Fitzgerald catch you with that fag. He'll go mad.'

'Fitzgerald used to be a sixty-a-day man.'

Riley was sliding the mouse around, clicking away. 'You know it's bad for you. Why don't you pack it in, Pez?'

'If we did everything the doctors told us we'd die from stress. Right?'

'I don't buy that . . . Take a look at this.'

'It looks like the sole of a foot – Samson's.'

Riley enlarged the image. 'The letters were written with a ballpoint. The gaps are areas where the pen either ran dry or the ink-flow was suppressed due to the characteristics of human skin.'

'You can't decipher the message.'

'I can. The gaps contain very faint ink traces which are easily filled in by using this fine piece of equipment. I shan't bother you with the technical details. . . . Here we have a composite of the two soles. Now I shall complete the message.'

Pez felt a surge of excitement. He leaned over Riley's shoulder and watched him fill the spaces, almost like doing a crossword puzzle.

'What the hell does it say?' he asked, his smoke drifting towards the screen.

Riley coughed and wafted the smoke away. 'It says, Allahu Akbar.'

'*Allahu Akbar* . . . Translation, please.'

'OK, my man. It's Arabic for God is Most Great.'

The penny dropped. Pez was stunned. The decapitation and Arabic writing were suggestive. 'A real clue, I wonder?' he muttered. 'Or is it meant to throw us off the scent?'

'That's for you to find out, my friend.'

'We have been waiting for you, inspector,' Spencer said, pointing to a seat close to Harv and Mack.

'Sorry, chief superintendent.'

The reply came with respect. Much of the room was taken up by plain clothes and uniform. Spencer waited for the general chatter to die down before addressing the team. 'The murder of Jack Samson remains unexplained,' he began. 'There is no obvious motive for the crime. The body was discovered on Wednesday morning. Harrison Draper's estimation of time of death is between nine and ten the previous evening.'

'Is that the closest estimate?' Pez asked.

'I'm afraid it is.'

'I'd say the murder occurred closer to ten. Nine-o-clock would be too light to commit such a crime, wouldn't you say? . . . Mack? . . . . Harv?'

His colleagues nodded.

'I'd go along with that,' Spencer said.

'Samson's wife said he left home at eight-thirty that evening,' Harv added. 'It would probably take about twenty minutes to drive from Mermaid's Bridge to the forest car-park. We have to assume he went there to meet somebody.'

Spencer reached for a thin folder and opened it. 'The team has traced most visitors who stayed at Glenmar Lodge during the crucial period. Let me see . . . This report tells us that a man was seen talking to somebody whose description matches that of Samson.'

'As yet, this person hasn't been traced.'

'That is correct, Harv. Information received recently suggests the man Samson was talking to could have been Billy Wright. Let's bring him in.'

At Spencer's request Harv gave a brief run-down on the Wright lead.

'If this Billy Wright character murdered Samson because of a dodgy car deal – which seems highly unlikely – then why go to the trouble of removing his head?' Pez asked.

'We can't afford to speculate,' Spencer answered.

Pez got up and stood alongside his boss. 'I've something important to say.'

'Go ahead.'

'Right, listen-up everybody. I have information regarding the writing on the victim's feet. I reckon they were written after death occurred. Why they were written is not yet clear. Some of the letters were missing. Our forensics department analysis of the writing has furnished us with the completed words: Allahu Akbar, which means God is Most Great.'

Quiet discussion rippled throughout the room. Harv and Mack exchanged glances.

'I've something to add to this,' Spencer said, quietly in his ear.

'The implications are obvious,' Pez continued. 'Last year anti-terrorist police arrested a suicide bomber. During extensive interrogation he said his actions were in the defence of Islam, and Muslims all over the world were victims of the infidels. He went on to say, "God is great . . . One day I will be a martyr."'

'You can't be serious!' PC Franks sounded. He was the first officer to arrive at the Glenmar crime scene.

'What do you mean?' Pez asked.

'You're saying a terrorist organization did it.'

Discussion erupted again.

'I'm not saying that at all, but what might be significant here is the nature of Jack Samson's job. He was, after all, a nuclear-plant worker.'

'Inspector Perry has made a valid point,' Spencer sounded. 'Eighteen months ago three Algerians were charged, under section 57 of the Terrorism Act, with possession of articles of value to a terrorist. They were also charged under the 1966 Chemical Weapons Act with being concerned in the development or production of chemical weapons.'

'Perhaps Samson was obtaining nuclear material and selling it to a terrorist,' Harv suggested.

'Maybe he couldn't, or wouldn't, steal the material they wanted. Exit J Samson,' Mack said.

'There's another possibility,' Pez said. 'Samson gets greedy and asks for more money, threatens to spill the beans.'

Loud discussion permeated the room. A voice rose above the rest saying, 'Wild speculation. There aren't any terrorists in Cumbria. It's all nonsense.'

A look of embarrassment came over Spencer. He waved his arms, trying to subdue the sudden uproar. Silence came, eventually.

'We had better remain focused,' he said. 'We have done our homework; make no mistake. The threat of terrorism is all around us. We can't be complacent, and we certainly cannot allow our Cumbrian isolation to exclude the idea that this could be a terrorist-related killing.'

Spencer switched on a projector and turned his attention to the screen on the wall. 'Pay attention now,' he said, focusing the image. 'After the initial assault the victim was dragged to a fallen tree. His neck was placed in a position over the trunk in order to create a chopping block. What you see here are the indentations in the bark. Harrison Draper is unable to determine the size of the axe used.'

'Has the murder weapon not been found yet?' Harv asked.

'No. Glenmar Forest consists of two to three thousand acres of woodland. The task of searching the entire area would take forever. We just haven't got enough men to do it . . . The next photo shows three different types of dog hair: three different breeds of dog, one of them white in colour. They were lifted from seats in Samson's car. We know he walked his dogs in the forest. He kept a German Shepherd and two Yorkshire Terriers. Who is the owner of the white dog?'

Pez flipped open his pad and jotted a couple of notes.

'Now, this final image is intriguing,' Spencer went on. 'It is a human hair of Afro-Caribbean origin. The pigmentation particles are larger than those of other racial groups. This single fibre was located on the driver's seat. Who does it belong to? What was the relationship between that person and the victim? . . . That's it for now. Off you go. Wear your boots out.'

The team started to disperse. Spencer asked Pez to accompany him to his office. When they arrived he opened the window and poured a glass of water. Pez was hoping for something a bit stronger. He smiled when the bottle of Night Owl whisky was lifted from a drawer. His boss poured a generous measure.

'Very kind of you, Spencer.'

Pez took two swallows. There was still plenty left. That seemed to brighten his day. Spencer searched inside the same drawer and took from it a silver pen with a gold band round the middle and gold pocket-clip. Pez took it from him.

'Nice pen,' he said, admiring it. 'What's special about it?'

'SOCO found it in undergrowth only a few yards from the body. It was missed at first. There were partial prints on it. Unfortunately, not nearly enough for any kind of comparison analysis.'

'Interesting. A minor clue, eh? So why not mention it to the team?'

'Take a closer look at it. Tell me what is different about that pen.'

He scrutinized it for a while. 'See what you mean. There's a little circular emblem attached to the clip part. It has some raised dots in the shape of a horseshoe.'

'*Seven* raised dots, to be precise.'

'A Seven Moons pen?'

'Correct.'

'Could have been Samson's,' Pez suggested.

'Could belong to the killer.'

'Then the killer can't be a terrorist. He wouldn't own such a pen.'

'But suppose he had been shown around the Seven Moons plant. He might have been given that pen as a token gesture.'

He emptied the glass in one gulp and tossed it to Spencer. A long silence followed, Pez deep in thought. 'There's another possibility,' he said. 'And a frightening one.'

'Let's hear it.'

'The murderer could be a terrorist who is a legitimate employee at Seven Moons.'

'An infiltrator in their midst. You could be right . . . I'm keen to keep this aspect of the investigation low-key, for obvious reasons.'

'Don't want to cause unnecessary alarm, eh?'

'Not at a time like this. Your next assignment should be clear to you.'

'A visit to Seven Moons?'

Spencer nodded slowly. A stern look crossed his face. 'Tread carefully, Pez. You understand?'

'I got ya.'

'What do you make of it all?' Harv asked Pez, relating to the case. The late afternoon found them in the gloom of Hadrian's Bar with two pints of beer sitting in front of them.

'I think the word is, *problematical.*'

'What are Spencer's views?'

'He thinks the terrorist angle is worthy of consideration.' Pez downed a third of his pint and told Harv about the Seven Moons pen. 'So, we don't know whether the pen belonged to Samson or his killer. Not that it matters much. It's the writing on his feet that concerns me.'

'Allahu Cacbar. Could be a red herring.'

Pez laughed. 'It's *Allahu Akbar*, you idiot. A red herring, maybe. Still, a visit to Seven Moons is on my list of priorities.'

'What are you hoping to discover?'

'I'm not sure. Security is tight. I know that for a fact. I can't imagine anybody being able to smuggle significant amounts of nuclear material out of the place and get away with it. Mack's already been there, and since his visit he discovered Samson had a conviction for theft.'

'Before he worked there, you mean?'

'Yeah. Inspector Brooks is in charge of security arrangements. He didn't mention Samson's conviction. He probably doesn't know about it.'

'What difference does it make?'

'Come on, Harv. A factory that makes fuel for nuclear reactors isn't going to employ a tea leaf . . . This one slipped through the net.'

Pez's phone rang. He spoke a few words and finished with a hostile 'goodbye.'

'What's up?' Harv asked.

'That was Laura. She's off to the gym again and wants me to keep an eye on Miranda.'

'How is home life, Pez; or shouldn't I ask?'

'Crap. She's become a right lazy cow this last few months. I do jobs around the house, look after the girl . . . I tell you what, I'm fuckin' sick of it.'

'Don't let it bother you, Pez. Let me buy you another drink.'

'Very good of you,' he replied, a look of sadness on his face.

'Well, cheer up old son. At least we have a suspect in our sights. The lads are looking for him this very moment.'

'Billy Wright?'

'He's the one. My money's on him!'

'Mine's on nobody. I want you to bring Prescott in for questioning. Put some pressure on him.'

'Might as well question Hazel Bamber, too.'

'I'll deal with that one, Harv. We'll pull the obvious ones first.'

Harv stood up. 'Then what?'

Pez looked up, eyes half-shut. 'Do you know Osama bin Laden's address?'

Six

Tara Drake had risen earlier than normal. She decided against the early morning run, took a refreshing shower instead. After drying herself she sat in front of the rectangular mirror and applied the dryer to her long auburn hair, at the same time admiring her shapely figure. Proud she was of her curves and well-toned, tanned body. She couldn't help but notice that faded scar on the biceps muscle of her left arm: a wound received several years earlier when she was attacked by a yob trying to steal her handbag. That almost imperceptible scar always seemed to bother her. She wouldn't have minded as much if the injury had occurred during a training exercise, or in the line of duty. Ironic, she thought. You live your life doing a precarious job, and become a victim of minority mindless youth that couldn't enjoy a meaningful existence.

She caught something on the radio and clicked the dryer off. The newsreader was speaking about the air strikes in Iran. Innocent civilian workers, in the uranium conversion plants, had been killed. Death reports were becoming commonplace, and she had paid little attention to them in the past . . . until Perbury. It was an incident that rocked the nation. Security agencies were on full alert, and top MI5 officials had good reason to involve SATA in the pursuit of those responsible. Little progress had been made. Drake was ready to throw her full weight into the investigation. She'd been in regular contact with Jason Bryce, who possessed sound knowledge of terrorist explosive devices, but his leads on the plastic explosive used to blow up the dog were fruitless. Nobody could say, with any certainty, from where it was obtained. As yet, the general public had not been informed as to the nature of the toxic chemical used in the attack.

The CCTV images kept surfacing in her mind's eye as she dressed herself. What kind of chemical had the bombers used? What was the nature of the choking white mist that burned the lungs of hundreds of protesters? She wondered if any link existed between what happened

41

in North London and an undisclosed quantity of uranium that had fallen off a nuclear transport lorry during a freak weather accident. Questions with no answers. One thing was certain: the uranium was still missing, not accounted for. Drake surmised that its disappearance had been hushed-up. If the terrorists had acquired it, how was it done?

The sound of the door buzzer broke into her thoughts. She clipped her bra strap together and glanced at the computer screen which was connected to a camera outside her flat. Daniel Meyers looked up and waved.

'Mr Arsehole,' she said under her breath. She slipped into T-shirt and pants before answering the door.

He followed her into the living room, totally knocked out by the sight of awesome boobs pushing against thin material.

'Good morning, Miss Drake,' he said, collapsing onto the settee. 'The early bird catches the terrorist.'

'Quit the crap, Daniel. Call me by my first name, and let's be serious for a change, especially when we're on a mission.'

'I wouldn't call it a mission. We're just going to question a suspect, but we have to be careful; we have to be ready if there's trouble.'

'Wait till I put the rest of my gear on.'

'Don't forget the Glock semi-auto . . . By the way, you have a very strong grip. My balls are still blue.'

'You poor man,' she said, with false pity.

Drake hurriedly put on her official-blue shirt, gun holster and black jacket. 'What exactly is happening?' she asked.

'Come and sit down. I'll tell you. We've time to spare,' he replied, slumping further on the settee. Drake poured two Hot Shots and gave him one.

'Shouldn't drink on duty. Naughty girl.' Meyers sipped some and let out a breath of pleasure. 'What we are doing is all part of the Police Anti-terror Action Alert Scheme . . . I call it PATAAS.'

'You would.'

'Please sit down, Tara.'

'I'd rather stand.'

'Fair enough . . . Well, it goes like this. SO13 has set up a unit comprising officers whose job is to visit and make telephone calls to Muslim youths in the South London area. Two detective sergeants, who were highly recommended for the job, have been making enquiries in relation to other members of their respective communities. And that's where the lead has come from.'

'What is the nature of the information?'

'There's been talk of hand grenades being smuggled in from Israel, as well as attacks on Westerners, in the defence of Islam.'

'You believe all that?'

'Come on, Tara. You know the score. We can't afford to overlook such things.'

'Is there any connection with the Perbury attack?'

'We're not sure. It seems unlikely. Anyway, we're going in with an Armed Response Unit in one hour.'

'One suspect, you say?'

'One in particular. There are others. They don't concern us at the moment.'

Drake finished her drink and headed for the door. Meyers followed. They took the lift to the gloomy underground car-park and walked purposefully to his vehicle.

Questioning Billy Wright had proved difficult, and ended up with him doing a runner. Harv and Mack were alerted by a patrol unit that chased him as far as Martyr Gate Bridge which crossed the glistening River Melt. They arrived in time to see suspect Wright skipping and splashing across the river at its shallowest point, laughing and jeering. Uniformed officers dashed along the slippery banks in readiness for him.

'He'll never escape,' Mack said, bemused. 'What the hell is he playing at?'

'Your guess is as good as mine. He's a bloody idiot, that's for sure.'

'Wonder what he's running from. What has he got to hide?' Mack asked, turning to look at the crowd which had formed along the bridge.

'Don't know . . . Oh, look! He's fallen in.'

They laughed together. A constable gingerly stepped into the rapid-flowing water and hoisted him up by his collar. 'Let's be having you!' he snarled. The crowd of onlookers gave a round of applause. Wright looked up and made the 'V' sign. After being cuffed he was taken to the Mushroom. When they arrived Wright got out of the car and yawned heavily. Harv squared up to him. 'Trying to act clever, eh Billy?' he said.

Wright spat on the squad car. 'You ain't pinning anythin' on me. I done nowt.'

Harv looked him over. He was short, stocky, square-shouldered. His green-and-white striped T-shirt was heavily stained with mud. A definite propeller-head, Harv thought. Shit for brains.

Hazel Bamber sat down to a bowl of Rice Crispies and cup of weak coffee. She was determined to crunch her way through them despite Pez's obvious irritation.

He couldn't make up his mind whether she was a lesbian or swung both ways. She was painfully thin, boyish in appearance. Her black hair was cut short-back-and-sides. Her angry-brown eyes added to the hostile look on her face. Her husband, Harry, carried a huge gut. His face was blood-pressure red, and the mass of grey hair on his head looked spongy like candy floss.

'Mrs Bamber, what were you doing during the evening of Tuesday the eleventh of June?' Pez asked loudly, hoping she would stop eating. He took the bowl from her. She pulled a face.

'I'm not sure what I was doing.'

'I need to know.'

'I've already told you. It's years since I last saw Jack.'

'Could you *try* and answer the question?'

'She was here,' Harry Bamber said. 'We rarely go out, you see.'

She reached for the bowl and finished the rest of her snap, crackle and pop breaky. Pez gave her a stern look which demanded a response.

'Well, yes,' she said. 'We were in all night, me and Harry.'

'Can anyone verify that?'

'Come on,' Harry said, placing a reassuring hand on his worried-looking wife's shoulder. 'You can't be serious, Perry . . . Look, this street is full of nosey buggers. Ask the neighbours if they saw either of us going out.'

'Thank you, Mr Bamber. I don't think I'll bother . . . What can you tell me about Jack Samson?' he asked, addressing the wife.

'Jesus! You're really struggling with this lot, aren't you?'

'Try and be helpful.'

She slurped some coffee and said, 'I remember lots when we were kids. As we grew older we had our differences. Every family has differences.'

'I'm sure they do . . . So, you wouldn't know if he had any enemies?'

'We wouldn't!' Harry said, with a hint of annoyance.

Pez thought for a while and recalled that she was an anti-nuclear campaigner. Might as well give it a go, he thought.

'I believe you are a Greenpeace protester.'

She raised her eyebrows as if to say, 'So what?'

'I can't see what it's got to do with Samson's murder,' Harry said.

'Greenpeace has been around for years,' she added, making a point. 'I'm keen on protests, take part in them. No doubt I'll take part in others.'

'Any particular reason?'

'It's just how I feel about it. Think of all the chemicals they use. They discharge pollutants into the sea and air.'

'I don't know what goes on at Seven Moons, but I do know they are answerable to the Environmental Agency. All discharges are monitored.'

'So they tell us,' she said, with disbelief in her voice. 'They lie, you know . . . Let me tell you, inspector, there're things going on that are kept secret. They can't be trusted.'

'What do you mean?'

'Stuff's gone missing from Seven Moons.'

'Explain yourself.'

'The public don't know – we're not supposed to . . . Some kind of uranium compound has gone missing.'

Pez vaguely remembered a newspaper report that covered details surrounding the spillage of a uranic compound from a lorry. Bamber's use of the word 'missing' intrigued him.

'If material has gone missing, how come you know about it?'

'Friends, inspector. I know people who have contacts, and people talk.'

'These contacts you speak of work at Seven Moons, I bet. You'd better tell me all you know. There could be something important that might help me push along this inquiry.'

'I uphold Greenpeace. I'm not mentioning names. I'm not going to say anything else. You'll have to find out for yourself.'

Pez gave her a lingering look. Hazel Bamber made a weak smile that spoke of defiance, and showed him to the door.

'Incidentally, are there any Afro-Caribbeans amongst your group of protesters?'

'No,' she replied, looking puzzled.

'Goodbye, then. See you around.'

Indus Valley was a big immaculate-looking house set in its own grounds in Croydon. Indus Valley was home to the Bhailoks; no kids, only man and wife. The ARU moved in quick as lightening. Mrs Bhailok, confused and distressed, was whisked away to a local police station, shouting words in her native tongue. The search team poured into the house and ransacked every room. Their dogs were happy enough sniffing around cupboards and under beds.

Mr Bhailok was arrested by Meyers, with Drake at his side. She was surprised by the suspect's cool composure and accommodating manner. She felt no urge to reach for the gun. Could have the wrong man, she thought. Nevertheless, they sandwiched him in the back seat of their vehicle and the swift journey began. Bhailok's breathing became heavier. When he started sweating both SAT agents could smell a horrible garlic odour. Meyers could also sense his fear. There was no doubt in his mind that this one would tell all he knew.

Back at the Yard they led him to an ultra-secure underground block of an SO13 department, a place where Drake had never been and didn't know existed.

'It's the Observation Room for us,' Meyers said.

'I think you should tell me what's going on. I thought we were taking him to an ordinary police station.'

'Henderson's instructions. He wants to try a new technique:

46

positron emission tomography. It tells you if a person is lying. If you ask me, we won't even need to use it.'

'Who's giving the interview?'

'McIver and Bryce.'

Harv and Mack were still questioning Wright when Pez left the Mushroom. In his mind an early breakthrough seemed unlikely. Spencer was monitoring the interview and, as Pez looked shattered, he asked him if he wanted to leave early and take a rest. Pez accepted. Now he had the chance to buy that DVD he'd promised Miranda: The Magic White Pony. He parked as close to the town centre shops as he could. He bought the disc, walked out of the shop and into a sudden heavy shower. His eyes slid across a row of shops on the other side of the road, finally resting on The Cube public house. Enough time for a quicky, he thought. In he went. The pub was busy, but he didn't fancy walking to Hadrian's Bar in the rain. He hated The Cube. It used to be called The White Lady, and was supposedly haunted. There was nothing left that could be related to its past appearance. All its character had gone since being modernised; probably the ghost too. It reminded him of an office rather than a pub. They served pathetic umbrella-drinks and over-decorated plates of tiny, over-priced sandwiches. Too prim and proper to Pez's mind. Not even a jukebox to give it atmosphere.

He purchased half-a-bitter. One slurp confirmed his expectation. It *did* taste like gnat's piss. He edged through the crowd and looked up at the huge flat screen. His attention was captured by the news flash. A man had been arrested on suspicion of planning a terrorist attack. An anti-terrorist operation had taken place on information received. Forensic detectives were searching for evidence at a house in Croydon. The Met's Commissioner came on screen. The ongoing investigation was in its early stages, he said. When he mentioned Perbury he was asked if the latest arrest could be connected with the Amama. He didn't know the answer, and wasn't sure if the elusive Amama group was an off-shoot of al-Qaeda. Pez was drawn into the events taking place. He placed his drink on a table and, without thinking, lit a cigarette. The background chatter faded from his ears. The reporter spoke about a growing fear of further terrorist attacks brought on by the bombings in Iran.

The news flash ended. A man turned round and gave Pez a dirty look.

'What's the matter?' Pez asked. 'Someone farted?'

'Worse than that. Don't you know you can be fined for smoking in public places?'

Pez downed his drink and smoked the remainder of his fag in the pouring rain. Should have gone to Hadrian's, he thought.

Back home Laura was cleaning in the kitchen. Miranda heard the car pull up and rushed outside to greet Pez.

'Hello little one,' he said, and gave her the film wrapped in gift paper. 'Come on. Let's go inside.'

When Miranda opened it her face lit up. 'Wow! It's The Magic White Pony . . . Look what dad's bought me, mummy,' she cried.

Pez went to sit in the living room. Seconds later his phone chirped. Harv on the line. Wright's alibi had been checked. He *was* drinking with friends at the time of the murder.

'You certain about the time-frame?'

'Positive. Wright tried to give us the slip. Our lads caught him on the Melt – literally.'

'I know. Spencer told me.'

'Well, some of the lads had a quick look round his house as there was nobody else in it. They found a substantial amount of canno.'

'Class B. Carries five years. Pass it to the drugs department.'

'Will do.'

Pez wasn't happy that Wright had been eliminated. Finding a viable suspect was like looking for the proverbial needle. For the next hour he rested and listened to the patter of rain against the windows. His imagination took him back to Glenmar. Had something obvious been missed? Could there be a mundane explanation for Samson's gruesome murder, or were there deeper and more sinister implications?

Henderson paced his office and glanced at his watch for the final time. Nick Sinclair breezed in, gave the impression that good news was at hand. 'Nothing yet,' he said. 'Bhailok was bemused at the suggestion he's an extremist planning an attack . . . and he denied any knowledge of the Perbury bombing.'

'Have they completed the scan?'

'Yes. Results are due any time now.'

'I can't wait much longer, Nick. The media are baying, as usual.'

Henderson felt answerable to the media. He knew there had to be some form of compromise. The press had been useful allies in the past. He couldn't afford to rebuff them at such a time.

His phone rang. He braced himself. McIver spoke. 'We'll have to release him, sir. The scan says he's telling the truth: no terrorist plotting, and has absolutely no connection with Perbury . . . Are you there, Commissioner?'

'Yes, McIver,' he answered, his voice filled with despondency. 'I want surveillance on Bhailok, and a phone tap for a month or two at least. I have to be sure.'

'But the results –'

'I shan't be swayed by a scanner. The technique is relatively new, hasn't been tried before.'

Henderson slowly replaced the handset.

The look on his face said it all.

Seven

29-year-old Colin Church looked like a boffin, and had a string of letters behind his name to prove he was. The National Crime Faculty was proud to have him as one of its lecturers.

Church's sloping shoulders could barely support the dowdy brown jacket – with elbow patches – which he was so fond of. He wore a grey shirt and amber-coloured tie. His hair was receding rather quickly for a young man.

He stared, through square spectacles, across the desk. Spencer ended his phone conversation and waited until the criminal profiler had finished his Orange Delight drink. He crushed the carton with both hands and looked for a bin.

'I'll take that,' Spencer said, and dropped it into a bin beneath his desk.

Church covered his mouth and yawned. 'Excuse me,' he said, his voice as youthful as a teenager's. 'I'm not used to travelling so far.'

Spencer grinned. 'PC Franks – the officer who escorted you this morning – was the first to arrive at the crime scene. I take it he allowed enough time for you to see everything you needed to?'

'Oh, yes – everything,' he said, with an almost childish appreciation. He closed his eyes for a few seconds, displaying an obvious eccentricity that didn't bother him. 'This murder occurred last week, between nine and ten on Tuesday evening?'

'Correct. Inspector Dave Perry is leading the hunt for the killer. He suggested we consult a profiler.'

'A judicious suggestion, sir . . . Well now, the murder scene itself is very interesting to say the least, and the time selected for the commission of the crime is significant.'

'Do carry on.'

'Time and place often reveal something about the victim and his, or her, killer. I would say they were both familiar with the location. The forest covers a large area. It was not a chance meeting.'

'Interesting you should say that. Inspector Perry has to consider the possibility of a lone psychopath being involved: a man out of control.'

'H'm. Yes. I certainly understand the inspector's dilemma. Is it a random killing? . . . Was it planned? . . . A lone psychopath with such a disturbed personality would have come to your attention by now. Have there been reports of extreme violence towards members of your community? Have any mentally disordered patients, belonging to a local institution, been reported as missing?'

'Nothing like that.'

'Well, you can rule out the lone psychopath.'

'Were you shown photographs of the victim's injuries before you left the station this morning?'

'Yes. I was also given access to the police surgeon's report . . . The murderer has prepared himself for this crime. There must have been an on-going relationship of some kind between the two men. Obvious as it may seem, the culprit is male. Some female killers have been known to use extreme violence.'

'The decapitation is most unusual. Any thoughts?'

'It's unheard of. The beheading seems unnecessary.'

Spencer cleared his throat. 'We have to consider the possibility of a terrorist connection because Jack Samson worked at the atomic plant known as Seven Moons. . . . How does one interpret the writing on the soles of his feet?'

'*Allahu Akbar* . . . Most unusual. I can only speculate. Is speculation good enough?'

'I don't mind some speculation, Mr Church. I'd rather it come from you than some novice.'

'Quite . . . We all know what *Allahu Akbar* means, but would a terrorist need to advertise himself in such a way? . . . Let me think about the writing itself.'

'The clue – call it what you will – could have been written on his forehead, or anywhere else for that matter.'

'If written on the forehead and it rained . . .'

'Obliteration.'

'Perhaps.' Church placed forefinger over pursed lips and thought for a moment. 'To go to the trouble of replacing the socks and trainers takes time. He's taken a risk . . . This crime has been planned.'

'Could a terrorist have done it?'

'Let's consider the decap . . . No terrorist would make such a messy job of removing a head. It was unprofessional; and I say again, was it really necessary?'

'I understand where you are coming from. We shall have to look at the nature of Samson's work, and we need to speak to an advisor on terrorist activities.'

'That wouldn't be a bad idea. The motive is unclear, but I'll say this: Jack Samson was seen as a threat. He had to be eliminated, had to be taken out of the equation. My instinct tells me that the writing was a false clue, created to drive you in the wrong direction. It has nothing to do with terrorism – but you need to consider it as a possibility.'

'I see.'

'There must have been walkers and the like in the vicinity of the murder scene. Any reports of suspicious characters?'

'I'm afraid not.'

'I shall send you a profile,' Church said, standing up, 'as soon as possible.'

'Are there any other details you can add before leaving?'

'You are looking for a man who lives in a radius of ten to twenty miles of the crime location. He is fairly strong, above average intelligence. His age would be mid-thirties to mid-forties.'

Spencer thanked him and received a limp handshake.

Colin Church had entered the dark side of the human mind. He came with high recommendations. Spencer made notes and pondered over the profiler's opinions. He had no intention of taking them lightly.

When Pez entered the house he heard laughter coming from the kitchen. He threw his damp coat over the one remaining wall-hook. He recognised Diana's voice. Laura must have taken the day off work, just as he thought she would. He listened to the chatter and giggles. They're talking like two school girls, he thought. There was mention of a handsome athletic young man who kept going to the bookshop where Laura worked. Pez couldn't believe someone actually fancied her. He felt hurt with the way the conversation was heading. If she wanted another man, why didn't she just say so?

He popped his head around the kitchen door. 'Life's full of surprises,' he said, with an undercurrent of aggression.

'You look really fagged. You work too hard,' Diana said.

A few steps took him to the sink where he washed his hands. Laura's expression turned sour.

'Not at work today?' he asked, stepping back and facing her.

She gave Diana a quick glance and said, 'What are *you* doing at home, then?'

'Checking you out.'

Laura's face took on a worried look. Her body tensed. 'What do you mean, Pez?'

'I like to know what's going on, darling,' he replied with a hint of sarcasm.

'Diana, you're looking beautiful as ever. What's the secret of keeping a marriage together? Having a good sex life, or what?'

Laura stared scornfully at him. 'That's uncalled for . . . Diana's right. You've been working too hard. We've *both* been a bit tired lately.'

'Come on, Pez. Don't be like that,' Diana said, with a broad piss-take grin he was accustomed to. He sat at the table, feeling a tad foolish. Laura started talking about their kids in an attempt to diffuse the tense atmosphere. Diana didn't take the hint.

'How's this case of yours?' she asked.

'I'm not supposed to say too much,' he replied.

'Oh, come on. I've heard talk, you know.'

Pez eyed her. 'Tell me what you've heard.'

'Diana, you shouldn't be taking notice of idle gossip,' Laura said.

'I'm not interested in idle gossip,' Pez sounded. 'But I'll make an exception.'

'They say . . . Well, they say this Samson fellow has been involved with drugs. He did a dirty deal and got paid back for it. He was helping a smack-head called Wright.'

'Do you know him?'

'No. But you should.'

'How's that?'

'Wright and Samson were supposedly selling stuff in that place where you go – Hadrian's Bar.'

Pez wasn't impressed. 'Don't you think I would have heard something by now, Diana?

'Maybe so . . . There's something else, too.' She gave Laura a sideways glance. 'But idle gossip doesn't interest you, does it?'

'I can't believe there's any truth in what you say. All the same . . .'

Diana smiled with her eyes. 'Other rumours say Samson was having an affair with some crack-kid. His wife found out and hired a hit man to kill him the same way a terrorist would.'

'Interesting speculation.'

'Do you think it could be true, then?'

'Don't know,' he said, with a quick shrug.

She asked Laura the same question. Without looking at Diana, she replied, 'A lot of people are talking nonsense, if you ask me.'

Pez looked up at her. 'Very sensible reply, Laura.'

'Well, there you go . . . Come on, Diana. It's time we weren't here.'

'Where are you going?' he asked loudly.

'To the swimming baths. Maybe you should take me sometime.'

'Yeah. Sure. You wouldn't give me the chance.'

Pez shot up and took solace in the front room. It wasn't long before a car stopped outside his house. He heard footsteps along the drive. The doorbell sounded. Laura answered. He recognised the voice. A few seconds later, Fletcher Mack breezed in.

'Mack! What brings you here?' Pez asked.

'I was passing. Thought I would drop in.'

Pez gave him a questioning glance. He couldn't remember him having to pass the house before. First time for everything, he thought.

'So, what news is there?'

Mack became aware that Laura had company. 'Let's talk at the Mushroom, Pez.'

'Whatever you say.'

Pez grabbed a dry jacket. They headed for HQ in Mack's car. Halfway down High Street there was some commotion. A group of town folk had assembled. A few of them were standing in the road and a press photographer was poised with camera at the ready.

'Slow down,' Pez commanded. 'What's going on here?'

'Red Coyote lap-dancing bar. It's opening soon. Locals are going ape.'

'They might as well be opening a strip joint,' Pez said slowly, his eyes searching the crowd . . . Jesus Christ!'

'What is it?'

'Hazel Bamber seems to be heading the protest.'

'Isn't she the one who mentioned uranic material having gone missing from Seven Moons?'

'Right. I bet she's got fingers in a lot of pies.'

Mack speeded up. 'I wonder what's been going on up there.'

'At Seven Moons?'

'Yes.'

'I mean to find out. Bamber knows an informant who works there, and she's not saying who it is. Her husband won't help either.'

'Married, eh?'

'So it would seem . . . The Bambers are a funny couple. I mean, *strange . . . odd . . .*'

They soon found themselves in the Major Incident Room, second floor of the Mushroom. Pez's desk was tucked away in a corner, a huge whiteboard behind it and, close to hand, a small table on wheels where he kept his coffee-making facilities.

He laid a hand on Mack's shoulder and told him to bring the file on Jack Samson. He sat down and logged onto the computer. When Mack returned he pointed at the screen.

'An e-mail from Spencer. He's fond of e-mails – our Spencer. Lazy toad.'

Mack sat next to him and read some of the message. 'So, Spencer's spoken to profiler, Colin Church. He's been on tele, you know. That's what I was going to discuss with you at your house: what Church had to say. I didn't really want to talk about the case with Laura being there.'

'Sound logic, Mack. I wouldn't want Laura's friend, Diana Gobshite, eavesdropping. Church has yet to send us a detailed report, but what he's come up with so far is interesting . . . Spencer asks: would a terrorist write in English?'

'It makes sense. He would hardly write in Arabic or something, would he? Nobody would understand it.'

'Good point . . . Church says the beheading was unprofessional and therefore not the action of a terrorist.'

'He made it look unprofessional to put us off the scent.'

'And write, Allahu Akbar?'

'I see what you mean.'

Pez read some more. '"The murderer does not have a mental disorder . . ." You'd have to be mental to commit a crime like that, surely. "The motive is unclear" . . . "Samson seen as a threat that has to be taken out of the equation" . . . "The terrorist aspect remains a possibility" . . . Great! We're back to square one.'

'Profiling isn't an exact science, Pez. What do you expect with these guys?'

'I suppose they can't afford to be too one-sided. Anyway, the press officer is arranging to have an e-fit placed in the Cumbria journals. We need to know the identity of the man who was talking to Samson.' He reached for Samson's file and opened it. 'Not much here, is there?'

'Read this bit,' Mack said, pointing.

Pez read most of Mack's report, based on his meeting with Victor Brooks. 'You reckon it's impossible to steal nuclear material that could be used to make a dirty bomb?'

'Inspector Brooks said so; but look at this bit, Pez. Samson was transferred from his regular job, ended up working in Analytical Services. Why?'

'I've absolutely no idea. Something bothers me. Samson was caught stealing at his previous job. It could have been a nasty habit that never left him . . . I see you've written the word, *criticality*.'

'Yes, because I don't know what it means.'

'Neither do I. I'll try and find out.'

'Why not take a trip to Seven Moons? Brooks was quite helpful. He might arrange for you to see what goes on there.'

'I intend to. Seven Moons could hold the key to solving this crime . . . Ah, Harv's arrived.'

Harv was out of breath and looked dishevelled.

'What news?' Pez asked.

'Prescott's wife can't confirm his alibi. She was with a friend for most of the evening. She did tell me that her husband and Samson were good mates. There was never any suggestion of ill feeling between them, and the locals said very much the same.'

'We can't charge him on the basis of an unconfirmed alibi. What else?'

'There's no lead on the white dog and Afro-Caribbean hairs.'

'Oh. Any more bad news?'

'I'm sure I can find some if I look hard enough.'

'I bet you can, Harv. Did you attend the press conference?'

'I did. Spencer didn't mention the writing, "God is Most Great."'

'Good. I told him not to. No need to create alarm.'

Pez gave Harv a rundown on Colin Church's evaluation. They discussed the profile. Pez was keen to hear their opinions. One question was uppermost in his mind.

'This is the big one: terrorist or not? Tell me what you think.'

'I go along with Church,' Harv said.

'Terrorist-related,' Mack opposed.

They looked at Pez for his opinion.

'I'm not sure. Can't make up my mind.'

He recounted the hit man and drug-dealing theories as told to him by Diana.

'Bloody nonsense,' Harv blurted. 'Samson's wife wouldn't know how to contact a hit man, nor would she have enough money to hire one.'

'I agree. Mack, what's your feelings about the Samson/Wright drugs link?'

'Not convinced. If Samson was into drug dealing, we would already know about it.'

'We need to have that aspect checked. Mack, ask the drugs squad if they'd mind looking into it . . . OK, lads. I've work to do.'

Mack followed Harv out of the incident room. Pez leaned back with his hands behind his head. He thought about Hazel Bamber – a woman with an axe to grind – and the protesters standing outside the Red Coyote.

Red Coyote, he said to himself. Must check it out.

Eight

Dr Herbert Conlon gently pressed the brake pedal, bringing his maroon-coloured Merc to a stop in the underground parking facility of Stone-Croft Apartments. He groaned as he got out, and slammed the door shut. The sounds reverberated eerily across empty spaces. Only a couple of dozen vehicles were visible in the weak glow from the blue wall-security lights. He spotted cameras pointing from high corners, recording his every move. Still, he felt vulnerable. At sixty years of age, and in poor health, he would be easy prey for a fast, hard-hitting mugger.

He moved swiftly to the lift and pressed hard on the call button, as if the extra pressure would make it descend faster. Relief came when the doors opened. Minutes later he was standing outside door Number 3.

Drake heard a beeping sound and jerked her head towards the screen's image. It was 10.30 p.m. He had arrived on time. When the door opened he said, 'Dr Herbert Conlon. You are, Miss Tara Drake?'

She nodded, stepped aside to allow entrance. He unfastened the buttons on his long black raincoat. She helped him take it off, and when he turned towards her she ran her eyes down his body. It was habit, really. All SAT agents were trained to look for signs of concealed weapons. Conlon was kosher. He felt a sense of unease, and gave her a reassuring smile. 'I'm terribly busy,' he began, 'but I understand this is a matter of some urgency.' His voice carried a quaint Irish tilt.

He followed her into the living quarters and lowered himself into a chair, expelling a long breath of air which spoke of a tiring day.

'I'm very grateful you took the time to come here. Would you like some refreshment?'

'No thanks,' he replied, raising open hands. 'You could have seen me in at the office, you know.'

'This won't take too much of your time. I'd like to show you something. The privacy of my apartment is the best place.'

'I have no problem with that, Miss Drake. You may be certain I'll help you as much as I am permitted . . . Do you mind if I smoke?'

'Feel free, Dr Conlon.'

He took a cherry-red curved pipe from inside his jacket, already half-filled. He struck a match and drew deeply on his Condor/Clan mix.

'I've waited hours for this,' he said, wafting plumes of grey smoke away from his face. Drake pretended not to mind, but the sweet smell wasn't exactly pleasing to her nasal senses. Conlon inhaled deeply and blew a final cloud into the air. He pressed a small piece of tissue paper into the bowl to extinguish the weed. 'I feel a lot better now . . . So, how can I help you?'

'What do you know about the Perbury attack?'

'Probably a little more than your average publican. Why?'

'I have some footage which I'd like you to see.'

He gave a look of discomfort. 'Miss Drake, I am aware that you work for SO13. I have to point out that I am a member of the National Radiological Advisory Committee. We are responsible for implementing plans to deal with *accidents* involving radioactive material.'

'But surely you would include some measure to counter the effects of a dirty bomb?' she asked sharply, knowing his answer would be affirmative.

'It goes without saying. You must be aware that it was the explosion itself that caused the fatalities.'

'I know. I have been informed that a toxic uranic compound was used in the attack. Do you know what it was?'

'No, I don't. Physicists at the scene detected extremely low levels of radiation; so low, in fact, as to render it harmless to human health . . . I feel as if there is an element of secrecy surrounding the Perbury incident.'

'A feeling I share with you. The uranium aspect is worrying, Dr Conlon. I can understand why the authorities want to suppress it . . . Have you heard of the Amama terrorist group?'

'I have.'

'We believe they may have secured substantial quantities of uranium from India or Pakistan.'

'Enough to make a nuclear weapon?' he asked, with a furrowed brow.

'We don't know.'

'It would be illogical to assume such a venture could be undertaken.'

'Illogical?' she said, a hint of disbelief in her voice.

'Yes. You need a particular form of uranium to make a bomb, if that's what you're thinking. Even if it was possible to acquire it, a terrorist would have to smuggle it out of its country of origin, transport it to a safe haven, prepare it for use and avoid detection long enough to detonate it at the target. In any case, the uranium used at Perbury is not the same as is used for nuclear weapons.'

'What is the difference?'

'Nuclear weapons, or a nuclear bomb, use fissile material.'

'Fissile material,' Drake repeated, searching her memory for a definition of *fissile*.

'Fission is the process that occurs when an atom's nucleus splits. A massive amount of energy is then released. Fissile material is matter that can sustain a fission chain reaction. The two fissile materials, or isotopes, used in nuclear weapons are uranium-235 and plutonium-239.'

'Uranium-235 is available from nuclear plants, isn't it?'

'Correct. It is stored here in the UK: Candwell Heights on the south coast, and Crown Point Nuclear Plant in Cumbria. The uranium-235 has to be extremely concentrated for a working nuclear bomb. Those levels of concentration are simply not permitted in our nuclear plants.'

'Very informative, Dr Conlon.'

'Talking of Perbury . . .' He leaned forward, rested his elbows on his knees and brought his hands together. 'Have you any ideas as to who did it? Any chatter?'

'I'm forbidden to discuss the current state of play.'

'Quite . . . Well, you had better show me this footage.'

Herbert Conlon settled back whilst she loaded the disc. The first images were of the 'suicide dog.' Conlon was riveted. 'I haven't seen this before.'

'You are one of a handful.' She slowed the speed. 'See the dog collar? It's made out of plastic explosive, just enough to kill civilians in close proximity to the animal.'

'I assume the toxic compound is concealed on the underside of the dog . . . Very clever.'

Drake altered the speed to normal. The protesters appeared. The path taken by the dog was difficult to follow. Its journey was halted by a sudden white flash. Scenes of horror and confusion were discernible amidst the deadly white fumes.

'How on earth would you train a dog to do that?' Conlon asked.

'German Shepherds can be trained; but watch this.' She resumed play from the beginning. 'This dog isn't just running along. It's following a powerful scent which was sprayed onto the road. A dark-coloured van was used to lay the trail, which was at 2 a.m., some twelve hours before the incident occurred. False registration was used.'

'They did their homework. Mind you, if it had rained . . .'

'They probably read the weather forecast.' Drake located the aftermath of the explosion. 'Look at them rubbing their eyes and coughing.'

'Smoke inhalation.'

Drake shook her head. 'I spoke to several doctors and consultants who attended to the casualties. Many of them developed red, sore patches on their skin and suffered from dyspnoea: extreme breathlessness. In some cases pulmonary oedema occurred, which can be life threatening.' She stopped the disc, switched off the TV and said, 'I want to know what caused those symptoms: the name of the compound they used. Will you help me?'

He stood up and said, 'I'm impressed by your diligence in this dreadful matter. I will try my best, Miss Drake. How would you like me to contact you?'

She wrote her mobile number and gave it to him.

'If you find out what it was, keep it to yourself.'

Their eyes met, and conveyed an understanding. She opened the door for him. He grabbed his coat, gave her a surprisingly weak handshake and departed.

Pez came up behind Jacob Riley. He noticed the newspaper in his lap. 'Mr Keeno. Putting in the overtime, eh?' he said.

Riley smiled cheekily. 'Some folk have to.'

Pez pulled up a chair. 'What's the gossip? Anything of interest in the news?'

'A planned wind farm is causing disruption. They refer to it as, "The gateway to the Lake District."'

'And?'

'The Cumbria Tourist Board chairman told the Ashdown Windfarm public inquiry that if the findings of a survey conducted in April prove to be true, more than a million visitors a year would stay away as a direct result of the controversial 27-turbine project.'

'And the town would lose money.'

Riley took an ashtray out of the drawer, the one he kept just for Pez. 'The town would lose a lot of money. The success of the project would hit Cumbria's tourist industry to the tune of seventy-five million pounds a year, and cause serious damage to the county's already fragile rural economy.'

'The energy company concerned has dismissed these claims,' Pez assured him. He lit a cigarette and said, 'So don't let it bother you.'

Riley shrugged and started coughing.

Pez rolled his eyes. 'And don't give me any of your smoking-is-bad-for-you crap.'

'Well, it's true.'

'Take a look at yourself, Jacob. You're long-haired and overweight. Your girlfriend is feeding you too much. Try the gym once in a while.'

Riley grinned. 'I believe you're trying to say I'm a fat bastard. All right. I agree. My weight and appearance isn't hurting anyone, is it? . . . Anyway, why are you hanging around here so late?'

'Our investigation is going nowhere. I'd appreciate your thoughts on the matter.'

'Me? You don't want *my* thoughts on a murder investigation.'

'Oh, but I do.'

Pez blasted him with the relevant details and asked for his opinion on the terrorist theory.

'*Terrorists in Cumbria*. Unheard of. Impossible. You ought to base your strategy on the profiler's conclusions. You could be making a mistake –'

Riley answered the phone. Pez blew smoke rings above his head and waited till he'd finished his conversation.

'A mistake about what?'

'Jack Samson. Some sicko cuts off his head after stabbing him, and writes some nonsense on his feet. The fact he worked at a nuclear plant is probably a coincidence. Stealing uranium is like trying to obtain rocking-horse shit. Believe me.'

'You reckon?'

'Think about it, man. They don't exactly give the stuff away. Uranium isn't left unguarded. It has to be accounted for. They have uranium accounts, don't they?'

'Must do, I suppose . . . Let's consider some of the clues: white dog hair.'

'Could have come from another dog-walker. Samson liked dogs. He probably knew someone who has a white dog.'

'Sounds feasible . . . Afro-Caribbean hair?'

'No idea . . . He went to Greece, didn't he? Maybe he spent time with an Afro tart and some of her hair ended up on his clothes.'

'Possible. The thought never occurred to me.'

'We could play the guessing game all night. Any luck with the e-fit?'

'We've taken a few calls. Nothing of particular interest.'

Riley turned in his chair and faced Pez. 'You mentioned a hit man and a drugs deal. It's absurd. Drugs and hit-man scenarios belong to TV and books.'

'Can't agree. The violence displayed in the murder was extreme.'

'A psychopath did it. Was any money stolen?'

'We don't know. His car wasn't taken.'

'The killer couldn't drive.'

'Nice one. I appreciate your comments,' Pez said, stubbing his cigarette. 'I'll be on my way.'

'Be seeing you.'

Pez wandered into the Control Centre after spotting the blonde hair. She was relatively new to the force. He'd passed her on the corridors a few times. She always said hello, always smiled. And what a smile.

It took her a while to realize someone was behind her. 'Inspector Perry,' she said, surprised. He asked her name and what she was doing.

'Emily Ross, sir. Town clean-up initiative.'

'Clean-up initiative?'

'I have to check CCTV records from various locations to find out who is throwing litter on the pavements.'

Pez was stunned, angry too. He wondered what it was all coming to when manpower was being wasted in such a way. She continued her duties. Pez left her to it. Minutes later he was driving along High Street towards the town centre. He didn't usually travel that way home. His usual journey comprised splendid woodland and country roads defined by stone walls. A convenient turn-off led to the estate where he lived.

He was thinking about Laura and his darling Miranda who was probably tucked away in bed. Home life was a strain. The long hours at work didn't help; neither did his frequent binges at Hadrian's bar. Was it any wonder him and Laura were drifting apart? Pez was almost past caring. He stopped opposite the recently-opened Red Coyote lap dancing venue that many people perceived as a blot on the town's character. He looked at the building, curious as to what it was like in there. The arched entrance had flashing red and blue lights. On each side were huge posters depicting scantily-clad girls with exaggerated curves, and long hair falling to waist level. Their stiletto shoes had ridiculously high heels. Single men and couples were drifting in. His interest in the Coyote started on the day he saw Hazel Bamber inciting animosity.

He began to realize how sad and lonely he was. What sort of consolation could he possibly expect from such a sordid establishment? Pez fired the engine and drove home.

Miranda was fast asleep. Laura was on the phone talking to a friend. She didn't greet him, said nothing, but at least there was food in the freezer.

After taking a shower and changing into comfy clothes he retired to the living room with his grub. He switched the TV on and started channel-hopping, finally settling for the 24-hour news programme. A segment was dedicated to SO13's terrorist investigation. Several suspects had been released, including Bhailok. A search of his home revealed nothing incriminating.

The newsreader concluded by quoting the Prime Minister as saying, 'Terrorism is a cancerous evil that can never be fully eliminated.'

Pez shuddered at the thought of a terror campaign involving the threat of a nuclear bomb, and a question was still festering in his mind: had Carron Green harboured these misguided believers of the so-called Holy War?

Nine

The previous night's showers had given way to a fine morning. Harv was shuffling along the curved corridor of the Mushroom wishing he was somewhere else, preferably by some still lake with fishing rod propped next to him. The time was 9 a.m. He was late. He noticed Spencer's door ajar and decided to take a sneaky look inside. The office was empty. Maybe Spencer had taken a day off, he thought. Fletcher Mack thought the same when he passed thirty minutes earlier. He uncapped his pen just as Harv came in. He placed a carrier bag next to his desk and said, 'Punctual Mack. How do you do it?''

'You're wrong. I was late too. What's in the bag?'

'Grub for later. I bought some ready-cooked sausages, a pasty, bread roll and carton of milk.'

'I thought as much. I'm sure I caught a whiff of you coming down the corridor.'

Harv gave a wide grin and switched his machine on. He munched an 'early' sausage and typed his password. 'Computers are supposed to be fast, are they not?' he said, the words coming out with bits of sausage. 'This one must have treacle inside . . . Come on, come on!'

Mack prepared two hot drinks, passed one to his partner.

'Cheers, Mack . . . Did you see those documentaries last night? Experts were examining the Trade Centre attacks. They reckon the temperature of the jet fuel wasn't great enough to melt the buildings' steel structures. Most of the fuel burned away at the point of initial impact. They said only controlled explosions from further down the buildings could have caused them to collapse the way they did, like a pack of cards.'

'Conspiracy hype. I suppose you believe Kennedy was killed by the Mafia.'

'No way; but the documentary really gripped me . . . The makers of the programmes believe terrorist funding is coming from Northern

Ireland. They also discovered there are minority extremists who are brainwashing young men to kill Westerners. It's all connected with the Jihad.'

'It's all been reported before. Nothing New.'

'People need reminding. We're living in a dangerous world. The Sunday Reporter carried out a survey and revealed that three out of ten British Muslims believe Osama bin Laden is justified in mounting his war against the Yanks.'

'Scaremongering. In any case, there hasn't been any terrorist activity in this country for years.'

'You're wrong. Don't forget what happened in London only a few months ago. Since then there have been rumblings. The politicians were right – it's not safe out there.'

'I don't have much faith in politicians . . . You'd better take a look at that lot over there: effects taken from Samson's house.'

A few steps took Harv to a table at the back of the room. All the items had been sealed in bags. Harv forced plastic gloves on and removed the painting from its covering. 'I remember seeing this when I went to question Mrs Samson,' he said, holding it at eye level.

'*High Street*, by William Stringer. It's an original.'

'No kidding? Must have cost a bob or two.'

'Seven hundred pounds, at least.'

'Can't understand why someone like Jack Samson would spend so much on a painting. Even I couldn't afford to spend so much.' Harv slid the bag over it and looked at other items. 'Have you seen these? Binoculars and camcorder.'

'Wellington zoom binoculars, Harv. A pair would cost a hundred quid. The camcorder is a DCR 2000XL Sony. It has eight programmed exposure modes, fantastic zoom-in, touch-panel function and super night-shot facility.'

'Impressive. And where is the Seven Moons pen?'

'The pen was a crime scene exhibit. I think Pez keeps it in his desk.'

'Or in his jacket,' Harv said, turning around with a knowing smile. He went back to his chair, slurped coffee and started clicking the mouse. 'I suspect that lot will be finger-printed. Could be stolen goods, especially when one considers Samson's involvement with a pillock like Billy Wright.'

'Pez isn't looking at it from a stolen goods perspective. Consider the facts –' The phone sounded. Mack took the call and jotted a note. 'Do you know much about cars?' he asked, replacing the handset.

'I can change a tyre and do an oil change.'

'That was Mason. He did a valuation on Samson's car. His Citroën C6 cost fourteen thousand pounds. The car was bought by Samson himself. Cash payment.'

'I'm beginning to see where Pez is coming from with all this. Samson had a lot of money to splash around.'

'Exactly. I'm waiting for an update on his bank records.'

Mack picked up a different phone as it rang. When he finished speaking he looked at Harv.

'The desk sergeant says we have a visitor. The man seen talking to Jack Samson, on the evening he was murdered, is waiting to speak to us.'

Pez had to suffer the same rigmarole as Mack did when visiting Seven Moons atomic plant. He flashed his ID card at the young Atomic Energy police constable. A pang of annoyance erupted when he was asked to release the boot of his vehicle. Pez asked why he had to nosy inside.

'A policeman should know the reason,' came the empty reply.

'Exactly the point. I'm the last person in the world likely to bring a bomb on site!'

The PC closed lid. 'Park over there. It's not going on site.'

Pez gritted his teeth and parked-up. He slammed the door shut and walked towards Victor Brooks who was standing outside the police lodge, displaying a cheerful look. Pez was six feet tall. He felt dwarfed as he shook the hand of the mighty inspector. 'I'm Inspector Dave Perry. Pleased to meet you.'

'Victor Brooks . . . Follow me. I'll get you signed-in and see if we can sort you out with a visitor's pass.'

Pez went through the formalities, and Brooks handed him the folder containing Samson's work records. He apologised for having to leave him. Some urgent matter had been brought to his attention. Whilst waiting Pez read the contents thoroughly and gave it back to Brooks on his return. The two of them then took a casual stroll along the site's main avenue. Pez stared up at the huge constructions, filtration towers and miles of glistening pipe work.

'I saw the e-fit,' Brooks said, by way of starting the conversation. 'Has there been any response?'

'No. There are so many visitors to the forest. The murderer, or murderers, wouldn't necessarily stand out.'

'I don't envy you, inspector. You have a difficult case on your hands.'

'I see it as a challenge . . . I need to know more about Jack Samson's work activities. I'm keen to know what sort of materials he had access to.'

'Your detective constable touched on the same thing. Samson worked with various uranic substances.'

'He asked whether such substances could be stolen from here, didn't he?'

'Aye. It's very unlikely to happen. My officers perform regular searches on employees leaving for home. Anyone caught with the smallest amount of radioactive material would face dismissal and possibly a jail sentence.'

'But they don't search everybody leaving work.'

'No. Imagine how long it would take . . . I know what you're surmising –'

'I'm surmising nothing,' Pez interrupted.

'Let me finish. There hasn't been any suspicious activity up here. We're a long way from London, I know. However, we receive regular updates from the Civil Nuclear Security's departments. Their updates come from MI5 . . . The idea of Samson being embroiled in some terrorist intrigue is ridiculous. Why pursue it?'

'I have to keep my options open. If some *intrigue* is connected with his murder, I'll find out.'

'Fair enough,' Brooks replied.

'Did you receive my message regarding Afro-Caribbeans?'

'I did. None work here.'

'And you are now aware of Samson's past history for thieving?'

A flush of embarrassment passed over Brooks' face. 'I can't offer an explanation.'

'You check every employee for *previous*?'

'Absolutely. I'm not personally responsible for all the checks. I'm sorry. Too late now . . . What else do you need to know?'

'My investigation begins at Seven Moons. I may have to spend some time here.'

'You need to have a photograph taken then. Identification purposes. Every employee must display a security pass at all times. There are no exceptions.' They walked on a   little further and Pez said, 'Somebody has altered the date of Samson's transfer to Analytical Services Department. Apparently, he was sent there at the beginning of April, not May.'

Brooks shrugged. 'Clerical error, I suppose.'

'Do employees have places to keep their personal belongings?'

'They have lockers assigned to them. Do you want me to have Samson's locker opened, find out what's in it?'

'It would be helpful.'

'I'll see to it, inspector . . . I'll show you where the main production units are if you like, and then you can meet Geraint Marshall. He's the Managing Director of this company.'

The man was waiting in one of the Mushroom's ground-floor rooms. The newspaper e-fit kept surfacing in his mind. His mouth was dry as a sandpit and the nerves of his stomach were tingling with a worried anticipation. His brow darkened at the sound of footsteps approaching the door.

Harv and Mack came in and noticed the strained look on his face.

'I'm Detective Constable Harvey. This is Detective Constable Mack.'

They took seats opposite him. Harv asked his name.

'Brian Pill. I work at Crown Point.'

Harv began the questioning. 'How long have you worked there?'

'Going on for twenty-five years. I'm a process worker.'

'You knew Jack Samson?'

'Yes. I worked with him in one of the plants some two or three years ago.'

'Tell me what you know about him.'

70

Pill puffed his lips out and thought for a while.

'I didn't know him well. Not really. He seemed a happy enough chap. He kept dogs, you know. Used to talk about them a lot.'

'Did he discuss his wife?'

'Not that I can remember . . . She made a good bagging for him, though.'

Harv gave Mack a sideways glance. 'What is, *bagging*?'

'It means grub, your lunch-box, or whatever you want to call it. Jack's was always packed solid.'

'Good worker?' Harv continued.

'Yes. Never late. Never had time off for illness. He was a down-to-earth bloke.'

Mack turned to Harv and said, 'This ties in with interviews conducted with his work colleagues.' To Pill, he asked, 'Was he into photography or filming with a video camera?'

'No idea.'

'Jack Samson was murdered just over two weeks ago. Why the delay?' A question from Harv, with a serious tone.

Pill looked down momentarily. 'I'm very sorry. You see it's true I saw him at Glenmar Forest but I only spoke to him for a few minutes. I didn't think it was important.'

Questions were rapidly forming in Harv's mind. 'Did you see him at work in more recent times?'

'No. The factory is a massive place.'

'What were you doing at the forest?'

A crucial question from Mack. Pill swallowed, realizing the implication of being at the right place, right time.

'I haven't been to the forest for ages.'

Wrong answer. Harv decided to pursue this line of questioning. 'Glenmar covers a vast area. Seems odd you should bump into an old workmate. What are the chances of that happening?'

'Look, I decided to go there for a walk. I parked at the same place as Jack. From what I can remember there are only a couple of car-parks. A coincidence happened. Do you think I'd come here if I'd killed him?'

Harv, concentrating on his body language and answers given, thought he was telling the truth. He asked what Samson was doing when he met him.

'He was pacing around.'

'What did you say to him?'

'I said I was surprised to see him. I asked how he was doing, and what building he was working in.'

'Did he seem anxious?'

'No.'

'Did you discover why he was there?'

'Well, he said something strange. He was waiting for a friend, and he said the words, *Knowledge is power* – more to himself than to me. I wished him well and then went home.'

'At what time?'

'After nine o' clock. I can't remember exactly.'

'Did you notice anyone else in the area? Anyone acting suspicious?'

'There were other people about. Can't say I noticed anything unusual.'

Harv shot up, stuffed his hands into his pockets and walked to the back of the room. He gave Mack a quick nod.

'Thanks for coming down,' Mack said. 'I'll take you to see the desk sergeant. We want a statement and some personal details.'

Mack returned to find Harv lying against the wall, arms folded. '*Knowledge is power*,' he said, looking Mack straight in the eye. 'I wonder what he meant by that?'

When Pez stepped into the plush air conditioned office Geraint Marshall rose from behind his tidy desk. Pez noticed his jelly-belly straining against his immaculate white shirt. Marshall was in his early fifties. His black hair carried wisps of grey and was styled with a spiky effect to make him look more trendy – something they both had in common. Unlike Pez, he was growing an extra chin, but his smile revealed a set of brilliant white teeth that obviously hadn't got that way by mere brushing.

Pez approached him, his feet sinking into an expensive pale-blue carpet. Marshall offered his hand. The shake was long and welcoming. When Pez was seated his attention was drawn to an artist's impression of the new AP1000 nuclear plant which was nearing completion. The AP1000 had a basic design: rectangular-shaped buildings and cylindrical towers. The site was partly surrounded by smooth green fields punctuated by plump trees. A blue sea stretched beyond the nuclear masterpiece, fading into a white-line horizon supporting fluffy clouds.

'Impressive, isn't it?' Marshall said, his voice smooth, his accent posh. 'You are, Inspector Perry?'

Pez nodded. 'A new design?' he asked, looking once more at the painting to his right.

'Indeed. The AP1000 is almost ready to take on the world. The design was approved by the NRC: the United States Regulatory Commission. It is based on the same pressurised water reactor technology that has amassed thousands of reactor-years of successful operation world-wide since the first PWR went into action in Pennsylvania in 1957.'

'I don't understand the jargon. It sounds wonderful, though,' Pez said nodding.

Marshall glanced at it with admiration. 'I'm very fond of that picture . . . I've been offered a senior post there, you see. The reactor sits on the Norfolk coast. Hopefully, my wife and I shall be taking residence there, perhaps later this year.'

'Good for you . . . Could I ask a technical question, Mr Marshall?'

'No doubt you have many questions. Go ahead.'

'When I came here I noticed signposts with the words, *Criticality Exit*. What is *criticality*?'

'It pertains to fission, inspector. Very briefly, nuclear fission is a reaction in which a heavy atomic nucleus, such as uranium, splits into two parts. Massive amounts of energy are released in the form of heat and radiation. If you have enough uranium stored in a particular shape and at a certain, shall we say, concentration, you end up with an uncontrolled release of energy involving levels of radiation such that anyone in close proximity would die. This would be classed as a criticality incident.'

'The principle behind the atomic bomb?'

'Yes. Of course, our activities with fissile uranium are very carefully controlled. Any clearer?'

'A bit clearer, yes.'

'But you have more serious questions to ask me.'

'I need to know exactly what kind of work Jack Samson was doing. Also, the possibility that uranium has gone missing from this site.'

Marshall's face tightened. He looked sternly at Pez. 'Missing uranium?'

'A line of inquiry I'm interested in. I've heard some talk of –'

'Talk can be misleading!' Marshall sounded. He let out a long breath of air. 'Sorry, inspector.'

Pez knew he had hit a nerve. Marshall suddenly became fidgety and made a performance of looking at his watch.

'If you are short on time I can come back again.' Pez said. He made a faint smile as if oblivious to his sudden mood change.

Marshall gave him a lingering look. 'I'm always here to help you, inspector. Unfortunately, I'm expected to be in the lecture theatre in ten minutes. It's inconvenient for you, I know.'

'Next time, I shall make an appointment,' Pez said cordially.

Marshall offered his hand again for a firm shake. Pez made his way out and stopped suddenly. 'There's something I was meaning to ask. Jack Samson worked in an AGR canning plant. What is *AGR*?'

'All these terms are confusing to the outsider . . . AGR means, *Advanced Gas-cooled Reactor*. We have only one AGR plant on this site: Building 300. It's over there.' He pointed through the window behind him. 'You must come for an educational tour, when it suits you best.'

'Good idea. Thanks for your time.'

He left the pristine office knowing Geraint Marshall had more to tell.

Ian McIver was hunched over, studying CCTV footage from areas surrounding the Perbury bomb attack. He knew Drake was hovering behind him waiting to speak. For the first time she noticed a bald patch on top of his head. She looked at him with disdain. In fact, she didn't like the look of him from the outset. A big lumbering man he was with a chest like a bull. She had only spoken to him on a couple of occasions and found him to be condescending, arrogant and dismissive. He eventually looked up and asked what she wanted.

'I saw Bryce yesterday,' she said. 'You could have told me you were trying to trace friends of the Toxic Terrorist.'

'You must have misheard him, Tara. We know who they are. Time is on our side. We'll bag them when we're ready.'

'Don't wait too long . . . Can I ask, have you made any inquiries into the nature of the uranic compound used at Perbury?'

'Never gave it much thought. We are more interested in the bomb mechanism they used.'

'You surprise me. I thought it would be top of your list.'

'You thought wrong. Have *you* made any progress?'

'Conlon telephoned me. He gave me the name of the compound used in the attack.'

'Well, don't keep me waiting. What was it?'

'Fluorohexane. It's commonly referred to as Flux by those who work in the nuclear industry.'

'First-class piece of information. Well done, Tara!' he said, with a look of surprise.

'Only one nuclear establishment in this country makes it.'

McIver stretched his neck, turned his head slightly and raised an eyebrow.

'Up north, in Cumbria,' she continued. 'A place called Crown Point. Everybody who works there refers to it as Seven Moons.'

McIver stood up and patted her cheek. 'Excellent news, young lady. Commissioner Henderson will be delighted when you acquaint him with this nugget of information.'

'SATA need to visit this nuclear establishment – without delay.'

'No doubt about it. At last there is hope of catching the men responsible for this atrocious crime.'

Ten

Spencer heard a gentle tapping on the window. He made a gap in the blinds and peered outside. Thirty minutes ago Carron Green was bathing in sunshine. The heavy clouds brought shadow and rain. He closed the window and turned the light on. The weather was as unpredictable as his stomach. Even though he'd given-up the traditional English breakfast for an air-filled bun and glass of pure orange juice the gurgling acid-bursts were still bothering him. He gave up on the orange juice, started drinking tea again; and felt better for doing so. His working-day, however, was just as tedious as it had always been.

A letter from a councillor lay on his desk. Its content was trivial, at least to Spencer. Local residents were complaining. Bored chavs were causing unrest. Why were police officers not responding to calls? Spencer wasn't at all in-tune with the problem. There again, he lived in a detached house on the outskirts of town. Chavs never ventured that far. He gave the letter a cursory glance and cast it into the bin. More important issues to resolve, he said to himself. He waited for that knock on the door. When the hands of the clock reached ten-thirty, he arrived.

Ken Rhodes, Counter Terrorism Security Advisor, introduced himself. Spencer took his hat and coat, and was surprised to see he was wearing brown leather gloves. Rhodes said he'd been sent in place of a colleague who was suffering with depression.

'I hope it's not serious.'

'I'm sure he'll survive,' Rhodes said. He was middle-aged. His composure captured the essence of a military man.

When the pleasantries were over they got to the point of the matter. Spencer gave him all the relevant details surrounding Samson's murder.

'Who is working the investigation?' Rhodes asked.

'Inspector Perry. He's thorough, astute. He absorbs minor details which often turn out important. His investigation has to cover all aspects. Your help would be invaluable'

'Has the inspector been to the victim's place of employment?'

'He went there a few days ago. Perry believes some form of uranium may have gone missing from the atomic plant.'

'He's very smart.'

'Really?' Spencer said, surprise in his voice. Pez was smarter than he'd given him credit for.

'Yesterday we received a call from the Met Commissioner. There was no mention of Jack Samson, but something significant has transpired which may have some bearing on the matter. What I'm about to tell you relates to the bombing which took place in London.'

'I remember it well. The first dirty bomb attack in our country.'

'I hope it's the last . . . MI5 suspect a terrorist group called the Amama. They are elusive, cunning, sophisticated. The attack at Perbury involved the use of a uranium-based compound known as Flux. It's highly toxic. The only place that makes it is –'

'Crown Point, here in Cumbria.'

Rhodes gave a quick nod. 'Nobody knows how they acquired this compound. The worrying part is, they may have enough left for a further attack.'

'What are the properties of Flux?'

'I have no specific information at present. The fact that Flux was used at Perbury has, undoubtedly, been suppressed.'

'A cover-up?'

'Well, not exactly. Imagine the panic and loss of confidence in the security of our nuclear establishments if this became public knowledge.'

'How much of it is unaccounted?'

'I have no idea. I've spoken to the Chief Constable, told him the facts of the matter. He's keen on confidentiality. You must be careful.'

'I understand.'

'And I need to speak to your inspector, the one in charge of your murder inquiry.'

Spencer phoned the incident room. Harv told him Pez would be arriving soon.

'Inspector Perry is on his way . . . Might I ask, what is the situation regarding terrorism in Cumbria?'

'As far as I know, there is no specific threat.'

'So, how would you view the murder of Jack Samson?'

'An execution by terrorists doesn't ring true. Any terrorist would almost certainly carry out such an atrocity behind closed doors.'

'I suppose, then, since the beheading was messy and unprofessional, it may have been done for reasons which exclude a terrorist connection.'

'Possibly. But don't let me sway you. I've seen numerous al-Qaeda websites. Believe me, these men can be extremely barbaric . . . What progress have you made?'

'Very little. The motive for the crime is unclear. If we can establish what it is, we may be in a position to progress further.'

'Help may be at hand. Have you heard of SATA?'

'No.'

'*Special Anti-Terrorist Agent.* They are specially trained officers, part of an elite branch of SO13. Two of their agents are travelling to the Crown Point nuclear site. They may be willing to trade information.'

The phone rang before Spencer could speak. He took the message and said, 'Inspector Perry has arrived. You can see him in the conference room. You take the lift to the top floor, or walk the stairs.'

'The stairs will be fine.'

The conference room was empty. Rhodes entered and clicked the lights on. He neatly folded his coat and laid it across one of the seats surrounding a huge table. With hat still in his hand, he walked slowly to the window and looked at the roof-tops and chimneys of Carron Green. Further in the distance he could see Hawes Fell sitting beneath a dark veil formed by the rain. It seemed such an unlikely setting for a gruesome murder. A terrorist connection seemed even more implausible.

The door opened. Pez came in quietly. He looked pale, tired and wet. His usually spiky hair was flat to his head. He introduced himself and went straight into the investigation, adding details which Spencer had omitted. He mentioned 'greenpeacer' Hazel Bamber, drug dealer Billy Wright, and the latest player in the drama, Brian Pill. Initially, Rhodes showed interest in Wright. Pez explained he was no longer a suspect, and was being dealt with under separate charges relating to drugs offences.

'And that's the story so far,' Pez said. 'Any thoughts?'

'Firstly, I told your chief super that an execution in Glenmar Forest is highly unlikely. Secondly, I don't think a terrorist would bother to write "Allahu Akbar" on the soles of a dead man's feet.'

'False clue?'

Rhodes fiddled with his hat and said, 'It's not for me to decide. I'm sorry I can't be more helpful.'

Rhodes then talked about the terrible events that occurred in England's capital. When he uttered the word 'uranium,' Pez felt an emotional jolt. Rhodes fuelled the conversation with talk of unaccounted Flux, and SATA's forthcoming trip to Cumbria.

'Let's get this straight,' Pez said. 'You're saying that Flux was used in the Perbury bomb?'

'Correct. There has been no publicity. Your chief super knows. He must keep it to himself. I'm saying the same to you.'

'You can trust me . . . I wonder if this missing Flux has any connection with the murder?'

'I'd say you're in a good position to find out. The murder of Samson doesn't fall within SATA's jurisdiction, but don't be surprised if you receive a call from them. Their inquiries could be vital in solving this case. It all depends on the relevance of the known details surrounding his death . . . Has anything occurred recently?'

'Today I ran a check on his bank account. Significant amounts of money have been deposited and withdrawn. He was spending heavily – new car, holiday to Greece, and he bought an expensive camcorder some six months ago. We don't know what he used it for.'

Rhodes became lost in thought. Something was developing in his mind. 'Knowledge is power,' he said to himself.

'What is it?' Pez asked. No reply came. 'Tell me.'

'I could be way off the mark . . . Is it feasible that Samson was using his camcorder at work?'

'Is filming permitted?'

'Absolutely forbidden. Employees at nuclear plants can't even take cameras to their place of work; but suppose he was filming the layout of his work place, or – I dread to think – the processes involved in the manufacture of uranium.'

'Or, Flux.'

'Powerful knowledge, wouldn't you say?'

'Knowledge that could be sold to a terrorist.'

It was mid-afternoon when Victor Brooks arrived at Seven Moons' Analytical Services Department. Manager, Andrew Sharpe, was a short rotund man, pompous and dignified. 'Nasty weather,' he said, leading him inside. 'We use swipe cards nowadays.'

'I know.'

'Sign the visitors' book, please; and put the date and time.'

'Extra security measures,' Brooks said, taking up the pen. 'It's as bad as that, is it?'

'You should know, inspector.'

Brooks made his entry and followed him to the lift. They exited at the fourth floor and walked down a long corridor running between laboratories, offices and a row of lockers.

'Here we are,' Sharpe said, stopping. 'Locker Number 25.' He inserted the key, couldn't work it properly. Brooks tried and immediately clicked it open. He stepped back, away from the stink of stale socks.

A pair of steel toe-capped shoes lay on top of a dark-blue, zip-up jumper showing the Seven Moons logo. The socks were festering beneath the jumper, as Brooks discovered. He checked articles which had been stuffed in an upper compartment. There were several booklets: Working with Radiation, Health and Safety at Work, ASD and What We Do.

'And what have we here?' Brooks flipped the pages of a musty girly mag called 'Knockers and Nipples.' He smiled and said, 'This must be ancient. Look at the price – one pound and fifty pence . . . Great Scott! You don't get many of those to the pound.'

He turned the mag towards Sharpe, who snatched it from his

hand. 'Exactly what are you looking for, inspector?' he asked, annoyed and embarrassed.

'Anything of interest . . . Let's see what else there is.'

Brooks came across a few coins, a crushed box of tissues and a pair of yellow plastic gloves. 'What are these used for?' he asked, holding them up.

'Laboratory kit. All my staff have to wear them when dealing with chemicals.'

'Very good. Thanks for your help, Mr Sharpe.'

Brooks walked back to the lift. A short visit, Sharpe thought, shaking his head in dismay. He put the mag inside the locker and slammed the door shut.

Pez slumped onto the settee after a long and tiring day. At least they're sending Special Agents to Cumbria, he thought, with some relief. *Special Agents*, he murmured. Sounds like the FBI.

He wondered who they would interview, what questions would be asked. Would they talk to Pez himself? A sense of mild inadequacy began to set in. He certainly wouldn't want them stealing his trophy of success. He thought hard about the clues and theories, trying to make sense of it all. A short while later a soft voice broke into his reverie.

'Daddy, look at this.'

Miranda made a beautiful smile and showed her colouring book to him.

'What a lovely picture. Have *you* coloured the church, or did mummy do it for you?'

'I did it myself. Our teacher wants us to write a story. Mine's about St Peter's church . . . We went there once, didn't we?'

'We did. And can you remember the name of the place?'

She stuck a finger in her mouth and shook her head. Pez gripped her little waist and pulled her up onto his knee. 'It is called Salter Bay . . . St Peter's is hundreds of years old.'

'Will you take me again, one day?'

'Of course I will . . . What are you going to write in your story?'

'*Spider*,' she cried. 'He's a little brown dog who lives in the church, and one day he finds a bone near a grave which has lots of pretty flowers growing on it.'

'I hope I can read it.'

'Yes, yes,' she said, grabbing the book and running off up the stairs. Pez went into the back room. Laura was reading.

'Are you going out tonight, or what?' he asked.

'Why do you ask?'

'I might go out myself.'

'It's not like you to venture out. Where are you going?'

'Not sure. I fancy a few beers. I might give Harv a ring.'

'Do whatever you want. Diana is coming round later.'

'That does it,' he said, his mind made up. 'I'll have a wash and get ready.'

Laura was annoyed. She had always wanted him to accept Diana as a welcome guest, but he hated it when she came to the house. All that talk and giggling would get on his tits, and the talking would become louder as they drank more cheap wine.

An hour later he was waiting for a taxi outside his house. He felt good in his blue-and-white striped T-shirt and black jeans, and he couldn't wait to sample the delights on offer at the Red Coyote.

At 10 p.m. the Mushroom was still buzzing with activity. Spencer made his way down the corridor towards the incident room, trying his best to avoid contact with other officers who passed by. His eye started twitching: a nervous twitch that only happened when the pressure was on. His pace was slow. When he reached Pez's desk he picked up a notepad, turned to the last page. Pez had underlined certain sentences: Samson's locker – nothing important found; question Marshall; missing flux; was JS involved with Flux? SATA to visit Seven Moons; what do they know?

Spencer took a deep breath and returned to his office. It was some time before he punched a number into his phone. 'Inspector Perry is interested,' he said. 'He's going to interview Marshall about the Flux . . . I'll monitor his activities . . . Don't worry. I'll be watching him.'

Eleven

27-year-old Susie Reynolds couldn't have landed herself a better position. As the managing director's secretary she did a first-class job, took pride in her work, and her appearance. Her slimness made her look taller than she actually was. Her blonde hair had lighter tints added and hung straight and sleek halfway down her back. She had clear blue eyes, high cheek bones and sensual lips. A real stunner. A head-turner.

At 11 a.m. Susie stopped writing, aware of a dull drilling sound coming from above. It must be them, she thought. She looked at her watch and realized they had arrived an hour later than scheduled.

Geraint Marshall was alone in the adjoining room. He rattled open the blinds but saw nothing. Susie was standing at the open door. 'I think they're here,' she said, watching for a reaction from him, any reaction. Marshall didn't speak to her. He immediately left the building and drove steadily to the police lodge. He could see the black helicopter now, hovering close to the main entrance. It descended slowly, disappearing from view. He could hear the police dogs barking when he arrived. Victor Brooks was waiting on the edge of the helipad. The blades eventually stopped spinning. Brooks moved forward and Marshall joined him. Two men, dressed in black, jumped onto the ground and stood side by side. Jason Bryce cleaned his glasses. Daniel Meyers yanked the lapels of his jacket to straighten the creases. Marshall swallowed as they approached, looking serious, looking tough.

The SAT agents showed their identity passes and said who they were. Brooks was already known to them. He shook their hands and introduced them to Geraint Marshall. That done, Brooks led the way to his office. Officers and civilians inside the police lodge looked upon the agents with respect, even awe. Meyers looked upon everyone with disdain, and it showed.

Brooks closed the door and asked how long they would be staying.

Bryce sniffed and looked at Meyers, who said, 'I shouldn't imagine it will take long. We need to clarify certain matters.'

Marshall became edgy. He breathed in deeply, quietly. 'What exactly is the purpose of your visit?'

'I thought you would have known, Mr Marshall,' Meyers replied, with an air of condescension. 'You must have known SATA were coming here.'

'Yes . . . Yes, I knew that, of course,' Marshall said, feeling a sudden tension in the air. 'You had better come to my office where we can talk in comfortable surroundings.'

'Your pilot might as well wait in here,' Brooks suggested.

'I *am* the pilot,' Meyers said. 'Let's go then.'

When they arrived Marshall arranged two comfy chairs. He left them alone for a moment and spoke to Susie who was still bemused by Meyers' insipid smile.

'I don't want any calls, no disturbance,' he said to her.

'What is it all about?'

'Susie, I haven't the time right now.'

Marshall left her and moved swiftly to his desk. Meyer's eyes followed him. 'What do you know about Flux?' he asked.

'Flux?' Marshall said, as if in ignorance.

'You heard me correctly.'

'It's an intermediary product. We make thousands of tonnes of the stuff.'

'You have machinery to make it?' Bryce asked, in a soft voice.

'How else do you think we make it?'

Meyers scowled. 'A quantity of Flux is missing. We want to know what happened. Where is it now? How could it have gone astray?'

Marshall wasn't sitting comfortably any more. His mouth was dry as sandpaper. He poured water into a glass, his hand shaking. He gave a reassuring smile. 'You must already know one of our Civil Nuclear Transport lorries was involved in an accident. It was carrying a consignment of varying forms of uranium to an enrichment plant in Eldridge, Cheshire.'

'We didn't know,' Meyers said, watching his facial expressions and body language. 'When did this happen?'

'Mid-February. The weather turned extremely nasty. The driver swerved to avoid a car crash. The lorry turned onto its side. Uranium, in liquid form, spilled onto the road. Fortunately, it was diluted and washed away by the heavy rain. So you see, there's no cause for alarm.'

Bryce threw a sideways glance at his colleague.

'The incident was reported in the nationals,' Marshall added.

'There was a cover-up, wasn't there?' No-nonsense Meyers asked.

'What do you mean?' said Marshall. He could barely contain his shock.

'Recently, we discovered that Flux was used to make a dirty bomb. You recall Perbury?' Bryce asked.

Marshall rubbed his forehead. 'Yes.'

'Dangerous chemical. When exposed to the atmosphere it produces poisonous fumes which can cause fatal injuries.'

'I know, Mr Meyers. Or is it, *Special Agent* Meyers?'

Jesus Christ, Bryce thought. Any second now he'll pounce on the smug bastard.

Meyers made no reply.

'You seem to be questioning me as if this company is in some way responsible,' he went on. 'You obviously do not understand the implications surrounding the loss of a toxic uranic compound. The full details of the accident have not been released. The reasons for this are fairly clear. We do not wish to create alarm . . . A relatively *small* amount of Flux is missing – some consolation, I think.'

'What quantity of Flux was the lorry carrying?' A pertinent question from Bryce.

'There were several drums. Each drum contained about a thousand grams. Only one drum could not be located. Heaven knows where it is! There has been secrecy, I'll admit. The highest levels of authority are intent on keeping it that way.'

'The worst has happened, Mr Marshall. It's our job to determine the circumstances surrounding the loss of this compound,' Bryce said, calm, composed. 'Who was the driver of the ill-fated lorry?'

'I don't know.'

'Don't know?' Meyers said loudly.

'Look, it's not my department. I do not supervise transportation of radioactive materials.'

'Who does?'

'Several people are involved. Their activities are governed by a complex series of guidelines laid down by Radioactive Materials Transport. I suppose, *Mr* Meyers, you'll be wanting to question the RMT manager?'

A long silence followed. Meyers was thinking the best way forward. Bryce watched Marshall pour more water. No trembling hand this time.

'Yes. And we would like to question him today.'

Marshall lifted the phone, spoke to Susie. 'Very well,' he said, replacing the handset. 'He's out at the moment, should be back soon . . . While you are here, I may as well tell you about a police visit.'

'Are you referring to your site constabulary?' Bryce asked.

'No. Inspector Perry called here recently. He is based at Carron Green, a small town some sixty miles from here.'

Bryce took the lead on this. 'Don't tell me he knows about the missing Flux.'

Marshall cleared his throat. 'He knows *something*. Unfortunately, one of our employees, Jack Samson, was murdered in Glenmar Forest three weeks ago. Perry is leading the hunt for the killer. Did you know?'

'We've heard about it on the news.'

'I'm certain this inspector will want to ask more questions.'

'Why should it concern us?'

'Samson spent some time in Analytical Services Department. More precisely, he worked in a laboratory dealing with Flux – and now he's dead.'

Bryce and Meyers exchanged glances. Meyers took over the conversation.

'How long did he work there?'

'Oh, let me think . . . Ten weeks, I'd say.'

'So, he had access to this compound?'

'Absolutely. It was a foolish thing to do, if he stole Flux from this site – more than his job was worth.'

'There is a problem here, isn't there? Either Samson stole Flux and sold it, or somebody else came across it at the scene of the accident and realized its potential in making a dirty bomb.'

'I see what you mean.'

'To my way of thinking, the accident seems to be the key to solving this problem,' Bryce came in. 'Samson may have known about the accident, may have known about the missing drum and gone to the scene himself.'

'A highly improbable theory. The whole business was camouflaged. Hardly anyone knows it's gone missing.'

'Not the case,' Meyers said. 'This inspector knows something. You said so yourself. There's been a leak of information, hasn't there?'

Marshall felt embarrassed and didn't answer. After speaking to Susie again he said, 'John Gregg is in charge of RMT. He's available to see you now. One of his team members is waiting outside. He will take you to him.'

The agents thanked him and left. On his way out Meyers took one last look at the delectable secretary. She did her best to ignore him but the heat of his stare compelled her to look up. He winked at her, slowed his pace, then speeded up when Bryce called his name.

Five minutes later Brooks knocked and entered. He said nothing to Susie, just pointed at Marshall's door. She showed surprise, and raised her hand as a gesture for him to proceed.

Marshall was facing the window, hands stuffed deep inside his trouser pockets. When he turned around the inspector was seated.

'Sit yourself down, Mr Marshall, and tell me everything they said to you . . . *Everything*.'

32-year-old John Gregg had no intention of giving his staff the chance to eavesdrop. When Meyers and Bryce arrived he led them to a quiet part of the department. Meyers looked at his watch, giving a distinct impression they wouldn't be there for long. He asked Gregg what he knew about the murder of Jack Samson. Gregg merely reiterated what the papers had revealed. Bryce took over from his colleague.

'Are you in charge of transport?' he asked.

'That's correct,' Gregg answered nervously.

'There has been a cover-up in relation to this consignment of Flux.

Who initiated it?'

'There's a question,' he said coyly. 'I can't answer it.'

'Can't, or won't?'

'Probably Geraint Marshall,' he guessed.

'I wouldn't have thought he was high enough in the chain of command.'

Gregg shrugged.

'It's of no consequence,' Bryce continued. 'Do you know of an inspector called Perry?'

'Not personally.'

'Has he been to this department?'

'No. Not to my knowledge.'

'How strange, because Perry may know about your missing Flux.'

'Really? . . . Nothing has leaked from my staff; and I can say for definite, Jack Samson had no connection whatsoever with this department.'

'He might have known someone who works in here.'

'I doubt it.'

'Could he have known the lorry driver involved in the accident?'

'No. Drivers are sub-contracted to us from further up north.'

'His name, please.'

Gregg looked at the computer's records and gave the name as, 'Thomas Wilding.'

'Are the lorries escorted by Transport Police?'

'It's not necessary, but our drivers must contact this office every half-hour during working-day hours. When the office is closed they contact the Emergency Control Centre. As an added security measure all transport vehicles are monitored by a satellite tracking system.'

'Very efficient. But suppose your driver decided to go a different way. What then?'

'All drivers must adhere to a specific route. They can't deviate from it unless granted special permission, and there has to be a very good reason for such a request.'

'Who attended the accident scene?'

Gregg lowered his head for a few seconds. 'Uh . . . The emergency services would be first at the scene. A Health Physicist would be called in to assess any potential risk to the public and give advice on the safest way to recover any damaged cylinders or drums.'

'So, any travellers passing the scene would realise the dangerous nature of these drums of nuclear material?'

'Some would, I dare say.'

'Could Jack Samson have been informed about the accident and gone there himself?' This was suggested to Marshall. Bryce was interested to see if his answer would be the same.

'He'd be one of the last people to be informed.'

'What if he had inside info?'

'Even if he went there, he wouldn't have been allowed to enter the safety cordon.'

Meyers nodded to Bryce, who said, 'Thank you, Mr Gregg. You've been a help to us.'

When they left Gregg gave a sigh of relief. Their presence carried a slight air of intimidation. He wondered if they'd had the same effect on Marshall.

It was late afternoon when Pez found himself traipsing down Bakers Alley, hands in pockets, looking at the ground. Subconsciously he turned left into one of Carron Green's oldest public houses. An appetizing odour hit his nasal senses. He turned left again and carefully descended the creaking narrow stairs leading to Hadrian's Bar. No nice smells here. Bad smells to some people. Beery vapours mixed with volumes of cigarette smoke permeated the dreadful atmosphere of the place. He bought a pint, went to sit in his usual place and lit a ciggy. He didn't need a ciggy at all. All he had to do was breathe the air. That would suffice. He inhaled deeply, and attacked his pint of Armitage Ale, the strongest beer on sale. It packed a punch. A second pint soon followed. Pez got to thinking about his lovely Miranda. She could never know mum and dad had drifted apart. Pez felt guilty over the nights he'd spent in the Red Coyote. Lots of women went there too. He'd already become friendly with a couple of girls in their late twenties. If Laura knew she'd go ape. He reached for his drink. His phone sounded. Harv on the line. Bad reception, but he got the message. Prescott had been questioned, his movements looked into. Nothing to report. One less suspect to deal with, he thought. More inquiries needed at Seven Moons. The key to the mystery must lie there. Then Pez remembered something the profiler said to Spencer. Jack Samson had to be eliminated from the equation. If only he knew what the equation was. His mind drifted to the horrific scene of the murder. Decapitation. A risky thing to do, even though the light was starting to fade. Who could have the presence of mind, and the desperation, to go so far?

Pez didn't realize somebody was sitting opposite.

'Lost in a dream, eh?' he said, expressionless.

Pez looked up and was struck by his mass of swept-back blond hair. 'Who are you?' he asked, aggression in his voice.

'Special Agent Meyers.'

'*Special Agent* . . . You from the FBI, then?'

'Very funny . . . What's an inspector doing in a law-breaking shit-hole like this?'

'It's as good a place as any. Can I buy you a drink?'

'Don't drink on duty.'

'How do you know who I am?'

'Never mind how.'

Pez crushed his ciggy in the ashtray. 'What have you discovered? he asked, straight to the point.

'It doesn't really concern you.'

'Look, I've an unsolved murder on my hands. I'd appreciate any help.'

'You're trying to link a murder with the loss of a uranic compound. Yes?'

'It's a possibility.'

'What do you know about Flux?' Meyers asked, with a searching glance.

'Nothing at all.'

'Geraint Marshall thinks you know something. The Perbury/Flux link has only recently come to our attention, but you already knew about it.'

Pez knew there had been a leak of sensitive information from what Hazel Bamber had told him. He could sense Meyers was giving nothing away. He decided to play the same game.

'I don't want to continue this conversation.'

'You poor lad,' Meyers said, with a wide grin. 'Floundering in a sea of uncertainty.' He got up and fastened his jacket. 'Fair enough, Perry. Just remember, SATA are investigating a serious matter. Whoever stole this Flux knew what he was doing. If you ask me, I'd say your murder victim was killed for reasons which have nothing to do with stolen Flux. Don't bother wasting your time.'

'Thanks for nothing.'

Meyers walked towards the stairs. Pez called his name.

'What is it?'

'Did you say, "SATA?"' he asked, tempting him to give a definition in the presence of the clientele. Meyers returned and leaned across the table. And now they were close up, eye to eye.

'You stupid? . . . *Special Anti-terrorist Agent*. What *Toys R Us* department do you work for?'

'Fast Action Response Team.'

'It makes sense. You're just about as much use as one.'

.

Twelve

Ian McIver perched himself on the steel climbing frame. He lowered his head and used his T-shirt to wipe the sweat from his forehead. Meanwhile, Tara Drake did thirty push-ups. She sat on the grass and waited for him to regain his breath. 'You can't be tired after such a short run,' she said.

'It's too hot for running,' he replied, still pulling air into his chest. 'I tried to catch up with you. No chance.'

Drake adjusted her sunglasses which had slipped further down her nose. 'Let's see you do a dozen push-ups.'

'Are you kidding?'

She laughed. 'Ian McIver, not-so-special anti-terrorist agent, is unfit!'

'I'm older than you . . . Anyway, in my younger days I could do a hundred push-ups and run twice as fast.'

'Wow! I already did a hundred before the run.' She smiled cheekily and stood up. 'See you later.'

'Wait a minute.' McIver dropped down from the frame. There was something he wanted to tell her and it was as good a time as any. She faced him, hands on hips, legs slightly apart. He waited until other officers had passed.

'How's work going down?' he asked.

'Listening to telephone conversations and spying on Internet users isn't exactly stimulating.'

'Nick Sinclair is aware of this. He has a special job for you.'

'I'm supposed to be concentrating on Perbury.'

'It's costing money. I think we can afford to relinquish you for a while.'

'Money shouldn't be an issue . . . Look, I was the one who homed-in on the Flux aspect. I'm keen to stay on this case.'

'I know, but hear me out. Special Agents in Pakistan believe a shipment of uranium may have found its way to Britain. What people don't realise is that Pakistan's intelligence services have extensive ties with the Taliban. The United States and Britain are on the alert. There might be a threat to this country. Perbury could be the beginning of a terror campaign.'

'It all sounds very nebulous, McIver.'

'MI5 don't think so. There's been domestic opposition in Pakistan. Their President has detained, questioned, and even imprisoned al-Qaeda sympathizers. His actions haven't exactly changed the minds and hearts of his people.'

'I thought he was pro-American.'

'It hasn't always been the case. He has a need to pacify Americans. And don't forget, his country depends on their financial support. A team of his Special Advisors are escorting him to Britain to discuss nuclear policies. You will head a team of bodyguards to protect him during his stay. Got it?'

'SO16 covers those kinds of assignments. Sinclair damn well knows I don't work for them.'

'All right, calm down . . . You belong to SATA now. You are amongst the elite. You have to obey orders, Drake, whether you like it or not.'

'I won't be pushed. Anyway, I hardly think anyone is going to assassinate the President of Pakistan.'

Drake turned and began jogging at a slow pace.

'Sinclair wants to see you, Drake,' he shouted. 'Don't let him down!'

Drake gave the one-finger sign.

'Obstinate bitch,' McIver said, through clenched teeth.

Mack felt itchy as he waited on the sofa in Eileen Samson's living room. The barking of the dogs started to get on his nerves. There must have been three, he thought: two with high-pitch barks and one with a deep, menacing growl.

Eileen brought tea into the room. She was wearing the same drab clothes as when Harv visited her. 'Sorry about the noise,' she said. 'I've put the dogs in the back garden. They'll shut up soon.'

Mack took the tea. It tasted as bad as the one she'd made for Harv. Either her husband never drank tea, or he had no sense of taste. Mack looked around. There was no plant pot to pour it in.

'What's it like in Carron Green?' she asked.

'Busy as ever.'

'Beautiful place. I haven't been there for ages. Jack and me used to spend a lot of time there. He'd often take me down Berry's Yard to a shop called the Boutique . . . I love that shop, but the stuff they sold was too expensive. Afterwards we'd have a drink in the George and Dragon . . . Fond memories.' She looked forlornly through the dirty window. Mack could sense the sadness that would stay with her for months to come. 'Have you discovered anything about his murder?' she asked wearily.

'We know he was receiving large sums of money, enough to go on holiday, buy a new car . . .'

'I don't know how he came by it. I didn't even know he had it . . . You should check his phone calls. They check phone calls on these detective programmes, you know.'

'His calls have been looked into, Mrs Samson . . . Your husband never gave any indication of the money he had?'

'Never.'

'You didn't become suspicious when he bought a new flashy car?'

She scratched her big nose and shook her head. 'I know nothing about cars.'

A simple soul, Mack thought. He knew he wouldn't get much out of her.

'What did he use his camcorder for?'

'He never said.'

'For goodness sake, Mrs Samson. Can't you tell me anything?'

She put her brain cell into action. 'H'm . . . . His sister has phoned a few times.'

'Hazel Bamber?'

'Yes.'

'What did she want?'

'She asked how the police were doing. I told her to mind her business.'

'Very wise, Mrs Samson. Has Eric Prescott been in touch?'

'He hasn't been anywhere near; and I haven't heard from him.'

'Thank you. I appreciate your help,' he said crisply.

'Can't you stay a bit longer?' she asked, following him to the front door.

'Sorry. No.'

Mack gave a quick wave and walked on.

'You will catch the murderer, won't you?'

'We'll do our best, Mrs Samson. Goodbye.'

'I can't believe he was so off-hand with you,' Harv said, stroking his beard.

Pez tidied a pile of papers on his cluttered desk, and looked up. 'He was. You'd expect highly trained *agents* to have a sense of decency and respect, but not this fucker.'

'He could be right in saying Samson's murder has nothing to do with the stolen Flux.'

'If that's the case he knows more than I do.'

'What's your next move?'

'To find out as much as I can about the theft of this compound . . . Something, somewhere, isn't clicking into place. I want to know what it is.'

'I agree; but you'd be stepping on SATA's toes, and from what you've told me about Meyers . . .'

'I know. He'd probably shoot his own granny for a promotion.'

'Go carefully, Pez. Remember, you're one man heading a relatively small team. Don't end up losing your authority by stepping into unknown territory.'

'I'll try not to . . . Has Spencer had much to say to you, lately?'

'Can't say he has. Why?'

'He's showing a lot more interest in this case than I would expect.'

'So he should. Let's face it, he put the reins into *your* hands.'

'True . . . He's been a bit edgy of late. Something's not quite right with him.'

'Don't worry too much. He's probably got a lot on his mind. If he wasn't showing any interest at all . . .'

Pez answered a call. 'Forensic Support. Sweaty Yeti's found something important. You coming?'

'Might as well.'

They took the stairs, Harv running behind Pez. Jacob Riley was staring at his computer screen. Harv looked over his shoulder and gave the thumbs-down sign, which meant Riley was stinking of BO. 'You lot still floundering with this case?' he asked.

'What do *you* think?' Harv replied.

Riley maximised two fingerprint images with numbers representing points of similarity. 'This may help you,' he said. 'Or, it might add more mystery to the tangled skein.'

'Two finger prints that look the same,' Pez said.

'Right you are, Holmes,' Riley said with an upper-class accent. 'They are identical. They're not Samson's, or his wife's. One of them was lifted from the Citroën C6. The other was found on the painting by William Stringer. There are other prints too, probably coming from the people who sold the painting.'

'Could it be important?' Harv to Pez.

'Possibly.'

'Perhaps we should obtain dabs from all of Samson's friends and work associates.'

'No, Harv. Even if we find a match, it doesn't prove anything. Thanks for letting us know, Jacob.'

Harv made his way back to his office. A short while later Pez came in and said, 'I've had a call from Mack. Mrs Samson doesn't know what the camcorder was used for, and Hazel Bamber has been asking her how we are progressing with the inquiry.'

'Hazel Bamber, the Greenpeace lesbo.'

'Maybe she is, but don't quote me . . . I want you to pay her a visit. Find out what you can regarding this stolen uranium compound. Whatever you do, don't mention the word *Flux*.'

'Anything else?'

'I want Mack to find out who bought the Stringer painting, or at least a description of the person.'

Deputy Assistant Commissioner Nick Sinclair was at his desk when a knock sounded. Tara Drake had been prompted to see him. When she reached his office door she cursed before entering. 'Sorry I'm late,' she said. She wasn't sorry at all, and she'd no intention of giving him an easy ride. He looked at her from behind his desk, with a face like thunder.

'I believe you have a new assignment for me, sir,' she said, standing proud, shoulders back, feet together in mock attention.

Sinclair ran over the same details as McIver had done earlier.

'What do you think?' he asked.

'All in all, it sounds interesting.'

'Good. You will have to attend a strategy briefing as soon as I've confirmed certain details. Any questions?'

She shook her head, with a look of disdain. 'You surprise me. I produce an important lead and you come up with this ridiculous body-guard assignment. There are other agents, better trained –'

'Drake!' he shouted.

'And that's just for starters,' she hissed, stepping forward. 'I've heard – on the grapevine, as usual – about a murder up in Cumbria. Nobody seems to attach any importance to it. Is everyone around here plain stupid?'

Sinclair sat bolt upright. 'My, my. You *are* outspoken, young lady. Watch what you're saying!'

'Sorry, sir.'

'The inquiry you refer to is under investigation by a competent police force. I can hardly imagine the circumstances surrounding the murder of an atomic plant worker to have any bearing on what has occurred in London.'

'I disagree.'

'I don't care what you think,' Sinclair snapped, banging the desk top with a clenched fist. He rose from his seat and got to within inches of her face. Drake showed no sign of intimidation.

'There's too much at stake here, sir. A man is dead. Murdered. He was involved with Flux, the same chemical used to make a dirty bomb.'

'I've already told you –'

97

'From what I can gather, this northern-county police force would appreciate the assistance of a special agent such as myself.'

Sinclair backed-off a few paces. 'Look, there is no threat of terrorism in that part of the country. There is no intelligence to suggest a cell may be operating up there. I'm giving you a new assignment. End of story.'

'I'm not happy. I'm going to speak to the Commissioner.'

Sinclair returned to his desk. He laid back in his chair, folded his arms and said, 'Do as you wish, Drake. I'm sure the Commissioner will reiterate what I have said to you.'

'He recommended me for this post, remember. I don't think he'll want to lose a good agent so quickly.'

Drake scowled at him and slammed the door on her way out.

Pez turned off the B road that ran from Mermaid's bridge to Seven Moons. The gravel beneath the tyres crackled and crunched as he moved slowly along, gazing up at the tunnel-like canopy of overhanging branches. The road curved sharply to the right and brought him to Geraint Marshall's house. A double-garage nuzzled against the house itself. The white-painted stonework contrasted well against black window frames and porch. The latticed windows must have cost a fortune, but they added a sense of grandeur that one would associate with a bygone era. A big managerial-grey Merc was parked in front of the garage. Pez got out of his modest vehicle, looked around and listened. He heard only rustling leaves, accentuated by the sheer isolation of the place. He noticed CCTV cameras strategically positioned. A dozen steps took him to the porch. He rang the bell. No answer. After the second ring he heard a noise from inside. The door opened. 'What do *you* want?' she asked with a hint of aggression, looking him up and down.

'I'm Inspector Perry. I'd like to speak to Geraint Marshall. This is the right house, isn't it?'

She raised her eyebrows, told him to come in, and went off to inform her husband. Mrs Marshall was in her early fifties. Even during the day she wore earrings which were like chandeliers. Her hair was muddy-brown in colour, probably dyed. Though she'd had a face lift, her wrinkled neck was a dead giveaway, not to mention the fake boobs that did little to enhance her appeal. Pez was amused by her appearance. He wondered how many rich middle-aged-saggy-bodied women had paid thousands of pounds to have a body like Jordan. At least she hadn't gone in for the sexy long-blonde-hair touch. That would have made her look even more ridiculous.

A minute later she returned. 'My husband is in the lounge,' she said, pointing the way. She walked off, probably to the kitchen judging by the smell of good home cooking.

The lounge was almost as big as the Mushroom's major incident room. The arched fireplace must have been ten feet across. In front of it lay a luxurious white rug, the size of a swimming pool. Pez walked across the room and sank into a grand leather chair with sturdy arms. Marshall was sitting opposite, his eyes intense and watchful. 'It's good to see you, inspector,' he said. 'By the way, my wife's name is Gina.'

Marshall looked smug in his slippers, blue jeans, open-neck white shirt and pale-blue cardigan. A rich, comfortable, home-loving man, Pez thought. The only things missing were a Labrador and a shelf supporting a collection of Val Doonican records. Pez looked at the mantelpiece and noticed several family photos. 'Any children, Mr Marshall?'

'Afraid not. Gina can't conceive . . . What about you?'

'A daughter. She's six.'

'How nice for you . . . I didn't realize you knew where I lived.'

'It's not difficult to find out such things.'

'Why visit me at home?' he asked, irritation in his voice.

'You're a busy man. I didn't fancy travelling all the way to Seven Moons to discover you'd been called to an important meeting.'

Marshall pulled his lips to one side.

'I should be granted more time here at your home, and I hope you don't have to leave me in order to devour that lovely steak your wife is preparing.'

'Of course not,' he replied, with a forced laugh. 'You are welcome here, but I'd rather you ring first . . . What's new on the Samson case?'

'Glad you asked. Frankly, we are baffled. The motive is unclear.'

'Help may be at hand. Two anti-terrorist officers came to see me at work. I mentioned your inquiry.'

'Special agents, I believe. Sounds American, doesn't it? . . . One of them tracked me down at my usual watering-hole in Carron Green. Most unpleasant man. He reckons Samson's murder has no terrorist connection. What's your opinion?'

'I've given the matter some thought. For a while, Jack Samson worked in one of our laboratories that deal with Fluorohexane.'

'You mean, Flux?'

He gave a quick nod. Pez immediately realized the implication of what he'd just said.

'Did you know Flux was used to make a dirty bomb that killed a number of protesters in London?'

'I was made aware of it. The Flux was made at Seven Moons. One of our transport vehicles was carrying several drums of the stuff. One drum is missing. Knowledge of its disappearance has been suppressed. Had to be. There was a spillage of uranium liquor, which was reported, and was deemed to have been non-threatening to public health.'

Pez asked the obvious question. 'Why didn't you inform us about the Flux? Didn't it occur to you Samson might somehow be connected to events in London?'

'It did. I thought it was impossible that Samson had anything to do with it, and I was very concerned about having to divulge sensitive information regarding the chemical component used in the bomb . . . Inspector, I am sworn to secrecy.'

'By who?'

'Initially, the Office of Civil Nuclear Security.'

'I need to make inquiries into this business with the missing Flux,' Pez said thoughtfully. 'Furthermore, I want to see the laboratory in which Samson worked.'

'But those officers from London are dealing with it now,' Marshall said defensively.

'Doesn't make my job any easier. I must follow wherever the scent takes me . . . Who is in charge of – how can I say – uranic transport?'

'John Gregg. He's responsible for all radioactive shipments. I wouldn't waste your time. He's already been questioned.'

'I never waste my time, Mr Marshall,' Pez said, making a note of the name.

Commissioner Henderson saw Drake hurrying towards him along one of SO13's busy corridors. She halted his course and said, 'I'm not happy with this new assignment, sir.'

'Steady on . . . What is it you want, Miss Drake?'

'To remain on the Perbury investigation. I'm not asking for much, am I?'

'Can't be done. Nick feels you would be better placed in diplomatic protection.'

'I won't do it, sir,' she said sternly, hands on hips. 'I should be in Cumbria, following the trail of this stolen compound.'

'They don't want SATA up there. Look, Miss Drake –'

'I insist!'

'You insist, do you?' he said, with indignation. 'You are relieved from your duties. I shall reconsider in a month from now whether you are fit to continue.'

Her mouth opened in disbelief. 'You can't be serious.'

'Deadly serious. Make no mistake.'

Thirteen

It was fairly cold, even for a morning in July. Victor Brooks fastened his jacket and walked towards Glenmar Forest, a place that offered a different kind of solitude to that of his coastal home. He hadn't been there for some months. Located amidst the Cumbrian Mountains – and managed by the Forestry Commission – the forest had undergone subtle changes over the years. Cycling and walking trails now weaved their way along selected areas, running from one to nine miles in length. Brooks had fond memories of the place. During his junior school days he could remember old Mrs Edmunson telling the class about farming in the area. In the eleventh century Cistercian monks from Hawes Abbey managed much of the estate. Some of the broadleaf woodland was cleared to make way for sheep pastures, and they coppiced chunks of the woodland for timber and firewood. Funny, he thought, how he'd remembered those little nuggets of information. His mind wandered to his secondary school years. He tried to recall the history teacher's name. He couldn't remember it, but the story of a certain Luftwaffe ace started to surface. It was during World War 2 when Glenmar Hall was converted into a Prisoner of War camp, and the ace pilot was confined there until his escape. He was recaptured three days later on Cranmere Fell.

Happy school days, Brooks thought, with a smile.

The coldness of present-day reality brought him to a standstill. He knew he was close to where Jack Samson had been murdered, and still he couldn't figure out why this heinous crime had taken place. The thought of it scarred the fond memories of the beautiful, breathtaking woodland that lay before him.

Hazel Bamber swore under her breath when she answered the door. Harv showed his ID card. She sighed and waved him to come in. There was no sign of her other half.

'Husband not at home?' he asked.

'What's it to you?'

'Come on, Hazel. No need to be awkward. I'm only doing my job.'

'He's gone out to do some shopping.'

'Right then . . . What do you know about this missing uranium?' Harv asked, not wanting to waste any time.

'Oh, not that again.'

'Well?'

'Some special officers have been to Seven Moons.'

'You may be right,' Harv said, not wanting to reveal SATA's identity or the purpose of their visit.

'So, why not ask *them*?'

'I'm asking *you*. Who's your informant?'

'For God's sake! I can't understand what the big deal is . . . Rumours were being spread. I don't know specific names.'

'Are you telling me the truth?'

'Yes, I am. Anyway, you know as well as I do it was covered on TV.'

'You mean, the uranium spillage from a lorry?'

'Yes.'

'But something else occurred, didn't it?'

'It's like I told your inspector – people talk. You should be asking these questions to those who work there. I don't know anything. Honestly, I don't.'

Harv shoved his hands into his pockets and leaned against the kitchen work-top. 'You've been in contact with Eileen Samson.'

'Yes.'

'Asking about the investigation, how it's progressing.'

'Me being inquisitive.'

'Why should you be interested?'

'Jack was my brother, don't forget. We didn't get on well, but when I heard what happened to him . . . Perhaps you can tell me something. Anything.'

'Sorry, Hazel. Nothing to tell.'

'Well, what's the meaning of those foreign words written on his feet?'

Harv was surprised, didn't realize anyone but the force knew. 'Who told you?'

'Details are passed round. It happens all the time . . . The word on the street is that Jack was selling information to extremists. He told them about the nasty uranium falling off a lorry. When they got what they wanted, Jack asked for more money to keep his silence . . . They made sure he would never tell a living soul.'

Mack was standing outside the antiques shop admiring some of the expensive furniture on sale. He turned, crossed the narrow cobbled street and gazed up at the shop's name: Willows Art Gallery. A buzzer sounded when he went in. He waited for a minute. An old man came up behind him, coughing softly. He wore square spectacles and had a long beard that tapered to a point.

'Apologies, sir, for keeping you waiting,' he said.

'No problem at all.'

'Are you browsing, or can I offer assistance?'

'You may be able to help me. I'm interested in William Stringer.'

'Ah, the great Stringer,' he said, looking up at Mack with his grey, benevolent eyes. 'He was a rum lad, but a genius, notwithstanding.'

The old man pointed to a doorway which led into another room. 'We have some prints of his work in there. They are very popular.'

'Actually, I'm more interested in the original you had. It must have been a few months ago when I saw it.'

'Gone now,' he said, shaking his head. 'A fine piece it was, too.'

'Oh. Gone now, you say? . . . Who did you sell it to, if you don't mind me asking?'

'You must be an art dealer.'

'No. Not exactly.'

'Wait here, please.'

He shuffled out of the room. Mack cast a glance at the paintings covering the walls. Moments later a plump woman appeared, wearing a long dress with a rose pattern. 'Good morning, sir,' she said cheerily. 'My grandfather tells me you're interested in *High Street*.'

'High Street?'

'By William Stringer.'

'Of course . . . Can you remember who you sold it to?'

'We don't keep records. Why do you need to know?'

'I'm a police officer. I didn't want to alarm your grandfather.' The ID card was shown. 'I can't explain the details, but it would help if I knew who the purchaser was.'

'I sold the painting some months ago . . . Oh, dear . . . Let me think . . . Stringer . . .' She started nibbling a fingernail, concentrating hard. 'Yes. It's coming back now. A young woman came into the shop one afternoon. She didn't stay very long. Paid with cash.'

'Have you seen her since?'

'No. And I can't remember having seen her before.'

'Can you describe her?'

'I would say, mid-to-late twenties . . . Not particularly attractive . . . Her hair was short and black. I think it was cut in a straight fringe.'

'White-skinned?'

'Yes.'

'Any accent?'

'No particular accent.'

'How was she dressed?'

'H'm . . . Can't help you on that one. Sorry.'

Mack made a note, thanked her and departed.

Laura turned away from the living-room window and said, 'You just don't care. You know Miranda wants to go to St Peter's.'

'When I have time, I'll take her,' Pez said, feeling the guilt.

She let out a long, slow breath before she spoke. 'Why not take her now?'

'No!'

'You've been at home for the last hour. You can't be busy, can you?'

Pez resisted the urge to slap her. Lately she'd really been getting on his nerves. He couldn't tell her the real reason for some of his unexpected home visits. Maybe he was paranoid. The emotional distance between them was oceans apart. Could it be she was seeing someone else? The suspicion had been with him for some time. Life was becoming increasingly difficult.

He decided to crack the biggy.

'Are you waiting for somebody? You've been hovering near that window for ages.'

She gave a look of disgust. 'Don't be ridiculous! Do you not think I would have warned him off by now? Do you think I'd let someone in the house whilst Miranda was here?'

He ignored her and stormed off into the adjoining back room. His mobile rang. Mack on the line. He ran over his visit to the art shop. Pez told him to initiate an inquiry into the 'William Stringer' purchaser. He thanked him for calling, and started pacing the room. If only he knew the identity of the woman with the short black hair. Could it have been Hazel Bamber? Unlikely, he thought; but Pez knew he couldn't afford to ignore any lead. He spoke to Mack again, told him to run a comparison check on Bamber's dabs with those found on the painting. He dropped the phone into his shirt pocket and thought about Bamber. Did she know more than she was prepared to tell? Was she involved in a plot to discredit the company her brother worked for?

So many questions with no answers.

Miranda shouted 'Daddy' from the back garden after she'd spotted him moving around. He went out to her. She pleaded with him to take her to St Peter's. He picked her up, planted a kiss on her cheek. 'I will, darling. Promise. As soon as I have some free time, I will.'

Laura was looking out from the doorway, arms folded. His phone rang again.

'Spencer's probably wondering where the hell you are,' she said.

The voice on the line wasn't immediately recognizable. It came as a pleasant surprise when Victor Brooks told him he was in Carron Green.

The meeting place was the outdoor seating area at Weaver's Restaurant, overlooking the fast-flowing River Melt. Pez recognised Brooks by his ginger hair. He sat opposite him and put on his rectangular shades to dull the glare from the white plastic table. Brooks had already ordered two pints of ale. 'Hope you like bitter,' he said.

'Thanks,' Pez replied. He picked up the glass, drank some and said, 'Cheers!'

'Cheers . . . Are you keeping busy?'

'Reasonably . . . We've made little progress, if truth be known. What's happening at your end?'

'We have a couple of new recruits starting soon. Qualified men. You have to be careful with them.'

'How do you mean?'

'If you take on people who are well qualified their aspirations for promotion cannot be met. Eventually, they become restless. Disillusion sets in, you see. I've seen it happen. There are so many degree-level policemen out there who are out of touch with reality.'

'Quite agree.'

'Look at me. I'm long-in-the-tooth. No axe to grind. I like things to be nice and simple. It never works out as you would like it to.'

'Tell me about it.'

'I'm hoping to retire at sixty,' he went on. 'Get away from it all.'

'What have you in mind?'

'I'd like to travel, spend time fishing, gardening . . . And when I look back, I'd like to be able to say I helped solve the murder of Jack Samson.'

'I'm surprised. You're not directly involved with inquiries, are you?'

Brooks gulped a couple of mouthfuls of ale. A third of the glass's contents went down in seconds. He gave a sigh of repletion and said, 'Security is at risk. My services have been called upon.'

'To help with the Samson inquiry?'

'More so, the missing Flux; but the two may be linked.'

'If the two are connected, I can't find the link . . . You told one of my officers a toxic chemical was used in the Perbury bomb. Did you know it was Flux?'

'I knew about the lorry accident and the missing drum of Flux.'

'You had to keep it secret?'

'Aye. Such a disastrous incident could harm the company's good reputation. At least, that's what I was told . . . Marshall is worried. Some of the Flux could have been retained for a further attack.'

'You've spoken to Marshall?'

'I have. A couple of so-called special agents from London interviewed him.'

'I know.'

'Well, he told them Samson worked with this Flux. One of the agents suggested Samson went to the accident scene to secure some of it.'

'Sounds implausible.'

'But consider this: a leak of information has occurred because – according to Marshall – you already knew the stuff was missing.'

'There's definitely been some kind of leak . . . Have you heard of Hazel Bamber?'

'You bet. She's a Greenpeacer. On several occasions we've had to move Bamber and her cronies away from the Seven Moons' perimeter fence.'

'Obviously, she's picked up some gossip. I wouldn't attach too much importance to anything she says, but she was Samson's sister.'

'I didn't know.'

'Apparently, they weren't friendly with each other.'

'Do you think she's connected to the murder?'

'My gut-feeling tells me she isn't . . . You can't rely on intuition and hunches . . . and yet, hunches sometimes pay dividends.'

Brooks finished his drink, waved at the waiter and ordered another two beers. Brooks came over as a friendly, down-to-earth kind of guy. Pez found him easy to talk to and felt he could trust him. It was an added advantage to have a Civil Nuclear Police Inspector working with him. Few would dare to challenge *his* authority.

Brooks clapped his hands together when the waiter returned with the beers. 'Do you know anything about Flux?' he asked.

'Can't say I do.'

'Well, those London agents are clued-up. Must have done their homework.'

'You reckon?'

'Marshall seemed to think so . . . I've done my homework too. You know, the company's been transporting Flux worldwide for years, and there's never been a major spill. The drums used to contain it undergo stringent tests. It's practically impossible for them to burst open, even in the most severe test crashes. They're easy enough to open, though. All you need are a couple of spanners . . . I'm thinking: whoever stole the drum either knew about the shipment, or he got lucky.'

'In what way?'

'Flux is normally transported in huge cylinders which are twelve feet in length. You need a crane to lift one. But these particular drums contained Flux stored in Gland tubes, which are made from special material that is not corroded by the Flux. You could carry several Gland tubes in your pocket!'

'But surely the terrorists must have known about its harmful effects.'

'Possibly. Remember, though, any kind of uranium – if used in a dirty bomb – would cause widespread panic.'

'Hence the cover-up. No panic, and the company name isn't blemished. Two birds with one stone, eh?'

Brooks shrugged. 'Inspector Perry, we live in a world where corruption occurs in companies and government offices. You have corrupt police chiefs in the force. It's common knowledge. I'm not saying the Flux cover-up falls within this category, but some people would undoubtedly interpret it that way.'

'I'm sure Hazel Bamber would . . . So, what makes Flux so dangerous?'

'Water vapour in the atmosphere converts it into another compound which can form a highly corrosive vapour known as HF. HF permeates the atmosphere, and can cause appalling injuries.'

'If used in conjunction with a bomb . . .'

'The HF would form a huge cloud in seconds. Any one breathing it in would suffer severe throat irritation, coughs, and worst of all lung injury and pulmonary oedema.'

Pez swallowed a mouthful of delicious beer, and visualized the Perbury bombing. The shocking images from the TV broadcasts had lingered in his memory.

Brooks leaned forward, preparing him for something important. Pez slowly put his glass down and listened.

'I've heard a whisper from the Office of Civil Nuclear Security. Anti-terrorist chiefs in London believe there could be another attack. Apparently, there are home-grown Muslim extremists whose blood-lust has been stirred by a group calling themselves the Amama. National security is being stepped-up, and we are still on high-alert status at Seven Moons.'

'I'm not surprised. Have these agents spoken to you recently?'

'No . . . But I'm sure they'll be in touch sooner or later.'

Fourteen

It was 11.30 p.m. when McIver glanced at his wristwatch. Meyers and Bryce were seated behind him, patiently waiting for the action to begin. The windscreen wipers came on intermittently, wiping away a fine drizzle obscuring their view of the 'Indian Delight' takeaway in front of them. They'd parked in a grimy alley opposite. Weston Town, East London, was the location. Weston Town, home to a vast Asian community.

'I can't believe Bhailok was stupid enough to contact Habra within one week of being arrested,' Meyers said. 'What an idiot.'

'Just as well he is,' McIver said, turning his head. 'We now have the information at our disposal. Don't forget, Bhailok's not our main priority. He's under surveillance and it stays that way until our superiors at Thames House say otherwise.'

'We could drill him about his interest in the Amama website. How many times has he been on it?'

'It doesn't matter, Danny. Our interest lies in the two men who are planning an attack on a major shopping precinct. We must find them before it's too late.'

The minutes dragged by. Bryce became restless. 'The Secondary Back-up Unit should have arrived by now,' he said. 'What's going on?'

'Stay cool, Jason,' McIver said calmly. 'They've probably been delayed.'

'But what if the Armed Response Unit moves in first?'

'They only move in when I give the signal.'

Meyers laughed to himself and said, 'I bet Tara Bitch would love to be in on this one. What do you think, Ian?'

'She's probably sitting in her flat bored to tears, wishing for a new assignment.'

'Let's hope Henderson doesn't transfer her to another department. She could be very useful to us.'

'You're talking nonsense, Danny,' Bryce came in. 'Everyone knows you just want to fuck her . . . I'm glad to see the back of her.'

'I wouldn't mind fucking her,' McIver said, looking at Meyers through the rear-view mirror. 'Rumour has it she's got a six-pack and nipples like King Eddy cigar butts.'

Meyers grinned. 'I bet old Henderson is at her flat right now, sweet-talking her with better prospects, hoping for a blow job in return. What say, Ian?'

'Henderson would have a heart attack. Mind you, I'd probably have a heart attack if it was my pork-sword she was sucking on.'

'For goodness sake! Pack it in, will ya?' Bryce sounded. 'You're behaving like a couple of school kids.'

Ten minutes later the radio bleeped. A voice told them the Secondary Unit was fast approaching. Suddenly the sirens belted out and flashing serious-blue lights reflected from the sweating walls of the assorted takeaways and shops. Four vehicles screeched to a halt: two from each direction. An inspector was first to exit. He cast a glance towards the SAT agents. Uniformed officers piled into the premises. Two of them stood at each side of the entrance. The commotion inside swelled to an inferno. The inspector went inside and McIver alerted the ARU. They arrived in seconds. The doors of the van burst open and a stream of heavily-equipped men crowded the area in front of the door next to Indian Delight. A few words were exchanged and the door was battered from its hinges. Officers scrambled up the stairs to the flat, screaming loudly. McIver rubbed his hands together. 'Time for action, boys,' he said excitedly 'Let's go get him!'

'Where are we taking him?' Bryce asked, pushing the door wide open with his foot.

'To the Dark House,' Meyers said. 'Where else?'

Analytical Services Manager, Andrew Sharpe, had almost forgotten his meeting with Brooks. He rushed out of his office and skipped down the stairs, ignoring the company's safety culture which included a 'hands on rail' policy. When he reached the ground floor he saw the inspector waiting outside, arms folded. The doors opened. He brushed past Sharpe and signed himself in.

Sharpe took him to a separate partitioned room inside the foyer, cosy and quiet.

'Sorry I kept you waiting,' he said, slightly out of breath from his rush down the stairs. 'I've been busy. You know how it is.'

'Frankly, I don't,' Brooks replied, letting his annoyance be known.

'Ah, well, I suppose your job runs a different course to mine.'

Brooks said nothing. His expressionless face put Sharpe on his guard.

'Now you are here, how can I help you?'

'Mr Sharpe, I e-mailed you a while ago and received no reply. I want to see what goes on in your Flux laboratory. Can I see it now?'

'Yes. Certainly.'

'Thank you . . . I need to clarify a few points before you take me there. Jack Samson was transferred from the canning plant, and came to this building. Right?'

'Yes.'

'By whose authority?'

'Er, let me think . . . The Group Leader who runs our Business Unit.'

'And your staff are well qualified?'

'They are indeed.'

'According to Samson's file, he wasn't particularly bright.'

'H'm . . . Perhaps his educational status wasn't taken into consideration. I must add, many employees were transferred to different jobs as part of a new strategy, you see. It's called *multi-skilling*, and has proved its worth in many major companies.'

'Has it been a success here at Seven Moons?'

'I'm not sure. There have been pitfalls. The strategy has been dropped.'

'Really? Thanks to your Business Unit Manager, eh?'

Sharpe resented the slur on higher management. He kept silent, though he couldn't quite sustain the expressionless look that came naturally to Brooks. He asked Sharpe if Samson had objected to his transfer into Analytical Services.

'I don't know, but he was a diligent and safe worker.'

'Was he the right man for the job?'

Sharpe looked down. His double-chin bubbled out. 'The right man?' he repeated.

'Would you have put a worker with his educational background into the Flux lab?'

A long pause followed. 'No, Inspector Brooks,' he said finally. 'I don't believe I would.'

'Is it possible he could have had a reason for wanting to work in there?'

'I wouldn't like to say . . . I shouldn't imagine he would have been in a position to make such a choice.'

'Thank you for being honest with me, Mr Sharpe. You can show me the laboratory now.'

The Flux laboratory was thirty feet square. It had a writing desk, rickety chair, and a work bench with an array of tools scattered on it. Along one side of the room were three granite sinks containing an assortment of glassware. When Brooks entered he was wearing a protective white coat and safety spectacles which Sharpe had given to him.

Sharpe made the introductions and slipped out of the room. Lab chemist Stuart Owen, an athletic-looking man in his mid-twenties, gave a brief overview of his activities.

'So, this is where Jack Samson worked?' Brooks said, taking in as much detail as he could. 'How long was he here for?'

'About five weeks. I trained him.'

'How well did you know him?'

'Not intimately. He was a decent sort of bloke. Didn't have much to say for himself, really . . . I was shocked when I heard he'd been murdered.'

'What can you tell me about his murder?'

'Only what I've read and seen on TV . . . I've heard he was selling uranium to a terrorist organisation.'

'It doesn't take long for rumours to spread, does it? . . . Let's suppose there's some truth in the rumour. This company sends tubes, containing Flux, to an enrichment plant. Jack Samson could have kept some for his own purpose, couldn't he?'

'The tubes you refer to are called Gland tubes. We didn't prepare any tubes during the time he spent with me.'

'He could have prepared them in your absence.'

'I was with him all the time. Even if he was left alone, he wouldn't have known how to prepare a Gland tube for shipment to another company.'

'You sure?'

'Positive.'

'All right. Is it possible to smuggle Flux, in any other containment, out of this laboratory?'

'Inspector, I work with Flux all the time. Flux reacts with water. The humidity in the air is enough to produce a reaction. Once this occurs a toxic grey-white cloud called HF is formed.'

Grey-white cloud, Brooks thought. For a second his memory of the Perbury attack was rekindled. 'Presumably, you store substantial amounts of Flux in here.'

Owen nodded. He unlocked a metal cupboard. Inside it were rows of large stainless steel bottles. 'Those bottles contain Flux. You couldn't very easily hide one on your person,' he said. 'Wait here a moment.' He left the room, returning moments later with a tomato in his hand. Brooks really thought he was going to eat it.

Using metal grips, Owen immersed the tomato into a clear liquid which appeared to start boiling. Ten seconds later he removed it from the liquid and threw it to the ground. To Brooks's amazement the tom shattered as if it was made from glass.

'How to freeze a tomato in ten seconds,' Owen said. 'The liquid is Cryo-7. Its boiling point is –160 degrees centigrade.'

'*Very cold,*' Brooks added.

'You can't carry Cryo-7 around with you, for obvious reasons . . . If you need to transfer Flux from one container to another, you need to freeze it down using Cryo-7. As soon as it's open to the atmosphere the solid Flux vaporises, forming this toxic grey-white compound I mentioned. Jack Samson wouldn't want to steal it, and if he did he would have run the risk of severe burns to his skin . . . Only calcium gluconate will treat such burns, and you can't buy it from your local pharmacy.'

The Dark House was sometimes used as a Safe House for victims of crime. Sometimes it was used as a counselling unit for those suffering from post-traumatic disorders or nervous exhaustion.

Situated between Beaconsfield and Amersham, the Dark House was well hidden from prying eyes. The land surrounding it was laced with numerous devices to warn occupants against intruders. The building itself was grey stone, scarred by a spreading yellow lichen. Peeling window frames contributed to its dilapidated appearance. It would cost thousands of pounds to transform it into something to be proud of. Surrounded by patches of forlorn trees and an abundance of weeds, it rested silently in an atmospheric eeriness. The Dark House would have been worthy of the 'Hammer Horror' seal of approval, and could easily have been dreamed-up by the great Poe himself.

Sudi Habra had no idea where he was. They'd left him in a comfy living room. He only saw it after he ripped away the blindfold and switched the light on. He'd been there for hours, listening for a voice, a noise – anything. The door was locked. The windows too; and they were protected by steel bars strong enough for the Bank of England.

Sudi Habra was twenty-six and came from Algeria. In the past, Scotland Yard officers had questioned him. Habra used aliases and different dates of birth. They could never pin him down, but anti-terrorism laws were different now. Suspects could be held for up to ninety days without charge.

He wondered how long they'd keep him. His stomach was churning with acidic nausea. He couldn't control the fear. Sweating fear. Dread. Nothing to eat or drink, but food was the last thing he wanted. A drink of water, maybe, to take the dryness away.

Nothing could quell a fear that deepened with every passing minute.

Habra couldn't understand why, but he suddenly felt less frightened when he heard footsteps approaching. *The moment had arrived*. The anguish of waiting was finally over, and now he prepared himself for an ordeal. He had to be careful what he said to them, couldn't afford to say a wrong word in case they became angry with him. Be helpful, he thought. Lie to them if necessary. Don't endanger your brothers.

The footsteps ceased. The door burst open, the force of impact weakening one of its hinges. Two men breezed in. Two men wearing white boiler suits. They looked down at the helpless, quivering figure huddled in the corner. They wore hideous rubber masks: a smiling George Bush and an expressionless Osama bin Laden with exaggerated lips. One was holding a large kitchen knife, the other was swinging a baseball bat. Habra swallowed hard and buried his face in trembling hands.

The President stepped forward, gently hitting his hand with the bat: an intimidating gesture that put Habra into defensive mode.

'I haven't done anything,' he whimpered. 'What do you want with me?'

The Leader said, 'Tell us about your friends. What are their names? Where do they live?'

Habra pushed himself up from the floor. 'I'll tell you nothing,' he spat.

The President felled him with a savage blow to the stomach.

'Bring him along,' the Leader ordered.

They dragged him out of the stale room and down a hallway leading to the rear of the house. He was violently pushed into another room, a room with a damp smell . . . and a large tin bath filled with water.

'Take your clothes off,' one of them screamed. 'Clothes off, now – everything!'

He obeyed, and without warning they plunged him into the freezing water. He struggled and fought, but the weight forcing him under was too great to overcome. Thirty long seconds went by before they raised him by his armpits.

'Friends of the Toxic terrorist! . . . Names . . . Addresses . . . You hear me, you fucker?'

Habra drew air into his lungs, and it all happened again. Longer this time. When they pulled him out they heard him sucking air into his oxygen-starved lungs. The shock was too great for him to speak. The torture went on relentlessly until his tormented cries signalled them to stop before it was too late.

They saw he was totally exhausted . . . but not broken. Not yet.

The Leader said, 'Tell us who they are and what they intend to do, and we'll let you go.'

Habra shook his head in reply. They lifted him out of the bath and pushed him onto a wooden chair.

'Tell us,' the Leader repeated, 'and we will release you.'

Habra took deep breaths. They waited patiently for him to speak. Finally, his dark eyes looked up at the ridiculous figures standing before him.

'I say nothing, you pigs, you bastards.'

Habra had done well to keep his mouth shut, and he knew it. He'd no intention of snitching on his brothers of the Holy War. Habra couldn't afford to let them foil the plan, the effects of which the government would take notice of.

'What are you going to do with me? Don't hurt me,' he pleaded.

The Leader suddenly left the room.

'You could be free in less than an hour,' the President said. 'We know your friends are planning an attack in our great country – and I don't mean the fucking USA . . . We will not allow our people to die at the hands of scum like you, perverted murderers who kill innocent people, like the ones who died in Perbury. I bet you enjoyed seeing it on TV, didn't you? Your friends must have been proud of what they did.'

'I don't care what happened in Perbury.'

'Well, we'll find them. Even without your help, we'll hunt them down . . . You want to be set free, don't you?'

Habra lowered his head and kept his silence.

The Leader returned, dragging with him an odd-looking metallic contraption.

They forced him to lean over a metal cross-piece. His wrists were tied together with rope and the other end fastened to the base. The President kicked his feet apart and snapped ceramic collars over them. No movement. Trapped. Naked. Vulnerable.

Habra thought he knew their next move.

Queer bastards, he thought.

His breathing became heavy again, due to his stomach pressing into the cross-piece. The scenario was ludicrous. How could he ever live with the memory of being shagged by boiler-suited men wearing rubber masks depicting the famous and infamous – depending on which way you looked at it. But Habra had got it wrong.

'Henry's hungry,' the President said.

'He's starving,' the Leader murmured.

'What are you talking about?' Habra said, his voice straining.

Henry trotted in. He was a loathsome creature, an appalling DNA mix-up. Henry was known to have eaten other dogs. Big ones too.

'Stand back,' the President cried. 'Keep out of his way! . . . Sudi Habra, I only need to say one word . . .'

Habra's mind filled with blind terror.

Henry was sniffing at his arse, and purring like a lion.

Fifteen

'Not William Stringer again?' the woman said.

'Fletcher Mack, as a matter of fact.'

There was a welcoming glint in her eyes. 'What can I do for you this time?' she asked, tilting her head. 'Or, have you come to buy something?'

'Official business, I'm sorry to say . . . We're trying to trace the young lady who purchased the painting. It's a long shot I know, but do you think you could help our police artist create a likeness?'

She cast her mind back whilst running her long fingers across a golden wicker chair. 'I really don't think I can help. I'm sorry. As you know, the sale took place a while ago. The lady was gone after a couple of minutes.'

'Pity . . . If you do recall anything you can contact the main police station. Sorry to trouble you.'

Mack left the shop feeling dejected. He would have to disappoint Pez, who was hoping for a breakthrough on the 'Stringer' lead.

He traipsed along, heading in the direction of High Street. His feeling of dejection was bordering on futility. He wondered if they'd ever solve the case. Were they simply not good enough to interpret the clues? Moreover, what was Spencer's stance in the investigation? Lately, he had taken to asking other officers about Pez's perspective and activities. Why not confront the man himself? Was he trying to hide something?

Mack started to re-think the motive for Samson's murder. At first, the terrorist-related scenario was favourite. Now, he wasn't so sure.

A few minutes of 'blind' walking took him to the entrance of Fenletty Street. He turned into it and strolled along, looking into the windows of the shops: JJB Sports, Contemporary Jewellery and Hillside Warehouse. When he looked ahead he saw her approaching

Ye Olde Fleece Inn. She saw him too, and stopped outside the entrance to the quaint pub with whitewashed walls. She looked up and down the narrow street in case somebody else had seen her, somebody who knew her. She slipped inside and sat in a secluded corner. Mack walked in and pretended he hadn't seen her. He went to the bar, purchased a pint of Bombardier and Bacardi with Coke. She smiled when he brought the drinks to the table.

'I didn't expect to see *you* today,' he said.

'Come and sit next to me,' Laura said quietly.

'In here?'

'We'll be OK. Nobody will see us.'

He sat next to her and said, 'I'm on duty. I shouldn't be doing this.'

'Stop worrying, Fletcher . . . Where have you been?'

'Willows Art Gallery.'

'Art and crime. I can't see the connection.'

'We're trying to trace a woman who bought an original painting.'

'What's so special about a painting?'

'It was expensive, and it turned up in Jack Samson's house.'

'I can't imagine why it should be so important.'

'Pez thinks it might be.'

'Pez has some strange ideas.'

'Don't underestimate him. We need to tie up the loose ends in order to see the bigger picture.'

'What other loose ends are there?'

'An Afro-Caribbean hair was found in Samson's car. We' need to know the identity of the person it came from . . . Anyway, how are you two getting on?'

'Same as always. We don't talk much, don't go anywhere together. I bet he doesn't talk about me at all.'

He moved his face closer to hers, trying to create some privacy in that public place. 'None of us talk about our wives,' he said, and then he whispered, 'When can you and I become intimate?'

'Fletcher!' she said, with an embarrassed laugh. 'We can't become *intimate.*'

'Yes, we can.'

'I hope you're not expecting us to do it down some back alley.'

'Don't be stupid.'

She was momentarily surprised. 'I thought you and I were friends. Susan not giving you enough?'

'You're embarrassing me.'

'You poor sod.'

'Look, Laura, I want to experience carnal delights.'

'*Carnal delights*. Sounds a bit poetic, or should I say, *pathetic*.'

'Don't you have any sexual feelings for me?'

'I might – when the time is right.'

'Fair comment . . . Who's looking after the little one?'

'My friend, Diana. And don't worry, she doesn't know we are seeing each other. If she did the whole town would know by now.'

'We'd better be careful, then. If Pez sniffs an assignation . . .'

Laura kept quiet, not wanting to alarm Mack by telling him Pez already had suspicions. The silence dragged on. 'What does he do with himself nowadays?' he asked, out of curiosity. 'In his spare time, I mean.'

'He's started going out more . . . to the Red Coyote.'

'He never said . . . The locals are playing hell over it.'

'I know. Pez has been seen in there by some of Diana's friends. I guess he's scouting the talent. Silly fool. He's too old.'

'From what I've heard, the Coyote attracts all kinds of people: the young, the middle aged –'

'The sex starved.'

'Sex starved, is he?'

'How do I know? He could be dipping his wick somewhere else. We haven't done it for ages.'

'If you want it, look no further,' he said, watching for a change of expression. Laura looked at him and said, 'Let's drink up. Diana will be wondering where I am.'

Looking down from the roof of the Mushroom Pez had a magnificent view of Carron Green, bathing momentarily in a sweeping blanket of sunlight. He coughed noisily and spat a ball of phlegm onto the car-park below.

'Nasty habit, Pez.'

The voice came from behind. Spencer was standing motionless and had a severe look on his face. Something was bothering him, and it wasn't the possibility that Pez's grolly-crunch might have landed on his car.

'It's not a habit, Spencer,' Pez said, turning to face him.

The chief walked slowly to his side and leaned against the concrete parapet. 'Nasty, all the same . . . Have you heard the latest regarding SATA?'

'The bright boys from London?'

'I detect a hint of sarcasm, my lad.'

'I've heard nothing.'

'They have detained a terrorist suspect. He's Algerian. MI5 have been watching him.'

'What's the big deal?'

'Anti-terrorist operatives believe the Algerian has connections. MI5 could be closer to identifying the Perbury bombers.'

'Why are you telling me this?'

Spencer was taken aback by Pez's indifference. 'Headline news, don't you know? And, I have to point out; your investigation hasn't shown a connection between Samson's murder and a terrorist attack.'

'How come you know what MI5 are doing?'

'Ken Rhodes receives the updates.'

'So, what do you want me to do?'

'I believe you have requested video footage of the lorry accident that occurred in February.'

'Rhodes told you.'

'Yes . . . I can't understand why you want to see it. You're losing focus, clutching at straws.'

'Look, Spencer, the murder of Jack Samson and the theft of Flux from a Civil Nuclear Transport lorry might be a coincidence, but until –'

'So, drop it! Life will be much easier.'

'I can't. Samson worked in a laboratory dealing with the very same compound used to make a dirty bomb.'

Spencer let out a long breath. 'For God's sake man, don't you think it's time for a rethink?'

'What do you expect me to do?' Pez replied, thrusting his hands forward.

'Let's be logical for once. All of Samson's friends and associates have been interviewed and cleared. Why not take a team up to Seven Moons and interview everybody?'

'A place that size! Are you bloody kidding?'

'Not at all.'

'They have their own police structure, you know.'

'But it's not their investigation.'

'Inspector Brooks is helping me.'

'I've heard about Brooks. He's unconventional, from what I can gather.'

'Makes no difference to me,' Pez said, aggression in his voice. 'Brooks is based there. He can enter any building, talk to who he wants. I can't go wandering about the place whenever I like. They have rules and regulations!'

Spencer turned his back on him and made off towards the Mushroom's central hub.

'I'm taking it further,' Pez shouted. 'The lorry accident intrigues me . . . I intend to find out exactly what happened.'

Spencer spun around. 'I can stop you if I like. The issue of stolen Flux doesn't concern you.'

'I disagree.'

'Very well. Do as you please, but don't expect to see the footage. Rhodes hasn't got it.'

Harv was making his way to the office when he caught sight of Spencer.

'A word please, Harv,' he said, an undercurrent of agitation in his voice.

'What is it, chief?'

'I've had words with Pez. He's hung-up on this terrorist aspect of the case. How far is he prepared to go with it?'

'I couldn't say. No idea, sir.'

'I see problems on the horizon. This inquiry is complicated enough. He's asked for footage of the lorry accident, would you believe?'

'I know. He told me.'

'I regret having assigned the case to him.'

'He's one of our best, sir. With all due respect, I wouldn't replace him if I were you. He's determined to solve it, and given enough time he will.'

'You think so?'

'I do.'

'Well, we'll see how it progresses. I'm keeping a close eye on this one. You can depend on it.'

Spencer retreated into silence and stared ahead. When he moved away Harv said, 'By the way, sir, the fingerprint inquiry is completed. Hazel Bamber's dabs don't match the ones on the Stringer painting. Thought you'd like to know.'

'I don't see the point, Harv.'

'Well, there are identical dabs on the Citroën car and the painting. They're not Samson's.'

'Rather confusing, isn't it?' he replied flippantly.

'At the moment, yes . . . There's a missing piece of jigsaw. When we find it, I'm sure all the clues at our disposal will fall into place.'

'Your optimism impresses me, Harv. Do you think the killer lives locally?'

'Not necessarily. Colin Church predicted a ten to twenty mile radius of the murder scene. I reckon he works at Seven Moons.'

'My thoughts exactly. Try telling Pez. See you later.'

Back inside his office, Harv started pondering over what Spencer had said. Everyone knew Pez was a competent detective. If there was fault in his method it was a reliance on gut-feeling rather than traditional policing tactics. Spencer often took a back seat and wouldn't interfere. For some unknown reason his mood had changed, and it carried an air of suspicion that could not be reconciled. Harv would hate to see Pez taken off the case because the investigation had lost impetus. And yet he couldn't look him in the eye and say, 'If those words hadn't been written on Samson's feet, you'd be closer to catching his killer.'

Eventually Harv settled into his work. Mack suddenly appeared, walked purposefully to the filing cabinet and fingered his way through tightly-packed files. Thoughts of Laura lingered in his mind. Harv said something. The words didn't register.

'What did you say?' he asked, slamming the drawer shut.

'Any luck with the art gallery?'

'No, no. The woman who works there can't help us.'

'Another setback.'

'Can't expect miracles, Harv. The chances of locating the purchaser are remote . . . What's Pez up to?'

'Couldn't tell you . . . Spencer pulled me on the corridor. He's not happy with the tenuous terrorist link. I think Pez is walking on thin ice.'

'*Tenuous* . . . I'm beginning to think so myself, but there's a real nuclear threat to this country according to one newspaper.'

'What have you read?'

'The article talks about al-Qaeda operatives in America. Apparently, they negotiated with Chechen separatists in Russia with a view to buying a nuclear warhead.'

'Your opinions on terrorism in this country have shifted a bit.'

'I admit, they have. The article was an eye-opener. More than half a million people occupy a half-mile radius of Times Square. According to the experts, the detonation of a ten-kiloton bomb would kill them all, and thousands of others would be crushed by collapsing buildings, not to mention fire and fallout. The electromagnetic pulse from the blast would fry cell phones, radios and other electronic communications.'

'Which would affect the emergency services.'

'And fire fighters would be battling against a sweeping wave of raging fires for days after the blast. You were right, Harv – it's not safe out there. The papers say the Amama is out to cause utter destruction by using nuclear materials. No wonder security is tight at Seven Moons, and presumably at all the other atomic sites.'

'The threat is all too real, but I'm convinced Pez's intuition is wrong. To my way of thinking, the Samson/terrorist link doesn't exist.'

'Well, I wouldn't like to see Pez derailed.'

'Neither would I.'

Pez parked close to the murder scene. The place was quiet, except for a gentle wind sweeping through the exuberant forest. He looked towards the spot where Samson's body was discovered. It was so different now, a serene magical location where one could wander without disturbance. He glanced at the landscape to his left. The early evening sun had cast a seductive pink hue across the sky. A beautiful sight, he thought. Miranda would love it here. He was beginning to hate himself for not taking her out more often. She wouldn't have to wait much longer. He couldn't allow that.

After studying the map Brooks had sent to him he went into the forest. A walk amidst a patch of small-leaved lime trees brought him to a path frequented by walkers and referred to as, 'The Silurian Trail.' The journey was truly relaxing, and if there ever was to be a *next time*, he wouldn't be wearing slip-on shoes and a suit. Eventually he came to a clearing partly flanked by scots pine trees. He looked at the map again and saw the broadleaved wood that Brooks had circled in red ink. Small blue circles indicated the location of two bird-hides. Brooks was waiting in one of them. His powerful voice rang out when Pez came into view. He climbed several creaky steps and entered a small room resembling an air-raid shelter made from wood. Brooks was seated, his arms resting on the windowless narrow slit that ran the perimeter of the hide.

'Welcome aboard,' Brooks said. 'Did you enjoy the walk?'

'Makes a change . . . What are you doing here?'

'This is my secret retreat. It's a wonderful place for peace and quiet. Nobody uses this hide any more, except me. There's a relatively new one not far away. You can't see it from here, especially this time of year. I don't like the newness of it. At least you can see out into the clearing from here . . . What do you know, inspector?'

'I wish I could tell you we were making progress. It's a dead-end inquiry, and to make matters worse the chief super isn't happy with me.'

'Why is that?'

'I'm trying to secure footage of the lorry accident. He thinks I'm on a wild goose chase.'

'You think Samson might have been involved with the stolen Flux?'

'Maybe.'

Brooks then related details of his visit to ASD. Pez began to realize not just the problems related to stealing Flux, but the difficulty in preparing it for use in a dirty bomb.

'What strikes me,' Brooks went on, 'is the unlikely coincidence of Samson stealing the Flux, and it being illegally taken from an accident location. But it does no harm to know exactly what one is dealing with. I think your murder victim was an ordinary sort of bloke. Before his stint in ASD he worked in the canning plant.'

'I know. Did anything unusual happen whilst he was there?'

'Nothing. I believe he did some overtime, cleaning floors and shelves on the first floor. Apparently, he made a meal of it. Some say he worked more slowly than usual so he could rake in more money.'

'Could he have used his camcorder for secret filming in the canning plant?'

'No uranium processes take place there, and I doubt he used it in the Flux laboratory. A terrorist wouldn't be able to gain any useful knowledge from seeing what goes on in there.'

'And yet somebody must have been present after the lorry swerved and spilled its load . . . How could they have found the Flux, inspector?'

'Beats me, but if I'm to help you we'd better drop the "inspector" stuff. My friends call me, Vic.'

'My nickname is, Pez.'

'Unusual, but I like it.'

Brooks reached for his hip-flask. 'The finest malt . . . Here's to a successful investigation.'

'I'll drink to that.'

Sixteen

Jason Bryce felt apprehensive after his phone conversation with Nick Sinclair. Operation *Fall Out* had entered its second phase. He peered over the shoulder of an officer who was waiting for events to unfold on the screen in front of him. The location was Belford, North-East London. Hidden cameras focused on a particular house in Neville Court, ready to relay the impending manoeuvre back to the incident room. Most residents of the court had been told to leave their homes. They knew some big operation was in progress when they saw CO19 firearms officers, known as 'Black Jacks,' preparing to take up their positions. Minutes later a message came through from the van's control centre. Bryce moved his head closer to the screen as The Black Jacks, accompanied by two SAT agents, advanced towards their target. The door of Number 14 crashed to the floor from the impact of the battering ram. The radio-link to the incident room picked up the screaming and shouting from inside the house. Bryce wished he could have been part of the action, which was soon over.

Kamal and Zahir Ahmadi were rushed away in separate vehicles escorted by squad cars. The Bomb Disposal Unit, headed by SAT agent Dash Cooper, rushed into the house. It didn't take long for Cooper to unearth a supply of ammonium nitrate fertiliser. The message came through. Everybody cheered, including Bryce, and he rubbed his hands together as the forensic team prepared to make a detailed search. An hour later McIver came into the room wearing a sly smile. 'We got 'em,' he said to Bryce, grabbing his hand for a congratulatory shake.

'Thanks to Henry,' Bryce said.

'Oh, yes! Good old Henry. He didn't get his tasty morsels after all.'

'But we got what we wanted, eh?'

'Certainly did. We have to make sure the journalists don't latch onto this – not until we're ready. If the Ahmadi brothers have contacts, we don't want them doing a runner.'

Pez looked up from his bed. He saw a clear blue sky through a gap in the curtains. The weather forecast was spot-on. He knew exactly what Miranda had in mind. She had talked about St Peter's church during the previous evening. He just had to take her, if only to stop her badgering him.

It was ten past nine when she trotted into the bedroom, proudly holding her drawing of the church. 'It's waiting for us, daddy,' she said, jumping onto the bed.

Pez sat upright. He planted kiss on her forehead and hugged her. 'What will you do for me, if I decide to take you?' he asked, eyebrows raised.

'I'll clean your car,' she replied excitedly.

'It's already clean.'

'Uh . . . I'll bring the newspaper.'

'Very good. And bring some toast and a nice cup of tea.'

When Miranda reached the kitchen she told Laura the good news. Pez listened. Laura seemed happy with their plan. He stretched his arms to their fullest extent and yawned. He felt happy. A day off work would help recharge his batteries. The fresh air would do him good.

Breakfast over, Pez went to the bathroom and sloshed his face in cold water. From the depth of the house he heard Laura calling him. He'd forgotten about his dental appointment.

'Oh, bollocks,' he said, looking at himself in the mirror. 'Ring them,' he shouted. 'Tell them something's cropped up!'

'You cancelled it last time, remember?' came the reply.

'Just do it, will you?'

'Oh, very well; but you can call them next time!'

Pez dressed himself and went into Miranda's bedroom. She was ready to leave, and looked lovely in her black pants and pink zip-up jacket with the fur-lined hood. Her blue eyes twinkled with the excitement of her little adventure. It hadn't occurred to her that mummy wasn't coming. Pez took it for granted she would stay at home. A day's shopping was on her list of priorities. So, off they went. On the way out of Carron Green they stopped at a corner shop. Miranda was already thirsty, and wanted chocolate and crisps, too. Pez went inside the shop and bought the goodies.

Some time later he was driving through Oak Valley when he spotted a worn sign with the depiction of St Peter's, easy to miss if you weren't looking for it. Pez followed the sign, entering a narrow road which took them out of the wood. After many sharp bends it became even narrower. Pez slowed down in case someone was coming the other way.

St Peter's church sat in its own ancient woodland. It soon came into view. Miranda stared unblinking and asked if it really was the same place she'd been to before. He assured her it was, and as they got closer she said, 'It's lovely, it's lovely.'

Pez managed to find a secluded spot to park. They strolled up a steep road and into a wood which, though small, was as idyllic as the vast Glenmar Forest. A narrow stream, punctuated by water forget-me-not flowers, flowed gently, and carpets of red campion added colour and a sense of grace. The path they followed ended at a single-stoned arched opening, once part of a tenth-century church. St Peter's stood before them. A grey sea, visible in the distance, shimmered below a cloudless sky. Miranda suddenly ran into the churchyard and stopped next to an ancient sarcophagus. 'This is where Spider found his bone,' she cried.

Pez left her to roam around. He went inside the tiny church and browsed at the postcards and booklets. Other visitors were there too. One man was peering through one of the windows at the sea beyond. Pez soon came out, aware that his atheistic belief had brought on a sense of unease.

Miranda was standing close to an elderly couple who were admiring an Anglo-Saxon cross ornamented with foliage scroll work. They discussed two figures on the cross, one of them depicting the haloed figure of Mary with baby Jesus in her arms. When they left, Miranda went up on her toes. Pez came up and lifted her off the ground. She ran her finger across the weather-worn Jesus. 'Put me down now, please,' she said. 'I want to see the cliffs.'

They made their way towards the top of the headland, to the site of a sixth-century chapel.

'What are these stones, daddy?' Miranda asked.

'I'm not sure . . . They could be the remains of another church, probably older than St Peter's . . . Oh, look Miranda, there's a plaque here . . . This area used to be a burial site.'

'Are people buried here?'

Pez read the words to her. '"Archaeologists found skeletons here . . . Carbon dating suggests they were not earlier than tenth century."'

'Which means they're very old, doesn't it, daddy?'

'Very good, Miranda.'

'I wish my teacher was here to see this.'

Miranda pulled a Mars Bar from her pocket and started running about the place. Pez sat down, took in the view, and breathed the bracing air. Eventually, she stood before him and asked to be taken a walk along the cliff edge.

The scant remains of the chapel faded behind them as they trudged along a barely visible path, fighting against winds that were unusually strong for a clear sunny day.

'We'd better move away from the edge,' Pez said, taking hold of her hand.

'What's wrong?' she asked, sensing danger.

'The cliffs here are very sandy, and the strong waves are wearing them away. Sooner or later they will fall into the sea – taking us with them if we're not careful.'

They returned to the church. Miranda wanted to stay longer. She pulled a small sketchpad and some crayons out of her coat pocket, along with sweet and chocolate-bar wrappers. Pez waited patiently whilst she drew a picture. He didn't have to prompt her to include her imaginary dog, Spider.

Two armed officers stood silently at the entrance to Neville Court. The residents were now back in their homes, and anxious to learn the reasons for the unexpected raid on Number 14. Journalists and agitated news reporters were standing around in groups, trying to prise information from officers who were too busy to help them. In any case, most of them knew very little apart from the obvious fact that members of the anti-terrorist squad had executed a raid.

Chief Forensic Officer Geoff Taylor was coordinating the search of the house. One of his officers rushed down from upstairs and joined him in the room facing the court. 'You'd better have a look at this,' he said, handing Taylor a clear folder containing photos and what appeared to be hand-drawn plans. He carefully removed the contents, his attention immediately drawn to the photos.

'It looks like a shopping centre,' his officer said.

Taylor read the handwritten notes. His eyes widened. 'Royle's Shopping Centres,' he said. 'London and Birmingham are the targets. Coordinated explosions were planned to go off in the two locations: same date, same time . . . Inform SATA immediately. Tell them to call Birmingham's headquarters, and make it clear they need to secure as much footage as possible from Royle's.'

Taylor handed him the folder and moved swiftly into the back room. 'Everything checked in here?' he asked.

'We're nearly finished,' came the reply from Dash Cooper who was examining TV and Hi-Fi equipment.

'I see the wall-unit has been emptied,' Taylor said, looking at the alcove where the unit was standing. 'Have you searched behind it?'

'Not yet,' one of the other officers replied.

'Let's have a look then.' Taylor forcefully dragged the unit forward. 'I'm sure I heard something drop behind it . . . All right, let's have it out.'

Two men dragged it away from the wall. Various items lay on the carpet: a couple of pens, a gas lighter and an eight-inch long package. Taylor got onto his knees and scrutinized it.

'What is it?' Cooper asked.

'Don't know,' he said, running his fingers along the hard objects inside. 'It has a "Radioactive" sticker on it.' He stood up and handed it to Cooper. 'Have it sent to the labs straight away, and keep it at arms length – just in case.'

At 10.30 p.m. Pez was strolling towards the Red Coyote. The red neon lights were flashing and punters were queuing outside. Pez noticed a couple of women offering handouts. He pulled his jacket-collar up and tried to sneak inside.

'Shouldn't you be at home with your wife, inspector?'

He recognised Hazel Bamber's voice. She pushed her way through a group of improperly-dressed young men who were about to be turned away by a burly doorman.

'What makes you think I'm married?' he asked calmly.

'Someone told me . . . I find it incredible that you – a serving police officer – should need to come to a disgusting, seedy place like this.'

'Oh, really? And how do you know it's disgusting and seedy? Been inside, have you?'

'I wouldn't breathe the air in there,' she said, with disdain. 'Does your wife know you come here?'

'None of your business.'

'Typical! I thought you, of all people, would be appalled with this kind of sordid entertainment. Carron Green is a decent town. We want it to stay that way.'

'Entertainment it is, whether you like it or not . . . Listen, Hazel. If I let you in on a secret, will you promise not to tell?'

'All right, then.'

Pez put his lips close to her ear. 'I'm working on an assignment, gathering evidence. Give me enough time, and I'll have this place closed down. Then you won't have to bother people with your protests and silly handouts.'

'Are you being serious?'

'Absolutely,' he said, with a quick wink.

She eyed him with suspicion and joined her friends. Pez slipped inside and paid his entrance fee.

The Coyote was alive with funky R and B music, flashing disco lights, and semi-naked dancers. Pez spotted two off-duty police officers standing in an area called 'Slippery Beaver.' A young, leggy pole-dancer posed in front of them. She blew a kiss, climbed the pole like a monkey up a tree, and slowly lowered herself, legs wide apart. Pez's attention was drawn to a gorgeous blonde in white bra, knickers and high-heels. What a fantastic place this is, he thought, teaming with boobs and booty. He went to the black marble-top bar, watching the blonde, devouring her fantastic body. She looked his way for a second, smiling. He wondered if she really did wink at him. It certainly was a night for winking.

The friendly young barman faced him and said, 'Hello, Pez. How are you tonight?'

'I'm fine, thanks.'

'Tell you what I'll do. As you are a regular customer, you can have a *special* for half price.'

'*Special*?'

'A *Nostradamus*. Normally, ten pounds. A fiver to you.'

'What's in it?'

'I'm not allowed to divulge the recipe.'

Pez gave him the nod and slapped a fiver on the bar. The drink came in a tall glass and had several different coloured layers. He took his first sip. Sweet, he thought. Not bad at all. The second layer was a bit stronger, tasted familiar, but the name escaped him.

Pez edged his way through an ever-swelling crowd. He emerged on the other side and made for the plush plum-coloured seats against a wall supporting framed drawings of famous actors. He recognised Bacon, Caine and Depp. The first actor, whose surname obviously began with an 'A,' had him stumped. He removed his jacket, sat down and explored his drink again.

He was surrounded by erotic sensuality. Six men were standing round one of the 'buzz rings,' where a girl would dance and tease. Pound coins were thrown onto the circular wooden floor. The clothes came off – all of them for the right amount. Pez swallowed more Nostradamus and tried to catch a glimpse of the naughty stripper.

Suddenly, a girl appeared wearing a wet-look, short black coat tied in the middle. 'Can I dance for you?' she said, swaying to the beat of Michael Jackson's 'Billie Jean.'

Pez gave her a wry smile and said, 'It's a bit early for that.'

'Come on! I'll do you a special.'

'Like this drink, full of surprises?'

She smiled back, revealing a set of Hollywood-white teeth. 'It's never too early.'

'Not now,' Pez declined, and he noticed the blonde woman close by, holding a tray of drinks. 'I want the blonde to dance for me,' he said pointing. 'Can you ask her?'

Her smile faded. 'Maybe . . . I'll see what she says.'

Pez waited a while, and drifted off to the bar. He paid full price for another Nostradamus, and returned to his seat beneath the actors. He still couldn't think of the name beginning with 'A.'

By midnight the place was packed. The alcohol had dulled his senses, and the fresh air at Salter Bay had put him in good stead for an early night. It was too late for early. Pez's eyelids became heavy. He thought about going home, but all that changed in a split second. She appeared in front of him, turning slowly so he could see all of her. The tight pink dress, just covering her New York arse, blasted his senses with renewed vitality. Hands raised above head, she gyrated her body. His eyes fell from her lips to her breasts. Jesus, what a pair, he thought. She turned away from him, bent her legs and pointed to the zip on her dress. Pez obliged. It came down easily enough. The dress fell apart. She stepped out of it to reveal lacy white underwear that had grabbed his attention earlier on.

'Twenty pounds,' she said, her lips touching his cheek, her silky hair caressing his face.

'I'll pay . . . when you've finished.'

She danced, thrusting her pelvis 'dirty-dancing' style. She spun round a couple of times, nice and slow, seductive and teasing. Oh, how he would love to run his hands across her delicious curves. He didn't think for a second that she would go all the way. Without any encouragement, she unfastened her bra and allowed him to pull it off with his teeth. He became a helpless child, and his brains turned into mush when the skimpy thong was peeled away. Pez feasted his eyes on her perfectly-trimmed landing strip. She lowered herself onto him and wrapped her arms around his shoulders. She could feel his throbber pressing into her womanhood. Their lips came closer. He prised her mouth open with his tongue, and they kissed avidly. His hand came up automatically. He felt her firm breast. This was extreme, even for the Red Coyote.

She gently pulled his hand away. 'We can go further, if you want to,' she said. 'What's your name?'

'Pez.'

'I'm called, Jade.'

'Well, Jade, if I'd known what you were going to do I would have paid a hundred quid.'

She spoke into his ear. 'Forget about the money. I finish at two . . . Your place or mine?'

Pez was too far gone to be rational; and little head was ruling big head.

Without thinking it through, he gave his answer.

Seventeen

'So, what are your thoughts on the Jack Samson/Flux connection?'

The RMT manager, John Gregg, stared into space after Brooks posed the question.

'Inspector, I haven't given any consideration to the matter.'

'Come on. You must have had *some* thoughts.' Gregg gave a weary sigh. Brooks then said, 'The inspector from Carron Green believes Samson picked up some knowledge regarding the Flux. You and I knew all along that a cover-up had been initiated.'

'What are you driving at?'

'I'm beginning to wonder if Samson's murder was deliberately made to look like an execution. Somebody – with secret knowledge – could easily have written a few misleading words on his feet.'

'Writing words is easy! I doubt it would be an easy matter for someone to take an axe and –' Gregg let out a sharp breath of air.

'And?'

'You know what happened, inspector . . . I see what you mean,' he said with a scowl. 'You think the murderer works here and it's somebody with *inside* knowledge.'

'Not many of us possess such *knowledge*. You are one of a privileged number.'

'I'm a suspect, then? Oh, I can't blame you for thinking it; but going by what you've said, the murderer could well be *you*.'

Brooks made a sarcastic smile. 'Let's talk about SATA.'

'Surely, they have spoken to you.'

'Yes . . . I'm asking *you*, what did they want to know?'

'They asked if I knew who initiated the cover-up.'

'That's all?'

'They wanted to know who the lorry driver was. I told them the name: Tom Wilding . . . They also mentioned Inspector Perry, insinuating he knew about the cover-up.'

'How did you respond?'

'Perry's knowledge of a cover-up did not come from my department. I told them so.'

'What else did they ask?'

'Let me think . . . They were interested to know if consignments were escorted by Transport Police, and who was present at the accident location.'

'Interesting. Could Wilding himself have arranged to have the Flux stolen?'

'Perhaps Perry can help you with that one,' Gregg said, in a dismissive manner.

'He might, Mr Gregg. Perry's on his way to Cheshire as we speak.'

'Is he, now?'

Brooks nodded. 'You know, I'm surprised you haven't called me. I mean, SATA must have spoken to you since their visit up here.'

'There's been no contact,' he replied, narrowing his eyes. 'And as far as I'm aware, Tom Wilding hasn't been questioned at all.'

'How very odd,' Brooks said, rubbing his big unshaven chin. 'Very odd indeed.'

'They may have spoken to Geraint Marshall. I would phone his secretary if I were you.'

'I may have to . . . Thanks for your time, Mr Gregg.'

'Let me know if you discover anything.'

Before he left, Brooks picked up a pen lying on the desk. 'Nice pen. I particularly like the Seven Moons emblem, the seven little dots in a horseshoe shape. I wish I had one.'

'I think they've stopped making them now. They were awarded to employees who'd put in twenty years service.'

'A long stint, wouldn't you say?'

'Yes. I've only been here for fifteen years. It was given to me by a friend who retired several years ago.'

'This is where it happened, inspector,' said Senior Health Physicist Ray Parish, brushing long brown hair away from his eyes. They were standing on the grass verge of an A road, some seven or eight miles from Eldridge Enrichment Plant. Parish was shivering under his ancient Parker coat. The weather was windy and cold for a morning in July. 'It was seven in the evening when the accident occurred,' he continued. 'If the driver had set off at the right time all of this would have been avoided. The delay was due to a fault with RMT's satellite tracking system.'

'RMT?'

'Radioactive Materials Transport, based at the nuclear plant where your murder victim was employed.'

Pez's attention was drawn to the broken fence, beyond which flat grassland ran for about forty yards before sloping down to a stream.

'Tell me about the accident.'

'Actually, there were two accidents. Initially, two cars collided. Visibility was poor because of the torrential rain. Wilding was driving a 36-foot flatbed trailer carrying two large cylinders of uranic material, a green drum containing uranium liquor, and six blue drums containing Flux. He must have swerved to avoid the cars. The trailer skidded and hit one of them. It turned over, taking Wilding's cab with it.'

'Was he seriously hurt?'

'Knocked unconscious. They rushed him to hospital and found he'd fractured his skull . . . The uranium liquor drum was cracked open from the impact. Fortunately, the spillage was relatively small and the heavy rain washed it away; but one of the cylinders broke free and smashed through the fence.'

'Big cylinders, then, too big to steal?'

'Twenty foot long and weigh a ton. The blue drums contained five Gland tubes in each. A Gland tube can hold up to two hundred grams of Flux.'

'I suppose you were astounded when you realized a drum was missing.'

'Absolutely; but we couldn't tell at first. I came here with a transport manager. One of our jobs was to check the consignment to make sure all the cylinders were intact and the drums accounted for. Wilding was in hospital by then, and the relevant documents were in his pocket.'

'What happened next?'

'The manager rang the duty officer at Crown Point –'

'Seven Moons, you mean?'

'Yes. He would have had access to RMT's database, which holds all details of shipments as well as destination, name of driver and so on. The database wasn't responding. We had to wait until the next day to be told there were six drums.'

'And all hell let loose.'

'The accident alone was serious enough. You know, accidents involving nuclear material must be reported to the Secretary of State. Once we knew a drum was missing, all sorts of bods came here: our own Civil Nuclear Officers, Transport Police, officers from the Cheshire Constabulary . . .'

'Were the roads blocked off?'

'Yes. We had to send one of our own lorries from the enrichment plant to take away the cylinders and drums. A crane was needed to lift the cylinders, and it was all done under armed police surveillance.'

'*Armed Police*. Extreme measures, I'd say.'

'You might think so, but after nine/eleven all procedures and security connected with radioactive materials transportation were reviewed.'

'Which makes the Perbury attack all the more embarrassing,' Pez said, realizing, too late, that he'd slipped up.

'Why Perbury?'

'It doesn't matter,' Pez replied, surveying the area. 'Could the drum have been stolen whilst Wilding stopped for a break?'

'No. Drivers work to Process Control Schedules. They are not allowed to leave their vehicle unsupervised in a place to which the public has access. If they do, there has to be an escort to keep an eye on the situation.'

Pez walked the forty yards to where the grassland started to dip. Parish followed close behind.

'What are you looking at?' he asked.

'This is like a ravine. One of those drums could have rolled into that stream.'

'The area was searched, inspector. No drum was found down there.'

'It could have been carried by the current.'

'Impossible. The stream isn't deep enough. Anyway, the drums probably wouldn't float.'

'*Probably.*'

'I really don't think a drum ended up in the stream, inspector.'

'Fair enough . . . What weight would one of those drums be?'

'Couldn't say, but light enough for a man to lift.'

'Would one fit into a car?'

'Definitely.'

'So, somebody must have come along in a car, or van, and taken one.'

Parish thought the matter over and said, 'Sounds feasible, but the contents would be worthless. You couldn't find a buyer, and you couldn't find a useful purpose for it . . . It's a mystery. Why should anyone want to steal a drum of uranic material?'

'In order to make a bomb, perhaps,' Pez said, interested to hear his response.

Parish made a croaky laughing sound and shook his head. 'You need about two tons of sufficiently enriched Flux to make a nuclear bomb.'

'Two tons? That's a huge amount.' Pez walked slowly away from Parish and said. 'I'm staying here for a while to have a look round.'

'It's pity you weren't here the day after the accident. You could have seen everything for yourself . . . Have you not viewed the footage?'

Pez stopped, spun around and shook his head.

'Have you not asked to see it?' Parish asked, walking up to him.

'Exactly what footage are you talking about?'

'Somebody from Crown Point's RMT department filmed the damaged vehicles, particularly the flatbed. It's standard procedure.'

'I had no idea. Thanks for telling me.'

'No problem . . . Good luck with your investigation.'

The two men walked in opposite directions. The 'feel good' factor was back in Pez's life. At least he had a chance to view the footage, and if that didn't provide any clues, he would have to consider other options.

He paused by the gently flowing stream and tried to picture the accident: the cab swerving to avoid the mangled cars, the flatbed overturning. What would be his first reaction as a passing motorist? Help the injured, he thought. Call the emergency services. Stealing a drum would be the last thing on his mind.

Pez trudged on for a couple of miles. His mind wandered to the previous evening, to Jade's small but comfy flat overlooking a narrow cobbled street lit by coloured lights. He visualised her getting undressed, and re-ran the scenes as if watching a porno movie. *She was naked, lying against the wall. They kissed for ages, their tongues wrestling uncontrollably. She fell onto the bed, legs wide open. He buried his face in her and began lapping like a thirsty dog. The arse-hair demon was ready to take control. He entered her, and in less than a minute the pumping became frantic. The demon had conquered. Minutes after spending his load, the nibbling, licking and kissing started again, shooting life into the little head . . . The demon claimed its second victory.*

And now, in the cold light of day, Pez's guilt evaporated. Little head was rising again, and Jade was only a phone call away. He tried to put her out of his mind. He trudged on, eventually stopping at a fork in the stream. A collection of branches and detritus lay on the embankment, much higher than the level of the water.

Pez reached for his phone and contacted Brooks.

Commissioner Henderson ran a clean handkerchief over the Queen's portrait hanging on the wall. He proudly looked at her before going to his desk. He flipped open a large black diary and looked at the notes he'd entered for the date of the Perbury blast some three months previous. A day to remember, he thought. A day he would never forget. He got up and paced the room, hands locked behind his back. An excited anticipation permeated the nerves of his body. At last, the phone rang. 'Henderson,' he said, before the mouthpiece was anywhere near his lips.

'The analysis is completed,' said the Chief Analytical Officer. 'The chemical compound contained in the tubes found at Neville Court contains uranium, and has been identified as Fluorohexane.'

'You are certain?'

'Positive.'

'Very good. Thank you for calling me.'

Henderson breathed a sigh of relief. The Perbury bombers had been caught.

During the following hour his phone was hot. The first calls were to Sinclair and McIver. Next, the Secretary of State received a call, and was informed of the discovery and identification of the compound. He, in turn, called the Prime Minister. There was a problem now. Henderson knew the authorities had hushed-up the fact that a highly toxic uranic compound was used to make a dirty bomb. There would be uproar if the public found out. The journalists were hungry for details of the Neville Court raid. Their persistence was becoming unbearable. SAT agent Dash Cooper was under the impression that police officers and members of the forensic team had been followed to their own homes. The situation was becoming volatile.

Henderson made a quick decision to arrange a meeting for his elite branch of SO13. He knew of one agent who would be grateful to hear the latest news. He punched the number into his phone and waited.

Drake came from the kitchen and into the living room. She grabbed the phone and said, 'Hello. Who is speaking?' Henderson gave a password before revealing his identity. He relayed details of the arrest and subsequent discovery of the Flux, and he urged her to say nothing in the unlikely event of being questioned by TV reporters or the tabloid men.

'I understand,' she said, her voice portraying a false reassurance. 'I'm back on the assignment, then?'

'Which one? You were supposed to be working on diplomatic protection.'

'Perbury. Or, is it too late for that?'

'You are too far removed from Perbury. We have other assignments involving undercover work amongst a newly discovered group of Muslim extremists. Or, if you like, I can extend your leave.'

'I think I'll take the extended leave, sir.'

'Very well. Take care, won't you?'

'I will. Could you send me details of the arrest?'

'I shall send you a secure e-mail. Goodbye for now.'

Drake finished preparing her meal. She ate a few mouthfuls before lying down with a soured appetite and perplexed mind. There were too many unanswered questions for her to feel any elation.

A big gap in the inquiry had been miraculously filled.

She thought deeply about unfolding events.

Somebody was playing a very dangerous game.

Laura pushed open the bathroom door and glared at him. Pez was rinsing soap from under his arms.

'You haven't spoken to me since coming home,' she said, trying to suppress her annoyance.

He dried himself and turned away from the mirror. 'I've been busy all day, and now Spencer wants to see me. What is it you want with me?

'You slept downstairs last night; and you were late coming home.'

'I'm a big boy now. Anyway, what's the point of sleeping with you?'

'The point is, you don't take me for a fool!'

Pez brushed past her and finished dressing in the bedroom. Laura breezed in and said, 'Did you sleep with someone else?'

'You've got some bloody cheek!' he shouted.

Pez stormed out of the house, couldn't get into his car fast enough. Laura followed him and banged her fist against the window, demanding an answer.

Pez fired the engine and gave her a look of anger. 'Fuck off! Go and find a toy-boy.'

'Fruitful day, Pez?' Spencer asked, from behind his desk.

'I think so,' he replied, still boiling-over from his altercation with Laura.

Spencer leaned forward and rested his elbows on the desk. 'I received a call from Rhodes. Officers from the anti-terrorist squad are questioning two Afghan suspects in relation to the bombing in London.'

'Interesting.'

'More than interesting,' he said, staring hard at Pez. 'A quantity of Flux was discovered at their home. It's restricted information, for the time being. The public will not be fully informed . . . You can forget the terrorist angle now, can't you?'

'I couldn't ignore it, Spencer. Thanks for telling me.'

He left the office with a feeling closer to defeat rather than relief. Harv bumped into him along the corridor and handed him a padded brown envelope. 'This was delivered today – by Brooks himself. Must be important.'

'Thanks, Harv.'

Pez walked away. Harv asked him if anything was all right.

'Not really. I'll speak to you later.'

When Pez reached his desk he lit a cigarette before ripping open the envelope. Brooks had responded to his request straight away. He took out the DVD of the accident footage that, until now, had been so important to him.

Perhaps Spencer was right in telling him to drop the terrorist lead. Pez thought long and hard about the options left open to him. He needed to take a fresh look at the investigation so far. The difficulties of the case seemed insurmountable.

Two questions were still uppermost in his mind.

Who murdered Jack Samson? And why?

Eighteen

John Gregg was munching hot toast dripping with butter. He looked outside again, beyond the bushes running the length of the pavement. 'Bloody hell. What does he want now?' he muttered. Victor Brooks looked straight at him. Gregg guessed he was coming his way. He gobbled the remainder of his snack and altered the computer screen from 'Market Place' to something that looked more appropriate for a manager.

Brooks knocked hard on the door and came in.

'Good morning, inspector. Are you going to arrest me?' he asked, leaning back.

'Not on a fine morning like this, Mr Gregg . . . I think you ought to wipe the butter from the side of your mouth. It does look unprofessional.'

Gregg snatched a tissue from its box and wiped away the smear. 'How can I help?'

'I'm interested in drums used for transporting Gland tubes.'

'Strange interest.'

'Aye, it is,' Brooks said, not wanting to counter his sarcasm. He kept quiet, forcing him to say something useful.

'What do you want to know, then?'

'Would such a drum float in water?'

Gregg straightened himself and said, 'I don't really know. Why do you ask?'

'Never mind why. Find out and let me know. I'll be at the police lodge.'

'Look here, inspector, we don't keep that kind of information.'

'You store these drums on site, don't you?'

'We do.'

'Then find one. Your physics GCSE should come in handy. The density of water is one gram per cubic centimetre –'

'I know.' Indignation from Gregg.

'And density equals mass divided by volume. If the density of the drum is less than one, it floats.'

'You don't have to tell me,' he said frowning.

'Very good, Mr Gregg . . . Very good.'

Harv was reading a handful of descriptions of a serial handbag-thief operating in the town centre. Spencer was making sure his officers were kept busy. The mundane tasks being dished out were proof enough that the Samson inquiry was slowly being stepped down. Mack's mood was pensive. He watched Harv going about his daily routine. Harv was OK, he thought. The banter and joking was the same as it had always been. Pez, on the other hand, was unusually quiet. He'd spoken to Harv, right enough, but seemed to have distanced himself from Mack. Did he have an inkling about him and Laura? Perhaps Mack's worry was unfounded. He tried to shrug it off. After all, nothing was going on between them. Not yet.

'What's on your mind?' Harv asked, noticing Mack's staring-into-space look.

'Oh, nothing . . . It's just, I resent having to work in conjunction with the RSPCA. What's it all coming to?'

'I know what you mean. We've an unsolved murder on our hands and I end up hunting petty criminals.'

Harv stood up from his desk. A pained expression came over his face.

'What's up, Harv?'

'I've got a curious turtle.'

'I'd head for the nearest toilet if I were you.'

Harv left the office immediately, walking as if he was holding a twenty pound note between the cheeks of his bum.

Mack laughed to himself and answered the phone. The desk sergeant wanted to know Pez's whereabouts. 'He's not here and I don't know where he is . . . A woman, you say? . . . I'd better come down. Tell her to wait.'

Jade had gone outside and was waiting in the sunbathed car-park. She was wearing cropped denim jeans and short-sleeve T-shirt, pale blue. Mack spotted her straight away. He slowed his pace, giving himself more time to look at her. She turned on hearing his approach, and looked at him through Replay visor-shades, well aware that he was weighing her up.

'What can I do for you, miss?'

'I'm looking for Inspector Perry.'

'Nobody knows where he is. Perhaps I can help.'

'When will he be back?'

'I couldn't tell you. Do you want me to pass a message on?'

'No. Can you give this to him?'

She handed a sealed envelope to him, smiled and walked away. Mack watched her disappear into the crowd of shoppers and tourists. He rushed back to the office and asked Harv if he was feeling better.

'I feel like a new man.'

'Good for you . . . Pez had a visitor. She was waiting outside, gave this envelope to me.'

'A letter?'

'Could be. She didn't explain the purpose of her visit.'

'Do we know her?'

'I certainly haven't seen her before. She was mid-thirties, attractive, athletic.'

'Attractive and athletic . . . I wonder if he's got a bit on the side.'

'Don't make assumptions, Harv.'

Mack fell into silence and began typing a report. He suddenly realized that he'd forgot to ask her name. He looked at the envelope. It had been well sealed.

He resisted the temptation to carefully open it, read its contents, and re-seal it.

'Here we are again,' Brooks said. He was nursing a pint of the finest cask ale, sitting at the same table at Weaver's Restaurant.

'Have you heard the latest?' Pez asked.

'The London arrests?'

'Yeah. I'm astounded. I mean, they arrest two men – presumably on the basis of information received – and they find Flux inside their home.'

'I'm thinking exactly the same as you.'

Brooks took a notebook from the pocket of his awful orange-and-red checked shirt. He turned to a particular page and said, 'Here we are. I've written down the density calculation as given to me by John Gregg, the RMT manager where I work. I like to note everything, no matter how trivial.'

'Just as I thought,' Pez said, looking at it. 'The density of the drum used to transport Flux is less than one. We have a drum that will float in water.'

'I'm confused.'

Pez recounted his trip to Cheshire. Brooks took it all in, occasionally interrupting him to ask a pertinent question.

'So, the consignment finally reached Eldridge – under armed escort,' he repeated to himself after Pez had finished speaking. 'I suspect that was a precautionary measure – they couldn't risk another mishap . . . Are you suggesting the drum floated downstream, and was stolen the day after the accident?'

'I can't think of anything more plausible . . . Ask yourself this question: what are the chances of a potential terrorist being there at the right time?'

'Might not have been a terrorist. There are a lot of strange people out there, Pez.'

'But they're dealing with a dangerous, highly toxic substance. How would they know how to prepare it?'

'Interesting observation, Pez. Cryo-7 is needed to freeze it down, otherwise the Flux wouldn't come out of the Gland tube so easily, and it would vaporise more readily causing serious damage to anybody who breathed it in. Perhaps they did their homework.'

'Maybe,' Pez said, nodding in agreement. 'Let's consider the facts . . . Who knew that Flux was used in the Perbury attack?'

'Geraint Marshall, John Gregg . . . Even I knew about it. So did lots of other people: higher management at the Eldridge enrichment plant and their own police inspector. Further up the chain you have the Office of Civil Nuclear Security, the Department of Trade and

Industry. I'm sure none of that lot have any connection with terrorism.'

After a long pause Pez said, 'I wonder how much SATA know about the accident.'

Brooks referred to his notebook again. 'According to my notes, Meyers asked Marshall how much Flux was on the trailer. He gave Marshall the impression that SATA didn't know an accident had occurred.'

'Hence their subsequent trip to Seven Moons.'

'And they didn't stay for very long. In fact, since they left there's been no contact whatsoever with myself, Marshall, Gregg or Tom Wilding the lorry driver. Is that curious, or what?'

'Doesn't make sense. Do you think they could have questioned Marshall again and told him to keep quiet?'

'I don't think so. All incoming calls to higher management are being monitored.' Brooks fingered the pages of his notebook. 'Here's another anomaly. Marshall said Jack Samson worked in the Flux lab for ten weeks . . . He didn't. Stuart Owen, who works in the lab, trained Samson for only five weeks. Samson's file – the one I showed you – has been altered. According to the handwritten alteration Samson was transferred to ASD at the beginning of April, when in fact he was transferred at the beginning of May. I suppose the mistake could be due to faulty memory or some kind of clerical error.'

Pez rose to his feet, leaned against the wall and stared into the River Melt. Brooks joined him. Pez rubbed his forehead. His stern expression evaporated.

'What is it, Pez?'

'Samson couldn't have any connection with Perbury. The bomb attack happened on April fourteen. According to what you've told me, he wasn't even working with Flux . . . Something else just occurred to me. He was on holiday in Greece from the eighth to the fifteenth of April.'

Brooks laughed a little and put his big hand on Pez's shoulder. 'Looks as if you've been chasing a ghost, my friend.'

'Yeah. Spencer said more or less the same thing, but for different reasons.'

'You still have various clues to consider. There's the Stringer painting, the dog hairs and the Afro-Caribbean hair, and let's not forget Samson's very own words, "Knowledge is power" . . . The motive for his murder could very well be blackmail, involving an employee at the plant.'

Pez carried on staring into the Melt.

'Are you going to re-focus your investigation now?'

'I'm not sure . . . Not sure at all.'

Later that day Pez was drinking in Ye Olde Fleece Inn. The whisky and half-pints of ale were slipping down nicely. He caught his reflection in the mirror behind the bar and was shocked at how pale and drawn he looked. Still, a whisky chaser wouldn't do any harm, he thought. Might even put some colour back into his cheeks. He placed the order and was distracted by a familiar voice.

'Hello, Pez. Is Laura with you?'

He slowly turned around. Diana was facing him, and by her side stood a gorgeous brunette.

'I'm on my own,' he replied, straight-faced.

'This is my friend, Louise,' she said, playing him along, trying to wind him up in her twisted way.

'Hello, Louise,' he said, with a one-second smile. He turned away from them and knocked the whisky back in one. 'Sorry, but I'm in a rush.'

'Off to the Red Coyote?' Diana said, condescension abounding.

'Yes, I am. The women are a lot more friendly there.'

He made his way out, feeling annoyed, but glad to escape the company of the nauseous bitch. The streets were busy and the warm night air was filled with merriment. He passed his car which was close to Jade's flat. Earlier, he didn't have the nerve to call on her, but now he felt relaxed from the alcohol seeping into his empty stomach.

The street-door was unlocked. He climbed the steep narrow stairs to her room. He knocked and waited for a reply. A voice said, 'Come in.'

She was sitting in front of the TV. He noticed the short, loose-fitting, purple bathrobe which barely covered her boobs and shapely legs.

'Pour yourself a drink. I'll have the gin.'

Gin and High Commissioner whisky were on offer. He filled two glasses and sat next to her.

'Before you ask, I didn't have your number,' she said.

'You should have waited for me to call you.'

'Sorry, Pez. I had to contact you one way or another.'

His slight annoyance melted away. His blood started running faster, and little head was stirring below deck. 'What will my colleagues back at the station think?'

She sipped gin, licked the rim of the glass and said, 'They're probably thinking what a lucky swine you are.'

'I'd have to agree with them, wouldn't I?'

Pez rested his hand on her thigh, then moved it under her robe. She made no attempt to stop him. Their lips met and their tongues wrestled. Little head stood to full attention as his fingers probed inside her warm moist valley. 'Not now, Pez,' she said, her voice breathless with excitement. 'Later.'

'What's the matter?'

'Well, it's just that I had to see you today because I'm leaving Carron Green.'

'How long have you been here?'

'A month or so. I'm returning back south.'

Pez was disappointed. Her words sobered him up. Perhaps her imminent departure was for the best.

'Are you angry with me?'

'Not at all. If you have to go . . .'

'I might return . . . someday.'

'Better opportunities and pay elsewhere, eh?'

'Maybe.'

Jade poured another drink and huddled next to him. 'Tell me about yourself.'

'You really want to know?' he said, his nose touching hers. She answered with her beautiful bright eyes, and if Pez had to tell the entire story of his life in order to get his 'leather,' so be it.

'My interest in police matters started at Leicester University where I enrolled for a course with the Department of Criminology . . . I have a degree in Criminal Psychology. To be honest, I can't say it's helped me very much.'

Pez spoke about his various jobs and eventual career change. She showed genuine interest and asked sensible questions.

'So, what are you working on at the moment? Anything spectacular?' she asked, when he'd finished talking.

'I've an unsolved murder on my hands. It's proving very difficult to solve; but I don't want to bore you with the details.'

'A murder! . . . Go on, tell me about it. I'm really interested.'

'I wouldn't have enough time to cover everything.'

'Excuses, Pez.'

'OK. I'll be as quick as I can.'

He took a swig of High Commissioner and began his story. After several more drinks he'd reached the Seven Moons/Flux scenario and his floating drum theory. He was slurring his words, and he wondered if the dreaded brewer's droop would be the anti-climax of the night.

Jade straightened herself. 'You actually have some footage?' she asked, with a surprising curiosity.

'Yeah, but it's in the car,' Pez said, hoping to attend to more important matters.

'I suppose I'm not allowed to see it – top secret, and all that.'

'Why should you want to see it?'

'You've got me interested, Pez.'

'I haven't even seen it myself. It's of no interest any more.'

'Tell you what – you go and get it while I make some coffee.'

Pez rolled his eyes and sighed. 'Do I have to?'

'You're more interested in my body,' she said, standing up and allowing her robe to come loose. 'Go and get it.'

He obeyed: anything to please her, anything to sign and seal his final session with the girl who had a New York arse.

Ten minutes later they were back together on the sofa. She flipped open the lid of the Arcura laptop, slid the disc into position and set it in motion. She leaned forward and sipped coffee. Pez waited patiently, frustrated at the possibility she was going to turn him down. Time was running out. Might as well watch it, too, he thought, wait till it's finished and try my luck.

The film began by focusing on the crashed cars, the overturned trailer, the huge cylinders and blue Flux drums. Pez recognised Parish talking to a yellow-jacketed police officer. Personnel from the emergency services team were mulling around in what appeared to be a state of confusion. The next scene featured the grassy slope and the stream. This was followed by a shot of the trailer from a different angle, and a sweeping view of the surrounding countryside.

Jade said something under her breath. She paused the sequence and ran the film backwards, pausing it again when the man appeared. She highlighted the head and shoulders, increased the picture size and resolution. Pez couldn't believe what he was seeing. He sat upright: an automatic response fuelled with adrenaline. His good time feeling quickly ebbed away as he sat there in silence, feeling threatened by the person sitting next to him.

'You know this man, don't you?' she said, sensing his mood change.

Pez shot up. 'Who are you?' he shouted. 'Well? . . . This is some kind of bloody trap, isn't it?'

She switched the machine off, stood up and faced him.

'I'm a Special-Anti-Terrorist Agent. My real name is Tara Drake.'

Nineteen

Pez had gone into the living room after a meagre breakfast. Something was obviously on his mind. All was quiet, except for the fact that Laura was hovering over him, her face stern enough to wilt a rose. He'd answered few of her questions at the breakfast table. His replies were not the ones she was expecting to hear.

'You say you were following a suspect in your investigation? How can you expect me to believe you?'

'For fuck's sake, Laura, I'm a detective!'

'Watch your mouth,' she snapped. 'Miranda can hear you.'

'Sorry.'

'Anyway, you don't follow suspects full of whisky.'

'I never said he'd had a drink.'

'You, I mean! . . . You lying swine. This is the second time you've come back late. I'm really fed up with it all.'

'Just shut up, will you?'

Miranda ran into the room. 'Stop shouting, mummy and daddy,' she said in a squeaky voice. She burst into tears.

'See what you've done, Pez?' Laura said, picking her up for a cuddle.

Pez shot up from the chair, mad as a bull, fists clenched. 'It's not all my fault,' he snarled.

Laura took Miranda out of the room and gently shut the door behind her. After ten minutes Pez walked to the window and stared into the street, not seeing anything but the previous night's events turning over in his mind. *She was damned clever,* he thought. Tara Drake must have known his movements in order to be at the right place; and the Red Coyote management must have been looking for new talent. How could they refuse her, a woman with stunning looks and a mind-blowing body? And how he fell for her. How many men could resist her sexual advances? Not many, he thought.

Pez realized that Tara Drake got more than she bargained for after seeing the footage, and now both of them were seeing the formation of a different kind of jigsaw which had nothing to do with the murder of Jack Samson. Drake had related some startling facts about the Perbury investigation. McIver gave her the impression he didn't know Flux was used in the bomb. Pez pondered over that one, then he remembered Brooks telling him that SATA had asked Marshall what quantity of Flux was on the trailer. *What were they hiding? Why the deception?* Both Pez and Drake came up with only one reason, and one which had a profound shock on their sense of justice. They couldn't begin to understand the motivation behind the dreadful attack on innocent civilians. Their theory was a time bomb. They needed answers, but who could they trust? Who would believe them? Pez could sense a malevolent force at work. Tara Drake was on her way back to London, hoping to gather more evidence to substantiate her suspicion. She was no longer a sex object to Pez, and he couldn't help but worry for her safety.

Laura came into the room and said, 'You're going to be late.'

Pez gave her a blank look. 'What did you say?'

She repeated her words and left him alone. He closed the door behind her and phoned Brooks. He told him, with some reluctance, about his sexual encounter with Drake at the Red Coyote, and their subsequent rendezvous where she revealed her true identity and the purpose of her self-appointed mission. Pez went on to explain their theory which came after viewing the accident footage. Brooks considered the situation. He urged Pez to be cautious in what he said to his subordinates and superiors, and he told him, in no uncertain terms, to watch over his shoulder until the matter was fully resolved.

A short while later Pez was sitting at his desk in the incident room. Before long, Harv joined him. 'I believe you had a visitor the other day?' he asked, his voice rising towards the end of the sentence. Pez just stared at the papers on his desk. Harv could tell he was worrying. 'You're not having *woman trouble*, are you?'

'She's helping me with the inquiry . . . Her name is Tara Drake.'

'Never heard of her . . . Are you sure about that? I mean, some of the lads saw you at the Coyote – in a close encounter.'

'Harv, what I do is my business.'

'Fair enough . . . I'll leave you to press on with your work.' Harv could sense Pez's agitation. He walked away and suddenly stopped. 'Oh, by the way,' he said, 'Spencer wants a word, in his office.'

'Tell him I'll be up on the roof.'

Harv gave a quick nod and walked away, knowing Spencer wouldn't be happy.

Pez was leaning against the roof's perimeter wall when his boss arrived. 'I wanted to see you in my office,' he said, his tone sharper than he intended.

'I fancied a fag.'

'I could have got you an ashtray, you know.'

'What do you want with me?' Pez said, his gaze sweeping over the town.

Spencer stood by his side and pretended to admire the view. 'It's really quite relaxing up here, isn't it?'

Pez didn't answer.

'The Samson inquiry has ground to a halt,' Spencer went on. He waited for a few seconds then said, 'I need someone else to review the case, perhaps head a new team. You may have overlooked something.'

'I'm hooked on the Perbury bombing. You must know that by now.'

Spencer lowered his head and said, 'I've seen the footage . . . Rhodes sent it, eventually. He must have been stalling, for whatever reason.'

'You should have told me.'

'I don't understand your interest in the lorry accident. The Flux incident is water under the bridge.'

'You're wrong, Spencer. I've seen it too . . . Somehow, SATA became involved with the accident investigation. They used it to their advantage.'

'What are you talking about, man?'

156

Pez squared up to him. 'These men – one of them is called Danny Meyers – planned and executed the attack in Perbury.'

Spencer's mouth opened in disbelief, and his eye started twitching. 'Jesus Christ, Pez. Have you lost your senses?'

'It sounds absurd, I know,' Pez admitted. 'But you must listen to me.'

Pez spoke of his floating drum theory, SATA's brief visit to Seven Moons and their apparent failure to follow up their inquiries. Finally, he posed the question: what was the purpose of Danny Meyers' presence at the accident scene?

'I suspect SATA are only answerable to their superiors. They are not obliged to lay all their cards on the table. And who, incidentally, is Tara Drake? I heard about your visitor, you know.'

'It's a long story.'

'I see . . . And what do you intend to do? Go to London yourself and arrest Meyers?' he said, hoping Pez would understand the difficulty inherent in his conspiracy theory.

'I'm open to suggestions.'

Spencer's mouth tightened. He snatched the cigarette from Pez's mouth and threw it to the ground. 'Listen-up, *inspector*. Concentrate on activities in Cumbria. Don't let your subjective feelings run riot.'

Pez grabbed Spencer's lapels and pulled him forward. 'I know what it is with you. You're afraid, aren't you?'

Spencer pushed him away. 'Don't presume you can judge me!' he said, eyeballing him. 'If you step out of line I'll give you a sideways transfer; and if that doesn't work, I'll suspend you – for a very long time.'

Later that day Drake reached London. She drove straight to her flat, took a shower and ate a simple meal. Her anxiety was deepening as she wondered who was on the right side of the law, and how many people knew the truth behind Perbury. She felt danger all around, and shuddered at the thought of the uncharted waters that lay ahead of her.

She quickly slipped into a sober outfit and drove to Thames House Headquarters. Nick Sinclair wanted to speak to her in her office. When she arrived, he was already there.

'Miss Drake, we're happy to have you back,' he said, with an insipid smile. 'What's with the blonde hair?'

'Oh, I fancied a change,' she replied, opening the blinds. She hoped he would say something trivial before departing, but he lingered. His presence was unwelcome, almost oppressive. She looked at him and said, 'I have several jobs to attend to, if you don't mind, sir.'

'We have your next assignment to consider, Miss Drake.'

'In that case, I'd like to see the Commissioner.'

'Why?'

'The Perbury investigation: I want to be part of it again.'

'You know, as well as I do, that the Ahmadi brothers have been arrested.'

'Where are they being held?'

'Belmarsh. Top security.'

'I need to speak to them.'

'No, you don't.'

'I do.'

Sinclair shook his head. 'What's going on, Miss Drake?'

'SAT agents have the right to pursue any lead that may be vital to the resolution of an inquiry.'

His lips widened into a seemingly friendly smile. 'I'll speak to the Commissioner and see what we can come up with . . . Good enough?'

'I suppose so.'

Detective Superintendent Brett was seated alongside his colleagues amongst the high-tech instruments in the Serious Crime Department of Birmingham's city centre headquarters. 'These are the two men who are currently under surveillance,' he said, handing out photographs of them. 'They are Algerians. Their names are Isli Zidane and Firhun Kensai. They were captured on CCTV at Royle's Shopping Centre which, as some of you know, is usually extremely busy. Intelligence from SATA has pinpointed an address in Solihull where they are thought to reside.'

An officer, wearing a baseball cap, held the two photos in front of his eyes.

'They're planning a bomb attack, are they?' he asked.

'Information at our disposal suggests an attack is imminent,' Brett replied.

'You can hardly tell them apart,' Baseball Cap said. 'When do we move in?'

'We have to liaise with SATA. They located the Ahmadi brothers via a series of contacts. We have to give them credit and, furthermore, our assistance.'

'Bloody Londoners,' Baseball retorted. 'We should be staging our own raid. Why wait for them to come up here? We don't need their help.'

'We can't move without them,' Brett replied, displaying open hands. 'You don't question MI5 . . . We wait.'

Drake was driving steadily down Hyeland Road. The early evening traffic was busier than usual. She was aching for another cool shower, and she thought about ordering a pizza and lifting a bottle of chilled wine out of the fridge. She turned left into the quieter Croftgate Street. A sharp right took her into the underground parking spaces of Stone-Croft Apartments.

When she reached her flat the phone was ringing. She slammed the door shut, dropped her handbag on the floor and snatched the handset. She had a feeling Sinclair would be on the line. She was right.

'How are you?' he asked.

'Fine, thank you.'

'Good . . . I've spoken to the Commissioner,' he went on. 'The Ahmadi brothers are being questioned by interrogation officers.'

'What's the bad news, then?'

'The news is good, Drake. You will be briefed very early tomorrow morning, and then travel to Solihull, Birmingham way.'

'What?' Drake sounded, confused.

Sinclair related details connected with Royle's, and the involvement of Zidane and Kensai.

'Do I have time to think it over? she asked.

'No. Take it or leave it. In your position, I wouldn't refuse. It would be another notch on your belt. If you decline, who knows what the Commissioner will do?'

'In that case . . .'

'Good for you.'

'Who am I working with?'

'Bryce and an agent called Dash Cooper. Cooper's an ace with booby traps and explosive devices. The two men are already there, making preparations. You will make an admirable back-up should anything go wrong.'

'Thank you, sir.'

At nine in the evening Drake was relaxing. Before long thoughts of Pez filled her mind, particularly how she snared him. She had to lure him somehow in order to gain his confidence and trust in her. Dirty way to do it, she thought; and she was surprised at not feeling ashamed. She knew he might not have cooperated if she had confronted him in an official capacity. Her plan had worked. And now Pez was probably her only ally . . . but more than that.

She wondered if he was missing her, too.

She felt the urge to ring him, so she could hear his voice. The distance between them, and his situation – a married police officer – made the possibility of a future romance highly remote. She decided, there and then, to see him again. She could spend a week up there, in that quaint town with its grey-stone narrow streets, ancient ruins and wonderful curiosities. It was so different to the bustle of London where every hour was rush hour.

Drake mulled over past events. She couldn't afford to say something that might alert Meyers or McIver to the possibility that their wall of deception was slowly crumbling.

And in an instant it dawned on her.

Why was she offered a job with McIver and his men in the first place? And why had Dash Cooper suddenly appeared on the scene?

The wheels of the organisation were turning in a new direction. Drake knew she was walking a tightrope. She tried relaxing with a magazine. It was difficult to concentrate. A minute elapsed. She heard a faint tapping sound, and saw that a droplet of sweat had landed on it, even though the room was cool.

Tara Drake couldn't escape the feeling of menace gnawing at her nerves.

After a while she gave up on the mag. Pez's face surfaced again, his blue eyes burning into her. Even if he was in London, there would be little he could do to help her. Eventually, two people came to mind.

Andrea Peters was high in the staff structure of SO13's IT department. Drake knew her well. Peters was well acquainted with Perbury and knew about the Amama. Drake called her, gave her the rundown. Nothing came as a surprise – not even the suggestion of bent SAT agents being amongst their very own. Peters could access phone records, itineraries and e-mail accounts. She gave the matter some thought and said she would help.

Dennis Farron was an old trusted friend. Farron: ex-Fleet Street journalist who fancied himself as a bit of a private detective, had his finger on the pulse. Drake ran the story, including details of what Pez had given her with regard to Seven Moons and the Flux lab where Samson worked. Farron took it on the chin. His intuition came from his experiences in life. When problems were presented, he saw them as shapes and patterns.

His gut-feeling told him Drake was in danger.

He told her so.

She took the same feeling to bed.

Twenty

McIver ushered Nick Sinclair into his drab living room. He unfastened the buttons of his horrible-green, waterproof macintosh and looked for somewhere to put it.

'Give it to me,' McIver said. He hung it on a loose nail that once supported a picture.

'Changeable weather we're having,' Sinclair said. He sat down and stared at the wall opposite.

Problems on the horizon, McIver thought. 'What's the matter, Nick? You've never called at my house before.'

'I'm worried about Drake.'

'You told me – earlier this evening – that she is to be briefed tomorrow morning.'

'I did. And she has accepted the situation. Bryce and Cooper are in Birmingham making preparations.'

'You have nothing to worry about, then.'

'Perhaps not, but she's requested an interview with the Ahmadis. It's been denied, of course'

'Job sorted. Let's have a drink.'

'Forget the drinks, and listen to me. Drake is intent on tracing their movements. If it can be shown they were nowhere near the accident, people will want to know how the Flux came to be in their possession.'

'I understand what you're saying, but it's all irrelevant now.'

Sinclair became tense, and it showed in his face. 'Drake has recently returned from Cumbria. Remember the murder up there? Jack Samson, an employee at a nuclear establishment, was murdered. Reports from the Cumbria security advisor suggest a possible terrorist link. The fact is, the man in question worked in a laboratory specifically designed to deal with Flux. Drake will have spotted the connection with Perbury.'

'But Samson's murder has nothing to do with Perbury.'

Sinclair stood up to face him. 'Inspector David Perry, of the Cumbria Constabulary, is the officer assigned to the case. I've been in touch with his boss, a helpful, discreet chap. He said, quite rightly, that Perry's investigation might take him into the realm of terrorism.'

'If Drake has liaised with this inspector . . .' McIver reflected, looking to the floor.

'Exactly! We have to be very careful. Drake is on to us, and we cannot afford to assume that Perry is ignorant of what really happened at Perbury . . . I shall speak to his boss again, see if he knows anything.'

A stunned McIver fell into his chair. Sinclair put his coat on, ready to leave.

'And Perry?' McIver said, showing him to the door. 'What are we going to do about him? I mean, if he suspects . . .'

'We shall have to wait and see . . . If worse comes to worse, eradicate the problem and hope for the best.'

'Eradicate? How?'

'By killing Perry.'

Detective Superintendent Brett had been pacing around the anti-terrorist incident room, biting his nails, for the past hour. When the convoy of armoured vehicles set off he seated himself in front of the monitor screen. An intermittent buzzing sounded from the monitor speakers, and the 'noise' on the screen evaporated into a clear image provided by a live camera sitting on the roof of a heavily-constructed Saxon Wagon. Brett was able to watch the unfolding journey to an area in Solihull known as Chesson Wood.

Chesson Wood was a no-go area – hell on Earth. It wreaked of 'poverty scummies', smackheads and chavs who looked pathetic pushing prams carrying babies. They lived in concrete breeze-block monstrosities and high-rise flats, some of them waiting to be demolished. Chesson Wood had a population of 40,000 and wasn't far from Birmingham's International Airport, making it handy for terrorists to escape – a fact that SATA were aware of.

Tara Drake was sitting quietly in the back of the Wagon, looking like Robocop in her American-style SWAT gear. Skinny, 30-year-old Dash Cooper hardly spoke a word. Jason Bryce was trying to melt her icy facade with his smooth talk. Even *he* fancied a dabble, and she could tell. His Richard Gere looks failed to impress her. She listened to him, nodding and gently smiling every now and again, but in her mind the words 'Fuck off little worm' kept popping up like irritating ads on the Internet.

The journey to Scumland took twenty minutes. Drake heard a voice coming from the driver's communication system. The Wagon came to a stop. Bryce fastened his head gear, checked his rifle, and slumped back against the van's interior. They had reached Raglan Road. A group of armed officers took up their positions in a rubbish-strewn field behind Number 96. The burned-out shell of a car, sitting amongst a mass of weeds, provided excellent cover. Two high-rise flats, surrounded by courtyards smothered in broken glass, overlooked the field. The whole vicinity was uninviting and depressing.

When the signal was given two Saxon Wagons raced forward from both ends of the road and screeched to a halt outside Zidane and Kensai's terraced house. The Saxons' rear doors cracked open. Drake jumped out, followed by Bryce and Cooper. Members of Brett's team were already charging towards the door of the house, wielding a battering ram heavy enough to shake the foundations of a castle. Drake ran up and joined them. The door caved in as if it was made from balsa wood. She made first entry and pounded her way up the stairs ahead of her. Bryce and Cooper yelled their way into the empty living room and kitchen. At the top of the stairs Drake kicked open the first door she came to. Nobody inside. Brett's team stormed into the remaining bedroom, swinging and pointing their rifles in eager anticipation. Nobody to be found. Drake faced the one remaining door. She raised her hand when the Brummies came up behind her. They stopped and listened. A faint voice could be heard above the panting of Brett's men. To Drake, it sounded like someone praying. She pushed the door with the butt of her rifle and looked down at the pitiful figure of Mrs Zidane, who had made it to the toilet just in time. Drake noticed her trembling hands and saw the fear in her dark eyes. The prayers stopped. The tears kept falling. She held out a feeble hand. Drake wanted to comfort her, but the sound of an explosion wrecked the nerves of her stomach. The old woman screamed loudly.

Confusion reigned. The Brummies immediately called for helicopter support, rushed downstairs and out into the smoke-filled field behind the house.

Bryce and Cooper searched in vain.

The terrorists were nowhere to be found.

Mrs Zidane suffered a heart attack that nearly killed her.

Harv and Mack were talking quietly to each other in the conference room. Pez was smoking a cigarette and staring out of the window towards Hawes Fell.

'Spencer will be here any minute. He doesn't like smoking in here,' Harv reminded him.

'Who cares? For all I know I might not be leading the investigation from now on.'

'Don't talk stupid,' Mack said. 'There is nobody else capable of taking over. Spencer will back off. You wait and see.'

'You'll be fine,' Harv added. 'Anyway, what's with this SAT agent, Drake?'

Pez flicked the butt out of an open window. 'How do you mean?'

'Have you heard anything?'

'Only what I told you. She was interested in the Samson case, came here to have a sniff around. That's all.'

'Are you sure?' Mack said, grinning.

'Yes, Mack . . . How's your work with the RSPCA coming along?'

'Don't rub it in.'

'Caught the handbag thief, Harv?'

'I don't want to talk about it.'

'One thing for sure – we ain't closer to catching Samson's killer . . . Spencer's here now.'

All eyes were on Spencer when he came in. He grabbed a chair and said, 'There's a trace of smoke in the air.'

'Sorry,' Pez said, with nonchalance. 'I only had a third of a fag.'

Spencer gave a look of disapproval. He moaned about his stomach ailment and then discussed the backgrounds of two new recruits. Pez guessed everything would be all right, and waited patiently for the moment of truth. Spencer looked directly at him. 'To more serious matters . . . We now know that Jack Samson had no connection whatsoever with the missing Flux. What we are looking at is almost certainly blackmail. Over to you, Pez.'

Pez was taken back. He composed himself. 'Right . . . The holiday in Greece, the new car, the Stringer painting . . .'

'You missed the camcorder,' Harv came in. 'It's my belief the camcorder is an integral part of the circumstances surrounding his death.'

'Yeah, but we haven't been able to discover what it was used for,' Pez said.

He felt immense relief. Their present conversation could only mean he was still in charge of the inquiry.

'The camcorder could have been used for *innocent* purposes,' Spencer suggested. 'I'm surprised we didn't locate the dark-haired lady who purchased the painting – a regrettable failure, gentlemen. However, we can focus on our main suspects . . . Brian Pill spoke to Samson shortly before he was murdered. In my opinion Pill is a viable suspect. The other players in this drama include the people who came into contact with Samson during the months prior to his death, and those who possess knowledge of the Flux/Perbury link.'

'What has that got to do with it?' Harv asked.

'The person who wrote *Allahu Akbar* on his feet was using Samson's experience of working with Flux as a way of implicating him with terrorism.'

'Who are the other suspects?' Mack asked.

'Geraint Marshall, John Gregg, Andrew Sharpe, Stuart Owen and Inspector Brooks.'

'Why Brooks?' Pez asked, alarmed.

'He knew the Flux had been stolen, and he kept it to himself.'

'Only because he was ordered to. Look, Spencer, I for one am not going to start throwing questions at Victor Brooks. He's helping me, remember. I can trust him.'

Spencer considered. Finally, he said, 'It's not a matter of trust.'

'Look, I would need his permission to question the other suspects. If he knows he's in the frame, how do you think he'll react? He's not going to offer any assistance at all, is he?'

'I see what you mean. All right, Pez. Omit Brooks for the time being.'

Pez pulled his bleeping phone from his trouser pocket. The news message read: Anti-terrorist officers in botched Solihull raid. Explosion hampers investigation.

'What is it?' Spencer asked.

Pez repeated the message and switched the phone off. After five minutes of further discussion they all left the conference room.

Back in his office Spencer paced up and down in worried contemplation. He gingerly picked up the phone, paused and replaced it. He could feel his stomach churning from mixed emotions. He waited, half-expecting the phone to ring. It didn't. The passing minutes were like hours. The tension became unbearable.

Finally, he dialled the number.

McIver's voice sounded from the other end.

It was 11 p.m. when Dennis Farron left Clancy's Bar in Grosvenor Square. The New Orleans-style music of the Yerba Buena Band was playing inside his head – great, uplifting music that, sadly, wasn't popular. His pace became slower when the telephone kiosk came into view.

Drake switched the hair dryer off and reached for the phone. She knew it was Farron by the sound of his rich, deep voice. She wasted no time in relaying the day's events to him.

'You say a bomb went off at the back of the house?'

'That's right. It wasn't big enough to cause serious damage.'

'The terrorists must have known about the raid. They might have been warned.'

'But how?'

'By who. And why detonate a bomb when they should be fleeing the country? It's suspicious, Tara. Highly suspicious.'

'Well, the airports are under observation and the news programmes are showing pictures of Zidane and Kensai, taken from Royle's CCTV records.' Silence followed. 'Are you there, Dennis?'

'Yes. I'm trying to work out what could be happening . . . Have you had any phone calls or visitors?'

'Come to think of it, I haven't.'

'Be careful. You're in the thick of it . . . By the way I spoke to your friend, Andrea Peters. I did some heavy research into the properties and uses of Flux, and Peters played detective for me. Are you ready for this?'

'As ready as I'll ever be.'

'In March, our friend Meyers took sick leave and went to see his own doctor. After some tedious leg-work I discovered he'd been to the London Hospital. The records for the date in question show that a certain Danny Seaton was treated for HF fume inhalation. They used some kind of Calcium Gluconate nebulizer for his damaged lungs; and remember, Perbury occurred in April. See what I'm getting at?'

'I do.'

'*Seaton* is his mother's maiden name. He used her address. So now you know. Keep the lid on it, Tara. Promise?'

'I promise. Anything else?'

'Dash Cooper was the first person of the Forensic Team to enter the house at Neville Court. That's all I can tell you about him.'

'Thanks for your help.'

'Take care. Bye.'

Farron continued his journey home, his job done. The Yerba Buena music started playing again. He erased it with thoughts of Drake, and how she'd been unwittingly sucked into a mesh of conspiracy and danger.

Later Drake switched her computer on. Several recent e-mails had been sent. Andrea Peter's innocuous subject title caught her eye: Women's Magazines. The message was short: Amama website is part English, part Arabic. Logo, on first page, has three small dragons incorporated into it. Could be wild coincidence, but Cooper's e-mail add. is, *dash_dragon3@hotmail.com*. Cooper is an exceptionally versatile SAT agent. He spent some time in Iraq working on house-clearing missions.

Drake, numbed by what she'd read, deleted the message. She took a bottle of wine to the settee and remained there till the early hours, trying to drink away the anxiety caused by her hopeless situation.

She longed for Pez to be with her.

He was the only person who could help her now.

Twenty-one

'I've read the report!' Sinclair barked. 'Bhailok is a minor player in the terrorist network. There is nothing we can charge him with, don't you see?'

'So, he's being deported?' McIver asked, incredulity in his voice.

Sinclair thrust his hands forward and said, 'If he is deported, it's one less to worry about.'

'We should have dealt with him in our own way.'

'Not a good idea, Ian. The situation is becoming critical, especially with Drake hanging around. Henderson's in a flap, and a thousand journalists are banging on our doors. They're practically coming down the chimneys. You must have noticed!'

Their conversation had started lightly, and gradually ascended to a sharpness that betrayed Sinclair's cool demeanour. McIver looked as if he was going to lose his temper. He gritted his teeth and said, 'Look, you've prepared a statement. Maybe that will be enough to pacify the media for the time being.'

Sinclair shook his head slowly and frowned. McIver calmed himself and said, 'Nick, stop worrying and listen. The Ahmadis haven't said a word to anybody, and even if they deny being the bombers, no one is going to believe them. We have Drake safely back in London and Danny is watching her every move. No sweat. No problem.'

Sinclair made a deadly smile. 'You think so? If it wasn't for the likes of her, Bryce and Cooper would probably have shot Zidane and Kensai. The raid took place two days ago, and already Forensics have discovered evidence which suggests they were positioned on the balcony of a high-rise flat overlooking their home. It doesn't take a genius to ask, "What were they doing there? How did they know a raid was imminent?"'

'Blame the terrorist network. Blame the Amama. Tell the press and our security officers how organised and cunning they are. People will have to accept what you say.'

'I shall have to give this special consideration. The last thing I want is for Henderson to conclude the Solihull terrorists were tipped-off.'

'When are we going to the church again, daddy?' Miranda asked, as she tried to pull the head off her teddy bear.

Pez was watching the news update, elbows on knees, hands cupped. 'What did you say, Miranda?'

'I want to go to Salter Bay again. '

'I'll take you, soon. Promise,' he replied, staring at the TV.

The house on Raglan Road was surrounded by armed police and detectives from Birmingham's CID. The camera man, situated on the wasteland behind the house, started filming the shell of the car where the bomb had been planted. His shots also captured the broken windows and the grey-coloured, high-rise flats that had been cordoned off. A news reporter, standing in front of the house, gave some background information that led to the planning of the raid. He quoted Sinclair as saying the terrorists were tipped-off by members of a cell operating in London and Birmingham.

Miranda started tugging Pez's shirt sleeve, saying she wanted to go to the shop. Her voice failed to penetrate his concentration. He knew Drake was involved in the raid, and her message to him gave some indication of the evil corruption surrounding her.

'Well?' Laura said in a high-pitched voice.

'What's the matter?' Pez said, lowering the volume.

'Are you going to take her to the shop, or what?'

'I want some of those new sweeties, daddy,' Miranda whined.

'I'll take you in a minute, sweetheart.' To Laura, he said, 'I thought you were supposed to be working today.'

'I am. Diana's coming here, but she's late.'

Laura's voice was strained. Pez scowled at her. She promptly left the room. Pez had an impression she wanted him to leave the house. Miranda provided the opportunity. She smiled at him when he stood up. 'Come on, then,' he said. 'What are these new sweeties called?'

'I think they're called Skellies. They have monsters' faces on them.'

Miranda ran out into the driveway and waited for Pez. When they passed the front of the house he caught something in his peripheral vision. He looked towards the window as the curtain fell back into place. He felt certain Laura was watching him, the cordless phone to her ear.

At Walker's Newsagent he bought some cigarettes and two packets of Skellies. Miranda couldn't wait to open one of them. On the way home she munched her sweeties and rambled on about her friend, Tom, and how he'd hurt his leg by falling off a trolley his dad had made for him. Once again, Pez wasn't listening. He could think only of Tara Drake and the terrible predicament she was in.

Diana was waiting for them in the front garden. 'Has Laura gone?' Pez asked.

'She left a few minutes ago,' she replied.

'I didn't see her at the bus stop,' he said suspiciously.

'The bus must have been early.'

Odd, he thought. 'I'd better be on my way. Look after Miranda.'

'Of course I will.'

Diana took Miranda into the house. Pez got into his car and answered his mobile. He was relieved to hear Drake's voice. 'Are you all right, Tara?' he asked.

'I'm fine. And you?'

'Not so bad, thanks. What's happening at the moment?'

'Right now, very little. I'm waiting for an update from Sinclair. I've been sitting around, pondering over the Perbury attack and the Ahmadi brothers. I wanted to talk to them, you know. No chance. Next minute, I find myself travelling to Birmingham to participate in a raid. The only person I came across was an aged Algerian woman who nearly died on us.'

'Don't worry yourself too much. I might be able to join you for a few days.'

'I'd really like to see you, Pez, but you should stay away for now. If Meyers or somebody sees you, anything could happen.'

'I understand. What you need is tangible evidence. Remember, I'm prepared to give you full support.'

'That's a comfort to know. I have something important to tell you . . .'

She relayed what Farron and Peters had unearthed.

'Have you told anybody else?' Pez asked.

'Not a soul.'

'Good. It might be better if you stay indoors. Should anything transpire, give me a call.'

'Pez, I have to do some shopping. Even SAT agents must eat. I shan't be out for long.'

'Well, take care . . . Bye for now.'

They walked down Fenletty Street, shouldering through the lunchtime rush.

'Have you time for a drink?' Mack asked.

'I guessed that was the general idea,' Laura replied, looking at her reflection in the shop windows, checking her hair was OK.

Ye Olde Fleece Inn was busy. She waited amongst the crowd whilst Mack tried to catch the barmaid's eye. After a few minutes he returned and gave her a glass of Coke.

'I don't think this is going to work,' she said, her eyes darting around.

Mack was accidentally pushed. 'Blast,' he said, looking at his beer-stained shirt. 'What do you mean?'

'You and me. Wherever we go in this town there's always someone I recognise.'

'You work in a shop. You're bound to see people you know.'

'I'm not happy with the way it's going; and don't think for one minute I'm going to let you bonk me in a car.'

A breakthrough for Mack. She *was* up for it. 'I can think of lots of quiet places,' he said, half joking.

'And when are we going to have time to do it? We're both very busy.'

'Brighten up, Laura. Don't put obstacles in the way . . . Anyway, how's Miranda these days? Enjoying the holidays?'

'*Holidays*. They last forever.'

'Can't be too bad. I mean, you've only got the one child to look after.'

'Mack, you don't even have any kids! How would you know what's involved?'

Mack shrugged, then said, 'We never planned to have any. Mind you, I do know how to handle them.'

'Of course you do,' she said with a sarcastic smile.

Mack looked around for a seat. 'It's a bit crowded in here. I think we'll try somewhere else next time.'

'Good idea . . . Mack, you haven't told me anything about Susan. What's she like?'

'There's not much I can say about Susan. She lives a life of luxury . . . Not much good in bed.'

'You're still having sex, then?' she said, feeling a pang of jealousy.

Mack was looking out of the window, his eyes narrowing with concentration.

'What is it? Somebody you know?'

Mack gave no reply. 'Here, hold this,' he said. She took the glass of ale and watched him worm his way out of the pub. She was left standing there, puzzled and wondering what to do next. She waited a couple of minutes and made her exit. Outside, she turned her head, looking in both directions. She caught sight of him at the bottom of the street. He waited for her to reach him.

'What the hell was all that about?' she asked.

Mack was slightly out of breath, and looking about the place trying to catch a glimpse of the woman. 'You must go, Laura. Pez is on his way.'

'Aren't you going to tell me who –'

'I can't explain now. Go before you end up in trouble.'

Laura walked away as quick as she could. Mack watched her melt into the shopping crowd. He managed to compose himself before Pez arrived, in record time.

'This is where you saw her?' he asked, looking everywhere.

'I saw her from further up the street. When I got here, she was gone. I looked in a couple of the shops . . .'

'You sure she was Afro-Caribbean?'

'Absolutely certain.'

'What was she wearing?'

'I think she had a white dress on.'

'Age?'

'Around thirty.'

'Build?'

173

'Slim.'

'You did well to spot her . . . Where, exactly, were you at the time?'

'I was, I was looking for a present for Susan's birthday,' he said, in a different voice.

'Susan's birthday is next month, isn't it?'

'You know what it's like, Pez. If I leave it to the last minute . . .'

'Yeah, I know what it's like . . . I remember you telling me that you never drank alone,' Pez said, feeling the damp, brown stain on Mack's shirt.

Drake could have heard a whisper when she got out of her car. She lifted her grocery bag off the back seat and locked the door. She looked and listened. A distant rattling noise smothered the electric buzzing from a faulty security light of the underground car-park. She moved uneasily towards the lift' doors and turned suddenly. What was that? she thought, her hand automatically reaching under her jacket for the holstered pistol. But sounds in there echoed. It was impossible to tell where they came from. The lift whined and halted. The doors slid open, the empty space offering temporary relief. That edgy, nervous feeling had started when she was driving back from the Late Shop. She felt certain someone was following her. She cursed for not having gone earlier.

Apart from speaking to Pez, the day had been ominously quiet. Drake knew she was trapped. She was a fly in a web, wondering which spider would come for her.

At 11.30 p.m. she cracked open a bottle of 57 Special red wine and listened to the soothing voice of Celia Johnson. Still, it made little difference. She couldn't escape the fear of uncertainty. She wondered what to do. Tell Henderson everything? But there was no way of knowing if Henderson himself was involved. Eventually, she succumbed to a tiredness that had been festering for days. Sleep came. And sleep went. The Visitor Signal sounded. She was half asleep and woke up startled. She looked towards the screen. A sickly feeling came over her. The wavy blond hair was immediately recognisable. *Was this the spider*?

He knocked instead of ringing the bell. 'Tara! Are you going to let me in?'

She opened the door and said, 'Have I any choice?' She turned and walked purposely slow, giving him time to ogle her delicious figure, just visible under a flimsy nightgown. 'Let me take your jacket.'

'Thanks. Hey, I love the hair colour.'

'Makes a change, doesn't it?'

Drake knew she had to play for time, and she knew Meyers would find her irresistible. *Her plan was already being hatched.*

'Sit down,' she said, pointing at the settee. 'I'll fix you a drink.'

Meyers made himself comfy. Celia Johnson was still playing in the background. He picked up a Health and Fitness magazine, flicked through the pages and tossed it to one side when she appeared. He took the glass from her hand. 'Jesus! I'm driving, you know.'

'Big lad like you can take it,' she said, falling into a chair opposite him. She crossed her leg, well aware that an acre of tempting succulent thigh was on view. 'What brings you here, Danny? Have the Solihull terrorists been arrested already?'

'It's early days. Every police force in Britain is on the alert. Calls are flooding into HQ, and Sinclair is staying in Birmingham for a day or two, working alongside their anti-terror boys.'

'That's all you've got to say?'

'I wanted to make sure you were OK.'

'Is there a problem, Danny?'

'Well, we believe the Amama are going to target SATA.'

She pulled a face. 'You kidding? No chance. How could they instigate such an operation?'

'It's happening, Tara . . . You were followed tonight.'

'What!' she gasped.

'I lost the target vehicle. Couldn't even get close enough to see the registration. Anyway, they probably use false plates . . . Fortunately, you're all right.'

She didn't believe him. She paused before taking a drink. He copied. That's what she wanted. She decided to play into his hands. 'Will you stay with me for a while? It's lonely up here.'

'I'll stay as long as you like,' he replied, with a conviction that betrayed his ulterior motive.

Drake had him where she wanted. She made friendly chatter, playing the game carefully, coaxing and teasing him with subtle, sexual innuendos. He took the bait, and the offer of another drink. They spoke all manner of things, and hardly any mention of ongoing

SATA activities came into the conversation. Meyers couldn't believe his luck. He drank slowly, running his eyes over her body again and again. Every so often her words fell on deaf ears. Meyers was overcome with visions of aggressive love making. He imagined himself pounding her with his sturdy throbber, and succumbing to the arse-hair demon.

More drinks came his way. Meyers asked if he could use her toilet. *The moment had arrived.* When he left the room she grabbed his jacket and frantically searched the pockets. She found what she hoped would be there. His phone was active. She selected *Menu, Messages,* and scrolled to *VTM (1 – New.)* She pressed *Enter.* Sinclair's face appeared on the Video Transmission Message. He spoke in monotone, saying the words, 'D Perry. T,H,O. Location – Glen. F. McIver Associate. Use initiative for rendezvous.'

She heard his footsteps and managed to slip the phone back into the pocket.

'What's up?' he asked, detecting a change in her expression.

'Nothing's the matter,' she said. Meyers' phone started ringing. Drake watched him fumble for it, and wondered if she'd put it in the right pocket. He took the call standing up. His face tightened. He gritted his teeth in anger. 'Damn,' he said loudly. 'They want me back at HQ.'

Drake tried not to show her relief. 'Are you fit to drive? You've had quite a lot to drink.'

'I'll be fine,' he said, picking up his coat. 'See you soon, hopefully.'

Meyers took the lift. Drake couldn't be sure he was really leaving. She ran barefoot down the stairs, slowly opened the door a little and peered into the parking area. Meyers started the engine. Through the gap she caught sight of him at the wheel. He drove off at speed. She opened the door fully and took several steps forward to verify that he'd left the apartments, and she thought about Sinclair's message. Its meaning became horribly clear to her.

THO – Take Him Out.

Pez was going to die.

Drake's heart started racing. She rushed back to her flat, completely unaware that Isli Zidane had been watching her from a dark corner.

Twenty-two

Victor Brooks' white cottage was situated a few miles north of Seven Moons. His wife had called it 'Sea Pink.' Victor never liked the name, but it was the only thing he didn't like about his quaint home. The house, situated close to the cliff edge, fell into their lap at the right time and for the right price. The isolation of the place offered serenity and a close relationship with nature.

Having returned from his morning walk, he found his pint-mug of tea waiting for him. He took it to his chair situated next to a window that presented a magnificent view of the sea, and began reading the newspaper.

Madge, his grey-haired plump wife came into the room. 'An inspector rang while you were out,' she said. 'I told him you'd gone for a walk. He said he'd ring back.'

'Did he say who he was?'

'I think he said, "Perry." Will you be wanting anything to eat?'

'Already eaten, Madge.'

He carried on reading, occasionally stopping to glance at the choppy waters and cloudy sky. On his days off he always tried to work out what the weather would be like. More often than not his predictions, though mainly guesswork, were correct. At 8.15 his reading was interrupted. He took a call from Pez who was at his desk at the Mushroom. Pez gave him the low-down on what Drake had told him. A numb disbelief kicked in, and the kind of feeling that emanates when one is told a close friend has died.

Brooks considered the situation.

'Are you there, Vic?'

'I'm here . . . So, they're sending two of them . . . What do you intend to do?'

'Not sure. I can't believe they'd go to such extremes. They'll be found out for sure. In any case, I could send all the known details to

MI5. Tara Drake would confirm everything.'

'I don't think it would work, Pez. These people are rotten to the core and, let's face it, we don't know how far up the chain the rot has reached. You've got to consider Drake, too. She's on her own, and vulnerable. What chance would she stand against such evil men?'

Pez thought hard about what he'd said. 'OK, Vic. I'm going to need your help. What do you say?'

'I'm on your side – all the way. What are your intentions?'

'I'll meet them head-on.'

'*We* will meet them head-on.'

'You do realize you're fighting a formidable enemy?'

'Aye, but we have an advantage – the lie of the land. I'm familiar with certain areas of Glenmar Forest.'

'Think about it carefully before you commit to anything. We're fighting big guns.'

'True. I don't need to think about it, Pez. Let's get ready to rumble.'

Pez ended the conversation. Brooks did think matters over. He was putting his life at risk; Pez too. And he'd made a valid point when he talked about *big guns*. What sort of fire power would they be up against? *Fire.* The word rang inside Brooks' mind. He grabbed the phone. Seconds later he was speaking to the Seven Moons fire chief.

'How are you doing, Victor?'

'I'm fine, Vincent. Sorry to bother you, but do you have any TFT left? I might be needing some.'

'We have loads of the stuff. You do know the use of it is banned?'

'I know. Do me a favour; have half a dozen cans ready to collect later today, will you?'

'Victor, that's a lot of TFT. You wanting to start a fire?'

'That's the general idea.'

'What the devil are you up to?'

'Got some rubbish to burn.'

'Don't believe you.'

'Come on Vincent! I'm desperate to have some.'

'All right. But this is between you and me. Remember not to breathe the fumes, otherwise you'll end up being sick and have a sore throat and headache to contend with.'

'Cheers! Catch you later.'

He shouted his wife into the living quarters. 'Madge, how many of those solar powered post lanterns do we have in the shed?'

She groaned her way into the armchair and said, 'A dozen, at least. Why?'

'It doesn't matter,' he replied, thumbing the pages of his personal telephone pad. 'I'm trying to find Harry Rendell's number. It doesn't seem to be here.'

'Harry Rendell, the locksmith? I'm sure he's dead.'

'Well he's not, woman.'

'Oh, you fuss-pot. His number used to be in the old pad, if we still have it.'

'Where is it?'

'In the sideboard, most likely.'

Brooks searched the drawers and found it. He wrote the number on the back of his hand and picked up a copy of the main telephone directory.'

'You fuss-pot,' she repeated. 'What are you looking for now?'

Brooks sank into his chair. 'The Chief Park Ranger's number. What's his name?'

'Ring directory inquiries.'

'No, no, woman. That means having to make two calls . . . Ah, here it is. Bayliss is the name. Must make a note of the number.'

'What do you want with all these numbers?'

'Preparing for a shoot-out, my dear.'

'You're not being serious, Victor.'

'But I am. It's to take place at Glenmar.'

'Is it a practice session?'

'You could call it a practice.'

'You use blank bullets, don't you?'

'We might use real ones for a change.'

'And what part does Harry Rendell play in all this? He must be in his eighties.'

'I'm hoping he'll provide the traps.'

'You don't make any sense at all.'

Brooks rang Rendell. Madge listened to the conversation and became even more confused.

Drake was excited by the call she received. Apparently, Henderson was happy with the way she'd conducted herself during the Solihull raid and now he wanted to see her at HQ.

She slid the coat hangers along the rail until she came to her black trouser suit. She decided on black stiletto shoes and white blouse to go with it. She sprayed Rio perfume onto her hand and rubbed it gently into her neck and cheeks. She tended to her hair, got dressed and looked at herself in the mirror. She pulled her jacket down at the back and adjusted the collar; and all the time the room was silent. All she could hear was Pez's voice echoing in her mind. She'd decided to tell Henderson all she knew, all she suspected; and if he wouldn't listen to her she would go straight to her flat and collect all she needed for a trip to Cumbria. She knew Pez couldn't beat them on his own. She had no idea that Brooks had offered to help. She had nothing to lose now. Her intentions were final.

Having got inside the high-tech SATA Merc she checked with the Control Centre to ensure there were no traffic problems. The all-clear was given. She put on her shades, fired the engine and sped up the ramp. She turned left into Croftgate Street. The car reached only twenty miles per hour. Drake came off the accelerator when a green Astra, parked further down the street, suddenly roared ahead, tires screeching, smoke bellowing from behind. She had little time to think, and no time to perform a manoeuvre. Having brought her car to a stop she waited, hoping the idiot would pass by. Her eyes widened as the Astra swerved and smashed into her. Drake was sprayed with pieces of glass. Her head fell forward, and as she sat there, temporarily numbed from the impact, a second vehicle raced along in pursuit of the first one. Within seconds Zidane and Kensai jumped out of the stolen Astra. Kensai, whose face was contorted with desperation, threw glances at terrified onlookers. He turned to his blood-crazed partner. Zidane took aim with his rifle and pumped several rounds into Drake's chest and abdomen. The other car stopped only yards from the ambush. Bryce got out and used the open door for protection. Kensai reached for the sky, pleading, 'Don't shoot! Don't shoot!' Bryce yelled at Zidane to drop his weapon, but he squeezed the trigger one last time. Drake's face imploded, and the back of her head erupted like an exploding can of tomatoes. Zidane dropped his rifle. The terrorists stood in silence, with death on their hands, and the hope of freedom in their hearts. Bryce slowly shook his head. The quick succession of shots reverberated along the deserted street.

Zidane and Kensai were despatched to their God.

'For heaven's sake, Pez, you're upsetting Miranda . . . Will you please tell me what's going on?'

Miranda was scared. She wrapped her arms around Laura's legs.

'Look, Laura, I can't explain,' he replied, his face full of sadness. You wouldn't understand.'

'Are you in some kind of trouble?'

'*Trouble* is not the right word. All I'm asking you to do is stay at Diana's for the night.'

'This is ridiculous!'

'I want you to go – right now.'

Miranda wiped her eyes and looked up at Pez. 'Daddy, please don't let anything bad happen.'

'Nothing bad will happen, sweetheart. Now, you get your pyjamas ready, and something to play with.'

Miranda ran out of the room. Laura moved closer to Pez and said, 'It's our safety you're worried about, isn't it?'

There was no reply. By the expression on his face she could tell that some terrible force was threatening him.

Harv felt a little awkward staring at the writing above a large window: Captain Paradise – Body Massage.

The front of the place had been recently painted and looked respectable. Harv wondered if it really was kosher. He felt certain there had been no dodgy goings-on, otherwise he would have heard something on the grapevine by now. In Carron Green it didn't take long for sordid goings-on to become common knowledge. The Red Coyote was a prime example. The activists and the local news media were always keen to highlight its 'activities.' The Coyote's days were undoubtedly numbered. Captain Paradise was still up and running. As far as Harv knew it had been operating for some years.

Joanne, a cheerful teenager, was taking the appointments that day. She noticed Harv coming in. Something told her he wasn't the usual type of customer.

'Good morning, sir,' she said, with a welcoming smile. 'What can we do for you?'

'I'm Detective Constable Harvey,' he said, showing his ID. 'I believe you have an Afro-Caribbean lady who works here?'

'Yes, we do. I think she's busy at the moment.'

'I'd like to speak to her.'

'Certainly. I'll give her a shout.'

What a nice, clean, civilised place, Harv thought. Nothing seedy or suggestive. That didn't mean the staff couldn't indulge in private 'sessions' for personal gain.

When Joanne returned she asked Harv if he wouldn't mind waiting in a side-room which was used for coffee breaks. He went inside and was shortly joined by the lady herself. She was wearing dark-blue trousers and a short-sleeve white jacket. She had big brown eyes, a dainty nose, full lips and smooth, perfect skin. They both sat down. 'You a detective, mister?' she asked.

'That's right.'

'You don't need to show me your ID card,' she said, her eyes smiling.

'We're investigating a murder at Glenmar Forest. It happened on June the eleventh.'

'I've heard about it.'

'The victim's name is Jack Samson.'

'Jack Samson,' she repeated, wishing she'd never met the man. 'I knew him.'

'Well, that's a relief. Our forensic team found human hairs in his car. One of them was of Afro-Caribbean origin. I reckon you're the only Afro-Caribbean living in Carron Green.'

'You reckon right, mister.'

'He was stabbed to death. Whoever killed him went on to cut off his head.'

She gasped and covered her mouth.

'Perhaps you could start by giving me your name, and tell me what you've been doing these last few months.'

'My name is Abi Boudir. I moved up here from London two years ago. Six weeks ago my mother fell ill. She lived in London. I went to look after her but she died . . . I came back here to carry on with my job.'

'You have my sympathy . . . How did you come to know Jack Samson?'

'He used to come here quite often.'

'For a massage?'

'Obviously, mister. That's what we're here for.'

'Did you spend any time with him outside this building?'

'Yes. Me and him became, sort of friends. He liked me a lot, always asked for me to do the massage. Sometimes, if it was late afternoon, he would wait and give me a lift home, or wherever I wanted to go.'

Harv leaned forward and said in a low voice, 'Does anything of a sexual nature happen here?'

'Nothing dirty, mister. Ask the other girls if you don't believe me.'

'Did Jack Samson ask for sexual favours?'

'Never . . . I don't like these sort of questions.'

She suddenly covered her mouth and looked to the floor. Harv had triggered something in her mind.

'What is it?' he asked.

'I'm trying to think back . . . A man started coming here. He wanted *me* to do the massage. Nobody else.'

'How long ago?'

'Not sure. Could have been a couple of months back. He asked, in a roundabout way, if I did extras. I told him, no. When he came back, at a later date, he offered me money in return for sex. The answer was the same.'

'Can you tell me his name, or anything about him?'

'I only remember he was a well dressed, bigish man in his forties . . . The very last time I saw him, he made an offer he thought I couldn't refuse.'

'Go on.'

'If I could seduce Jack Samson into having sex with me, he said ten thousand pounds would be mine. I was shocked and told him to leave. He never came back.'

'After this happened, did you see Samson again?'

'No. I told Joanne I didn't want to see him again so as to avoid any embarrassing situation. Anyway, I ended up having to go away to look after my mother.'

'Would you recognise this well-dressed man if you were to see him again?'

'Yes. I think I would.'

Twenty-three

Spencer looked up in surprise when the office-door suddenly burst open. 'It's customary to knock first,' he said, startled.

'Sorry,' Pez muttered, leaning against the door to shut it. 'I can't relax . . . I feel bloody sick.'

Spencer glared at him. 'You look terrible. You need a shave. And, might I ask, why are you dressed in black?'

Pez's breathing became irregular. 'They're coming for me, Spencer. They're going to kill me.'

'I don't understand,' Spencer said, leaning back and pulling a face.

Pez shook his head and wiped his sweating hands against his shirt. 'I reckon there'll be a shoot-out at the forest. I'm wearing these dark clothes for protection . . . You don't believe me.'

'You are over-reacting. Who, exactly, is going to kill you?'

'SATA. I had a call from Drake last night. The Deputy Assistant Commissioner, Nick Sinclair, has given specific orders to certain members of his team . . . They're going to wipe me out.'

'If it's true what you say, you only have to stay away from Glenmar.'

'I want this to be over with as soon as possible. Those crazy bastards will stop at nothing.'

'Look, Pez, let's be sensible –'

'Listen to me! . . . Sinclair and his agents are walking on a tightrope. If they don't kill me today, they'll come looking for me tomorrow. If I run, they will run after me. I have to consider the safety of my wife and child.'

'Surely you can't believe –'

'Fanatics! That's what they are. These are the men who allow a dog to follow a scent into an innocent crowd of protesters – a dog rigged with a bomb and a package containing Flux which was stolen from a lorry involved in a freak weather accident. They frame two terrorist-brothers by planting the remainder of the Flux in their house. Don't you see what has happened Spencer? A small section of SATA invent the Amama for reasons which I'm not entirely sure, and so their mission is justified, their future is secured. They become terrorists for a while, then let the real ones do the rest!'

'You have a wild imagination. You're over-reacting!'

'You won't help me?'

'How do you expect me to help you?'

'Provide me with an armed escort. I'll deploy them in the woods.'

'It can't be done. Impossible.'

'Do you want to see me killed?' Pez snarled.

'Don't be ridiculous. If this is all true, Drake would be dead by now!'

'She is far better equipped than I am. She can look after herself.'

Spencer bounced from his chair. 'Meaning?'

'I need a fucking gun!'

'If you think this is gangland Manchester, you are very much mistaken.'

Pez stormed out of the room leaving the door wide open. Spencer slowly closed it, returned to his desk, and fell into deep contemplation.

'Come away from the window, Laura,' Diana said, her voice soft and coaxing. 'Nothing can happen in broad daylight'

'You're probably right,' Laura said, turning to face her friend. 'You can almost see our house from here. I was watching for any sign of a disturbance.'

Diana wrapped her arm around her shoulder. 'You really are worried, aren't you? . . . I'm sure everything will be fine.'

'Oh, I hope so. I can't seem to settle down.'

Diana smiled. 'It's six o' clock and you haven't eaten . . . Come with me. Let's make the kids something to eat.'

Laura followed her into the dining room. Miranda was there playing with Diana's son, Ben.

'Come on you two,' Diana said. 'Take your toys upstairs whilst me and Laura make your tea.'

Miranda helped Ben gather his plastic cars and garage. 'All done,' she said, and they happily ran off to Ben's room, laughing and chuckling.

Diana started preparing their meals. After a long silence Laura said, 'Funny isn't it Diana? I thought I couldn't care less about Pez, and now I'm worried sick over him.'

'You still have feelings for him, ' Diana said, handing her the potato peeler.

Laura looked tearful. She made no comment.

Harv found Pez in the major incident room looking at the crime-scene photos secured to the notice board. 'What is it, Harv?' he said, his voice almost a whisper.

'I've been talking to Spencer, told him about my visit to Captain Paradise. He was distant, disinterested.'

Harv got the feeling that Pez was in a world of his own.

'He probably is disinterested.'

'But this is the breakthrough we've been waiting for.'

Pez was in two minds whether to ask Harv if he would help him. He knew he could depend on him. There again, he had a wife and kids of his own. Why should Pez put his life in jeopardy?

'Pez, are you listening to me?'

'Sorry, Harv. Yes, I am listening . . . and I'm sure the end is in sight.'

'So, what happens next?'

'Don't do anything for now,' he said, rubbing his chin. 'We need photographs for Abi Boudir to look at. Yeah?'

'Well, yes. She said she would recognise the man if she saw him again.'

'You phone Seven Moons, tomorrow. Make sure you speak to the appropriate department. They must have promotional booklets showing their management structure.'

'*Management.*'

'Samson's killer is a man of means, a man who has a lot to lose.'

Pez's phone bleeped. He read a text message sent by Brooks. Having donned his black leather jacket he said, 'Sorry, Harv. I've got to go somewhere.'

Harv followed him out of the incident room and said, 'And all because the lady loves Milk Tray.'

'I wish.'

Brooks was already at Glenmar Forest when he received Pez's reply. The car-parks had been sealed off with police tape, and the area surrounding the Silurian Trail was completely devoid of any human activity. Brooks was relieved – thankful that Park Ranger Bayliss had followed his instructions. As he walked the many twisting paths he kept his eyes and ears open for any sign of movement. His weather prediction was correct, and he wondered if the recent rainfall would subdue the potency of the TFT he'd poured over a stretch of woodland earlier that day. And so the waiting continued. Pez would be due to arrive in another thirty or so minutes. Brooks jogged towards the parking area where Samson's body had been discovered. For once, he had no interest in the beautiful scenery. His heaven on Earth would soon become a battle ground.

He stopped about forty yards short of the parking area, dropped his large canvas bag onto the ground and concealed himself in the shrubbery. He carefully lifted the MP5 Heckler and Koch submachine gun, ready to fire should the need arise. Brooks didn't know if SATA were already there waiting for Pez to make his appearance. He wasn't going to let his friend walk straight into a trap. No doubt they could annihilate Pez in a split second if they wanted to . . . and anyone else who posed a threat. Brooks knew they could both be dead before dusk. Giant of a man that he was, he could do nothing to stop the sick feeling in his stomach. He could walk away from it all, turn his back on Pez. Not Brooks. He could never forgive himself, not in a million years.

At 7 p.m. he heard the sound of a vehicle. Pez had made it. Brooks caught sight of him through the gaps in the foliage. He ran forward, gun at the ready. Pez crouched down, afraid he was about to be attacked.

'Pez! It's me, Victor Brooks.'

Pez kept low and scurried into the wood.

'Am I happy to see you,' Brooks said. 'Follow me.'

Brooks led him to the canvas bag. He pulled out a bullet-proof vest and helped him put it on; then the MP5 Heckler and Koch came out. 'I've never fired a submachine gun,' Pez said, feeling the weight.

'I have to admit, it's been years since I fired one.'

'Where did you get them from?'

'The Seven Moons armoury. I'll end up losing my job for doing this . . . What time is Drake due to arrive?'

'Nine o' clock, according to her text message.'

'How is she going to help us?'

'Don't know. I haven't been able to contact her. We'll have to wait and see what happens . . . If Tara arrives at nine, we can expect the others shortly after . . . By the way, Vic, you stink!'

'It's the TFT I'm using as part of my plan. Highly flammable stuff, TFT.'

'You have a plan?'

Brooks nodded. 'When they arrive, we lie low until dark falls. That way we stand a better chance.'

'They'll be equipped with night-vision binoculars,' Pez said, his voice straining.

'Maybe. Just make sure you keep close to me when we run back to the hide.'

'The bird hide, you mean?'

'Aye. We'll try and hold them back from there. When I ignite the TFT, a firewall will run half the perimeter of the open space. It should cause confusion, and might give us the chance to open fire at them.'

'You know what, Vic? The Forestry Commission will kill you if *they* don't.'

'The fire won't spread. We've had rain.'

'Any other surprises I should know about?'

'I visited Harry Rendell, an old acquaintance. He's a retired locksmith who has an unusual collection of traps.'

'I'm intrigued,' Pez said, aiming the gun at his car in mock practice for the confrontation.

'Harry collects some weird and wonderful things.'

'Takes all sorts to make a world.'

Another two and a half hours elapsed before they were alerted by the noise from an approaching vehicle. The light was fading, and the sound of singing birds had ceased, giving way to an eerie silence.

A dark-blue van, marked 'Paramedics,' came into view and pulled-up alongside Pez's car. The two men sank back into the gloom of the wood.

'They've travelled in a hospital van,' Brooks said softly. 'Crafty . . . We should be able to bang the first few shots in from here.'

'Stay off the trigger,' Pez responded, his voice low and coarse. 'Let's wait and see who gets out.'

A figure emerged, wearing a white cap and laboratory-style white coat.

'Who's that?' Brooks asked.

'No idea. Keep quiet.'

The man looked around furtively, then reached into the open rear-end of the van. Pez's heart sank when he heard a muffled scream. Tara's in there, he thought. Bound and gagged.

'He's taken something out of the van,' Brooks observed. 'I can't make out what it is . . . Now he's bending down next to your car . . . Oh, I've got it . . .'

'So have I. He's securing a bomb underneath.'

A movement sounded from inside the van. Another white-coated figure emerged. Pez spotted the khaki combat trousers and assault boots. Another scream sounded, louder and clearer than the previous one.

'Perry! We know you're hiding in there!' Khaki shouted. 'We want to speak to you . . . Come out. There's nothing to fear.'

Brooks whispered, 'Are you going to talk to them?'

'No chance. They'll blast us as soon as they hear my voice.'

'What are we going to do? Drake's being held captive.'

Khaki stepped forward and peered into the wood towards them. He knew they were hiding in there. Pez pushed his back hard against a tree and kept absolutely silent. His fear was almost unbearable.

Moments later metallic sounds could be heard coming from inside the van, followed by a female voice crying out in pain and anguish. Pez became blood-crazed. A strong urge came over him. Should he run at them, expelling the ammunition at his disposal?

'Don't do something stupid,' Brooks said, sensing his agitation.

'Perry! Come out of there, or she will die!'

This time it was the voice of an older man. 'We'll explain the situation to you,' he said, 'and perhaps you will understand why the Amama is so necessary for the protection of our country . . . Do you want to see our country ruined by soft-option politicians?'

'Crazy bastard,' Pez said, under his breath.

'This doesn't need to end in bloodshed . . . Do you hear? . . . Five minutes to go – and she dies if you don't come out.'

'They're bluffing,' Brooks whispered.

'No, they're not . . . Time is running out. It'll be dark soon . . . Listen – when I give the signal, we attack. It's our only chance. We've got to save her.'

Khaki and the older man suddenly jumped into the van. The engine started. Pez and Brooks rushed forward as it sped off.

The diversion had worked.

Meyers saw their shadowy figures cutting through the forest. He gritted his teeth, squeezed the trigger of the Uzi 9mm and released a sweeping blanket of bullets.

Twenty-four

'You know what the plan is,' McIver said, after driving the van back to the parking area. Skinny Dash Cooper ripped off his white coat, ready for action. He looked like a stick insect dressed in his green-and-brown combat gear. McIver climber over the seat and joined him. 'I thought Perry would have made some attempt to save Drake's life,' he said.

'Maybe he knew we were playing a recording,' Cooper suggested.

'I doubt it.'

McIver kicked open the lid of the metal box. He reached for the two remaining Uzi submachine guns. Cooper armed himself with several magazines. He took the gun from McIver and said, 'No terrorist should be without one.'

'I don't regard myself as a terrorist; and neither should you. If we pull this off, we can regard ourselves as extremely lucky.'

Cooper threw him a couldn't-care-less glance, and jumped outside. Suddenly, a dark shape appeared. Cooper eased his finger off the trigger when he realized it was Meyers.

'You could be dead now, Danny. We use code words and signals, don't forget . . . Well, did you see him, or what?'

'There's two of them. I fired –'

'And you missed.'

'They were some distance away. It's not easy to hit a target in this kind of environment. Anyway, we'll see how you perform, won't we?'

Cooper sneered. McIver joined them. 'I wonder who the other one is?' he said to himself. 'We fucked up, didn't we?'

'How?' Cooper asked.

'It's practically dark. We should have planned it for earlier.'

'We wouldn't have made it in time,' Meyers said.

'The darkness is no problem after all,' McIver responded. 'We have our SATA issue night vision/communication system, don't we?'

They equipped themselves, and became predators of the night, no longer recognisable. Their sturdy headgear, supporting long eye-pieces, gave them a formidable appearance, and now they had all they needed to execute a deadly assault. Meyers, though, wasn't satisfied. He reached into the van and dragged out the cumbersome rocket grenade launcher.

'You can't be serious,' McIver said, shaking his head.

'We haven't travelled all this way for nothing.'

'I didn't know we were up against an army,' Cooper said. There had always been an element of rivalry between the two of them.

Meyers pointed the weapon at him. 'I like to be sure, that's all.'

They didn't notice the grin on McIver's face. He knew all along that Meyers wanted to totally destroy the one man who possessed enough knowledge to expose them; but the threat of exposure was even bigger now. Andrea Peters and Dennis Farron had provided crucial details which Drake had passed to Pez during her tapped landline telephone conversation. He could only hope that Drake's horrific death would scare Peters and Farron into silence.

He gave his final instructions. The three men parted company and disappeared into the blackness of Glenmar Forest.

After a frantic dash, Brooks and Pez made it safely to 'old' bird hide. Five minutes passed before Pez was sufficiently stable to be able to speak normally. Brooks was breathing heavily.

'We can't stay here too long,' Pez said, peering through the narrow slit in the hide. 'Are you OK, Vic?'

'I'll be all right in a few minutes . . . I thought I was a good runner. Not any more.'

Pez kept his eyes peeled and listened for any unusual sounds. He tapped Brooks' shoulder.

'What is it, Pez?'

'I can see lights shining dimly. What are they up to?'

'It's nothing to do with them. The lights are my post lanterns. People use them in their gardens, but I placed them there for a different purpose. I planted several bear traps in the area surrounding those lights.'

'Bear traps?'

'Aye. Got them from Harry Rendell, remember. There's more of them en route to where my Range Rover is parked. Make sure you stay close to me if we have to make a run for it.'

'I will . . . I doubt a set of lights will entice them, though.'

'If I was in their shoes I'd be curious, and I'll tell you –'

'Shush! Listen . . . I think they're here.'

Brooks pulled hard on Pez's jacket and said, 'Get down.'

Having ascertained the positions of Cooper and Meyers, McIver emptied a full magazine into the area surrounding the hide. Pez was alerted by splinters of wood falling from the roof, and the dull sound of bullets punching into trees. McIver was shooting blind, firing indiscriminately.

'They're using silencers,' Pez whispered.

They were lying on the floor. Pez closed his eyes tightly as the second assault commenced. This time Cooper and Meyers unleashed sweeping arcs of bullets. Cooper – comfortably positioned on a sloping rock - spotted the post lanterns and managed to destroy three of them. Meyers had adopted the weight-forward stance. He grinned as the Uzi rattled and vibrated in his hands; but his so-called revenge could never be satiated by using mere bullets. Every so often he ran his fingers across the bag of rocket-assisted heat grenades. The taking of innocent lives meant nothing to him. Unlike his partners, he was prepared to die if he had to.

'They have us pinned down,' Pez said, when the firing stopped. Brooks was breathing heavily again, more from fear than exhaustion. Pez was trying to stay calm. The thought of death was on his mind, and yet, somehow, the urge to survive provided an inner strength that negated any notion of helplessness and defeat.

Brooks stood up. 'Remember the other hide I told you about?'

'The one not far from here?'

'Aye. There's half a dozen paraffin lamps in there . . . I'm going to light them, fire a magazine towards the flat ground, and come back here. If you have to shoot, aim north, that way.' He indicated the direction. 'That's where the shooting is coming from.'

'Be careful, Vic,' Pez said, his gun at the ready.

Brooks crept down the wooden steps. 'If I don't return, head south, or you might end up in one of Rendell's traps.'

'Head south – in this darkness?'

'Let's hope it doesn't come to that. I'm going.'

'Good luck.'

Brooks arched his back and ran into the thick woodland. A ditch and The Ancient Forester – a man-made sculpture – were landmarks that enabled him to reach the second hide. He lit the lamps with a shaking hand, and suspended them from hooks he'd hammered into the roof. On his way out he slipped on the damp steps. He lay motionless, his left side aching; but there was no time to rest, no time for pain. He got up, ran for fifty or so yards to a forest clearing. He knelt like a soldier in combat and released the safety catch of his MP5. He listened. A noise came from his left, the breaking of a branch, perhaps. Dash Cooper was on the move, and had reached the area dotted with post lanterns.

Brooks' body stiffened as he fired a magazine of 3-round bursts into the open space before him. The magazine empty, he made his way back to Pez. Meyers and McIver had fallen flat on the ground at the sound of staccato raps, but they were soon up on their feet, blasting at the dim light of the paraffin lamps. Brooks used a tree for cover, and all around him silent missiles ripped into lush foliage and delicate leaves. The attack lasted seconds. Cooper, not wanting to be hit by one of his own, had called a cease-fire. Brooks ran on, unaware that Cooper was gaining ground. But his advance wouldn't be stopped by a bullet. The bone-crunching teeth of Rendell's bear trap snapped onto his leg. A white flash of searing pain exploded before his eyes. He lay in agony, his gun out of reach, his communication system disabled. Pez heard the scream. He wondered if Brooks had been hit by a lucky shot. He turned sharply at the sound of footsteps, ready to shoot.

'Take it easy. It's only me,' Brooks said.

'What was that scream?'

'I reckon someone's suffering with a very sore leg . . . Get back to your position, Pez.'

Brooks squirted lighter fluid onto a rag and scuttled outside. He ignited the TFT and went back inside. 'Get ready,' he shouted. 'Keep the gun as steady as possible.'

A roaring river of flames raced along the eastern perimeter of the open space. Meyers, who was some distance away, sprayed his ammo towards the second hide.

'There! Over there!' Pez bellowed.

Exposed by the light of the firewall, McIver had no option but to run. The MP5's were fired simultaneously. McIver kept running, desperately trying to reach the cover of darkness. Suddenly, he fell. Brooks wondered if he had taken cover. They stopped firing and tried to locate him in the fading glow. They heard only their own breathing, and there was no telling of what they had achieved.

McIver's brains were lying next to him.

He would never see the morning sun.

Meyers' partners weren't responding to his transmissions. He thought he was the only one left. Fuelled with anger, he threw his Uzi to the ground and lifted the seven-kilogram grenade launcher. The Big Daddy will flush 'em out, he thought. He took careful aim, and released the deadly demon. Brooks saw the flash in the corner of his eye. Before he could speak, a loud explosion shattered the momentary peace of Glenmar. Pez's stomach caved in from the shock of it. Brooks dropped to the floor, his head buried in his huge hands; and realization came: whoever was out there would have seen the muzzle flare of their guns.

'Quick, Pez! Let's get out!'

They jumped onto the leafy ground. The running was arduous, as if in a dream when your legs feel like lead.

The second grenade exploded behind them, sending slivers of wood flying in all directions. Brooks followed a path surrounded with more bear traps. Pez kept close to him. They ran for all they were worth, eventually coming out of the cover of woodland. A steep hill lay before them.

'Not far to go,' Brooks said, panting heavily. 'My Range Rover is on the other side.'

Meyers had left the launcher behind and was running over open ground much faster than his prey. To his right, the hides were cracking and spitting. He stopped to rest, and through his night-vision glasses he saw them making their escape, struggling from sheer exhaustion as they fought the steep incline. Meyers fired relentlessly. They made it to the top. The Range Rover was visible in the moonlight shining from a gap in the cloudy sky. The bullets kept coming. Pez let out a sharp cry. His left arm felt as if it had been jabbed with a red hot poker. The burning pain took the strength out of his legs. Brooks wrapped his arm around him and helped him along the downwards slope and into the Rover. He started the engine and stamped on the accelerator.

'Where are we going?' Pez asked, his voice cracking with pain.

'The hospital at Carron Green . . . How do you feel?'

'Hurts like a bastard.'

'Hang in there, Pez. Let's hope there's no more SATA waiting for us, or we're as good as dead.'

The wheels went over a log. Pez screamed in agony. He was clutching his arm, and became aware of warm blood running down to his hand. He took deep breaths and tried to console himself. If he believed in God, he would be praying now.

Brooks reached the main road that led to Carron Green. He turned right and breathed an inward sigh of relief.

'You OK, Pez?'

'Hangin' in.'

'We should make it in thirty minutes.'

Pez's breathing became deeper. The more he worried, the worse he felt. Brooks knew the road well. He drove fast, slowing down for treacherous bends. After five minutes Pez's voice interrupted his concentration.

'I can't go on like this, Vic. I need your help.'

He stopped the vehicle and switched the interior light on. Pez was white as a sheet and sweating heavily. Brooks helped him remove his jacket and bullet-proof vest. He then cut off the shirt sleeve with a pocket-knife. The damage looked serious. The absence of an exit wound meant the bullet was embedded in his arm. Brooks used an old tea towel to stem the bleeding. He made Pez as comfortable as possible, and continued the journey. The road ran straight for a few miles. He reached eighty miles an hour, and had to brake hard to negotiate a notorious accident black spot known as 'Devil's Hook.' Pez leaned to his right to avoid being thrown into the door. The road straightened again. Brooks hit the accelerator. Seconds later, he stamped on the brake pedal.

'Why have you stopped?' Pez asked wearily.

'Isn't that the van we saw earlier?'

The van crept out of an opening to a field. Pez recognised the white lettering on its side. Brooks performed the quickest three-point turn of his life.

The Rover sped off, and now they were hopelessly trapped between Devil's Hook and Meyers' deadly grenade launcher. Having seen Brooks make his retreat, he grabbed the weapon, positioned himself in the middle of the road and fired his last missile. Brooks saw the white fireball screaming towards them. The Hook was upon them. He pulled heavily on the steering wheel. The Rover scraped along a stone wall, its side melting into a spray of red sparks. The missile missed them by inches and carried on over fields, eventually pounding its way into a hillside

The chase was on.

Ace-driver Meyers jumped into his van and followed in hot pursuit. Brooks kept pumping the pedals, taking the straights and the curves like a racing car driver. Meyers' headlights were in view. Pez fumbled for his mobile and tried to contact the Mushroom. No reception. Brooks shouted the Seven Moons security number to him. No reception.

Fifteen minutes of horrendous driving passed by. They reached Oak Valley. A quick mirror check showed that Meyers had closed the gap.

'They're catching up,' Brooks said.

'There might . . . There might only be one of them. We would have been shot at by now.'

'We can only head for Seven Moons,' Brooks said, his voice fuelled with distress. 'I don't think we're gonna make it! And you're in no fit condition to shoot from the rear.'

'There is one thing we can do . . . When I give the word, slow right down and turn left.'

'What!'

'Trust me, Vic. Just do as I tell you.'

Within minutes the barely visible church-sign shone in the headlights.

'Now. Slow down and turn left.'

'Are you crazy, Pez? This road takes us to St Peter's!'

'I know . . . Can you see the van?'

'Can't see it . . . Now I can.'

'Keep going as fast as you can. Come on, come on . . . I think there's a gate up this road, on the left. Drive through it. Smash it down if you have to.'

'You *are* crazy. You're delirious.'

'You must do what I say.'

Brooks saw the wooden gate. The Rover cracked through it with ease.

'Bear left,' Pez groaned. 'Drive towards the cliff edge.'

'Pez, this is madness!'

The Rover rumbled over rough ground, and started climbing a hill.

'When we go over the hill, put it in neutral. Jump out when I tell you; and make sure you stay flat on the ground.'

Brooks drove over the hill. The vehicle picked up speed. He snapped open their safety belts.

Pez took a deep breath and shouted, 'Jump!'

Brooks didn't hear his Range Rover plunge into the water below the cliff. A knock to his head rendered him unconscious. Pez was lying on his back, mouthing silent screams of agony as his conscious mind began to close down. Luckily, his timing had been perfect.

Meyers came over the rise. He put his van into a low gear and stared ahead. No vehicle. Nothing. They must have gone over the edge, he thought. They're dead. He stopped the van only feet away from the cliff edge and got out in time to see the metallic black mass sinking into the icy sea. A smile crossed his face. 'I did it,' he said, and he suddenly became aware of a familiar sound. Seconds later Meyers jerked his head upwards. He squinted at the powerful light beaming from the helicopter hovering over him. *And the inevitable happened.* The weight of the van was too much, of course. Meyers' eyes widened. He struggled to keep his balance. The ground surrounding him sank and split open. Before he could attempt an escape, part of the cliff broke away. The pilot watched in disbelief. Meyers clawed at fresh air, his futile screams for help smothered by the drilling sound of the helicopter. Down he went, along with his 'Paramedics' van, the sand, the soil.

And now the sea would forever vanquish the madness, the corruption, and the misguided self-preservation.

Pez was still conscious when the Armed Response Unit arrived. An immediate search was undertaken.

'Over here, sir!' an officer shouted.

Spencer ran to the spot and knelt beside him. 'Can you hear me, Pez?'

He moved his lips in response. 'I'm Sorry for not getting here sooner,' Spencer went on. 'We'll have you in hospital in no time. Don't worry. Armed officers are sweeping the forest right now.'

Pez mumbled some words. Spencer gently raised his head. 'What is it? What are you trying to tell me?'

'Tell them . . . Tell them my car has a bomb attached to it. Forest car-park.'

'I'll do it now.'

Spencer stood up. A voice shouted to him. 'There's another body here, sir. Can't tell if he's alive or not.'

'Let's get them into the helicopter right away!' Spencer commanded.

Before the pilot attempted a landing he spoke into the loud-speaker system and ordered all officers to stay away from the cliff edge.

Everything that had happened seemed surreal.

Spencer now knew the unpalatable truth.

He regretted not offering Pez any assistance.

At least he was still alive.

Twenty-five

The Mushroom was bustling with activity. It was midday, the day after the unbelievable events at Glenmar Forest. Every officer had picked up some detail concerning Pez's activities. Confusion reigned. Many questions were asked, and many unlikely answers would later compound the ensuing cover-up.

Mack rushed into his office and said to Harv, 'There's a hell of a commotion outside.'

'Reporters, you mean?'

'Not just them. Locals from Mermaid's Bridge are asking all kinds of questions. Spencer's out there, believe it or not, trying to quell the furore. He's trying to fob them off with some story about a training exercise.'

'Training exercise,' Harv said, shaking his head in disbelief.

'Well, what do you know about it?'

'Very little, Mack . . . It's my belief that Pez has opened a can of very nasty worms.'

'Maybe you're right. Any news on his recovery?'

'Don't know. I asked Spencer a couple of hours ago but he was busy coordinating operations at Salter Bay and Glenmar . . . Did you know that Rhodes has been with him all morning?'

'Yes. Rhodes is counter-terrorism. It must be serious.'

'Serious enough to warrant a visit from the Chief Constable . . . Anyway, we still have a job to do. Have a look at those.' Harv gave him a set of printouts. 'Copies of mug shots of the management structure at Seven Moons, excluding the last one.'

Mack looked at it and asked, 'Who is he?'

'Stuart Owen. He trained Samson in the Flux lab. I don't think he's the man we're looking for. He's too young.'

Harv took the printouts from Mack and walked towards the door.

'Where are you going, Harv?'

'I need to talk to Abi Boudir.'

Mack waited till he'd gone. He thought about ringing Laura. It was ironic that he should want to ring her to see if Pez was OK. Something told him not to bother, and at that moment in time he realized how foolish he had been. An affair with Laura would never have worked out.

Sir Douglas Henderson was standing in the rain, addressing TV reporters and journalists. It was amazing how fast information was being passed around. Henderson wasn't sure if they'd heard about events further north, in Cumbria. Rhodes telephoned him to say a SAT agent had been taken to hospital in Carron Green, and was being questioned with regard to the shoot-out. The situation couldn't be worse. He shuddered to think what plotting and scheming had gone on behind his back, and now he had the murder of Tara Drake to contend with. For the time being, reporters were pressing him for details surrounding the shooting of the two men who came close to blowing up Royle's shopping centres.

Henderson raised his hands in frustration at the quick-fire questions coming at him. 'I can confirm that the two terrorists, who were shot yesterday morning, lived in Birmingham. They had connections with a cell operating here in London.'

'Can you give us the name of the officer who shot them?' a Telegraph reporter asked.

'I can't reveal his name.'

'Were these men responsible for the attack in Perbury?'

'We believe they were members of the same group who claimed responsibility for the atrocity at Perbury. As you already know, two men are awaiting trial as a result of our investigation. I have nothing else to add at this stage. Thank you.'

Henderson and his entourage of high-ranking officials and body guards turned to leave. A man in the crowd asked, 'Commissioner, it seems incredible that two terror suspects should know the whereabouts of a Special Anti-terrorist Agent. Why was she allowed to die in such a way?'

Henderson paused momentarily. Realizing the implications of the question, he made a speedy exit.

The man shuffled along, deep in thought. He felt a hand on his shoulder and turned around to face a stranger. 'Interesting question,' he said.

'Who are you?'

'It doesn't matter, for now,' he replied, adjusting his trilby. 'How do you know Tara Drake was a Special Agent? You see, not many people, including the press, know about SATA.'

'She was a friend.'

'You said, she was *allowed* to die.'

'She knew too much. They had to get rid of her.'

'You mean, the Amama had to get rid of her?'

'You could say so.'

'I don't understand.'

'Look here, I don't know who you are. I'm sorry, but I must be on my way.'

'Just a minute! I am Commander Pennick of Special Branch. I might be interested in what you have to say. The circumstances surrounding Drake's death are suspicious.'

'Commander Pennick? I'll talk to you, then, but only in the presence of Commissioner Henderson.'

A long silence followed. Finally, Pennick nodded.

Harv heard Abi Boudir's distinctive voice before he saw her. She opened a door and entered the reception area of Captain Paradise. She looked at Joanne, then Harv. 'Mister Detective,' she said, 'let's go and talk in the little room.'

He followed her into the side-room, and bursting with optimism, he eagerly took the printouts out of a folder and passed them to her. 'Remember the conversation we had last time? A man offered you a bribe . . .'

Abi remembered all right. She started looking at the mug shots. They were small and the definition wasn't good.

'Take your time,' Harv said. He watched her big brown eyes moving down the page, just hoping she'd focus on a particular one.

A minute went by. She frowned and said, 'I'm not sure.'

'Please look again.'

'Very well.'

She tried to visualise the man she'd seen. The image that came to mind wasn't as clear any more. Harv's optimism was dwindling by the second.

'Some of these faces look alike,' she said. She studied them a while longer, and said, 'I don't recognise any of them.'

'You sure?'

'I'm certain, mister; and I'm sorry to disappoint you.'

'No problem. Thanks for your time, miss.'

Before he left, Harv asked Joanne to look at the faces. Her response was the same. All hope of solving the mystery evaporated. Harv went on his way feeling dejected. Back to the drawing board, he thought.

'Ex-journalist, you say?' Henderson said, when Farron had finished his story.

'That's right, Commissioner. It could be one of the biggest scoops of the century,' Farron replied, knowing his veiled threat would stir them.

Henderson's heart was racing. He tried to stay calm. 'The full details of Drake's death, and events that have taken place in Cumbria, will not reach the media.'

'Because you intend to camouflage the truth,' Farron said sharply.

'There will be an internal inquiry, of course.'

'Just as I thought – a cover-up.'

'Mr Farron, we must consider the public. The confidence of our people would be irreparably scarred,' Pennick said calmly.

'*Your people.* I suppose it's one way of looking at it . . . You make me sick. How can anyone justify what your officers have done?'

'Their actions can never be justified,' Pennick said.

'I don't believe a word you say.'

Henderson wiped his forehead with a neatly-folded handkerchief. His mind was in turmoil. He had to find some way of assuaging Farron's anger, some way of diluting his mistrust. 'So, who else knows?' he asked.

'Only Andrea Peters.'

'I shall speak to her at the first opportunity.'

'Why not offer her a promotion?' Farron condescended.

'Your attitude is becoming offensive.'

'Is it, Commissioner? You can take it I am offended! SO13 has much to answer for . . . Before I go, I want to know why certain members of SATA saw fit to execute such a devastating attack on innocent civilians.'

'Mr Farron . . . I really don't know; and that is the truth.'

'Well, when you discover the truth you will personally tell me . . . The agents responsible should be severely dealt with. If they are not, you have my word I will make public everything I know.'

Farron breezed out of the room. Pennick looked to Henderson and said, 'Is it all true, Commissioner?'

'Farron's account parallels information received from the Cumbrian force.' Henderson nervously rubbed his face with both hands. 'I recommended her for the Perbury inquiry. Drake was a brilliant officer . . .'

'Where do we go from here?' Pennick asked, urgency in his voice.

'We shall organise a top security meeting. All of the sub-rank commissioners must be informed of what has happened.'

'And who else?'

'Our security coordinator, DCS John Armond; the National Coordinator of Terrorist Investigations; the Chief Constable of the Civil Nuclear Constabulary, and the Permanent Secretary of the Department of Trade and Industry,' he replied, his chin falling onto his chest, his voice fading to a whisper.

'Why the DTI?'

'Because the CNC comes under their remit. Meanwhile, I have a job for you. Find Nick Sinclair and bring him to me. Use force if you have to.'

'Sinclair?'

'I have reason to believe he's involved. I also want you to make arrangements for Bryce to be escorted here – armed escort, you understand. You will find him at the Dark House. He's under protection from this so-called Amama. He'll be charged for murder, and related offences under the Terrorism Act.'

Miranda ran towards Pez when she saw him walk out of the hospital. He knelt on one leg. She wrapped her arms around his neck. He kissed her cheek. 'Be careful,' he said. 'I've got a very sore arm.'

She backed off and looked at the splint and arm sling. 'Mummy said you had an accident,' she said, rather cheerily.

'I did. It's nothing to worry about, sweetheart.'

Laura was waiting for him with a smile on her face. She kissed him full on the lips. He noticed tears in her eyes. She noticed sadness in his.

'Thank goodness you're safe and well,' she said. 'We were so worried. I didn't sleep a wink thinking about you.'

'I'll be fine in a month or two.'

'You'll tell me all about it: what happened and everything?'

'I will, in my own time,' he replied, but he had no intention of telling her the complete chain of events.

On the way home Pez told Laura to drop him off at the Mushroom. She wasn't happy. 'Pez, you should be resting,' she said. 'You're in no fit state to be working.'

'I know, but I need to speak to Harv.'

Pez was silent and morose during the journey to HQ. Laura assumed the sore arm was bothering him. She couldn't have been further from the truth.

During the afternoon he had gone to the hospital's TV room. A news bulletin revealed the names of the two Algerians who were shot dead after killing an anti-terrorist officer. Drake was named. Her face appeared briefly on screen. Pez was devastated. It wouldn't be easy to conceal his pain and sorrow.

Spencer was standing inside the entrance to the Mushroom amongst several officials. Pez didn't recognise any of them. He waited until his boss saw him.

'Pez, I'm delighted to see you,' he said. 'You should be at home, really.'

'Just popped in to see Harv.'

'You will find him in the incident room . . . By the way, Inspector Brooks is fine. Minor concussion. I suspect you already know that.'

Spencer told him who was involved in the shoot-out, and who

died. Pez felt some satisfaction. 'Where is Cooper?' he asked.

'At the hospital. I shouldn't imagine it will be long before he is taken to London for further questioning. You and I will have to make the trip, as soon as you're feeling better.'

'No problem. Tell me, Spencer, what brought you to my rescue?'

'Reports of gunshots coming from the forest. I knew something was terribly wrong . . . I owe you an apology.'

'For what?'

'For allowing all of this to happen. I simply could not believe that SO13 officers would bomb British citizens. Why did they do it? Why?'

'They were fanatics. Terrorism breeds terrorists.'

Spencer lowered his head in a moment of shame. 'I was keeping in touch with McIver, for quite some time.'

'What!'

'I should have told you, I know. He wanted me to keep him informed of your investigation into the missing Flux. Initially, I spoke to DAC Sinclair. He seemed to be concerned about your suspicions. I told him your inquiries might legitimately involve some aspect of terrorism, and I wasn't prepared to take you off the case. I gave them a watered-down account of your activities.'

'You must have sensed something was amiss.'

'I had my doubts . . . I'm sorry, Pez . . . Anyway, I must leave you now.'

Pez walked into the incident room with his head high. A momentous round of applause sounded. They couldn't have known the full story, the true events. Not yet. He walked slowly to his desk, nodding appreciation and thanks to as many as he could. Harv and Mack were standing by his desk, looking proud.

'Well done, Pez,' Harv said. 'It's bloody good to see you.'

'Nice one, boss,' Mack said. 'You're a hero.'

Pez waited for the bustle to die down. 'What's the verdict?' he asked Harv.

'She didn't recognise any of them. You know what? I don't think we'll ever solve this case.'

'We deserve more than this,' Pez said. He turned to Mack. 'You called Spencer, told him I was in danger.'

'That's right, Pez.'

'But you couldn't have known I was in danger. I never said anything to you. Even Harv didn't know.'

Mack's mouth fell open. He couldn't get round that one. He had to tell the truth. 'Laura rang me and said there was a problem.'

'The problem is, Laura should have spoken to Spencer. Why did she tell *you*?'

'Don't know, Pez. She probably wasn't thinking straight, that's all.'

'I think you've been seeing her.'

'Honestly, Pez, you worry over the most trivial things. You're talking nonsense.'

'Maybe I am.'

Pez walked away, leaving them standing in silence. Mack walked off. Harv grabbed his arm. 'I hope he is talking nonsense, Mack. You'll end up working on dog-shit DNA if you're not careful . . . Or something worse.'

A detective chief superintendent was the first to enter the garage attached to a magnificent detached house called Embers.

Mrs Sinclair told him her husband wasn't to be disturbed. She was perplexed as to why he'd ignored the constantly ringing phone. He seemed depressed, she told the detective; but she didn't think he was ill. She assured him there was nothing to worry about. Nevertheless, she started chewing her nails when she spotted several uniformed coppers waiting in the driveway and outside the garage.

Sinclair's lifeless body was hanging from one of the roof beams.

He'd made a good job of kicking the chair away.

He had even taken the trouble of wearing his uniform for the occasion.

Twenty-six

Seven Moons was fast becoming a world leader in uranium conversion technology. Its directors had signed a lucrative contract to make nuclear fuel for a Japanese company. The workers' jobs became even more secure, and a batch of new employees was being primed to face the challenges of a constantly changing and competitive market.

Rodney Adams was one such employee. He watched his foreman of AGR canning plant fasten the buttons on his long industrial-grey coat, and press a hard hat firmly onto his head.

'Right, Rodney. Let's see if we can find somewhere for you to put your gear,' he said, grabbing a clipboard.

The two men sauntered along several brightly-lit corridors until they reached the one that Rodney would become very familiar with. This particular corridor was lined with dozens of grey lockers. The foreman ran his eyes down the list of names and locker numbers, trying to find a spare one.

'Ah, what's going on here?' the foreman asked himself. 'Locker 37 is listed as being in use, and it shouldn't be . . . Let's go and see.'

He located locker 37, turned to Rodney and said, 'Do you know who Jack Samson was?'

'I've heard of him. He was the guy who was murdered a few months back.'

'Yes. And this was his locker. Wait here. I'll get the key.'

The foreman left him and soon returned, swinging a bunch of keys. 'You will have to use my spare key for the time being. I suspect Samson kept the other one when he was transferred to Analytical Services.' He separated the key from the bunch and inserted it. 'A bit stiff this one,' he said. He forced the key, the lock clicked open. He came across the usual items: safety glasses, a union handbook, a few coins, work-issue pants and jumper. The DVD wasn't so usual. He removed it from its sleeve. 'H'm. I wonder what's on this.'

Rodney looked over his shoulder and tried to read the writing on it.

'It's a copy of something,' the foreman muttered. 'The title is unusual, though – *Knowledge is Power.*'

Three days after the forest shoot-out Dash Cooper was taken under armed escort to a police station at Paddington Green. He tried to be 'pally' with anyone who spoke to him. Commander Pennick and security coordinator Chief Superintendent Ormond were having none of it. The interview room was covered by a live video-link to another room. Henderson and officers from the anti-terrorist branch were anxiously watching and listening, hoping to learn the reasons for the extraordinary and tragic events that threatened the integrity of Britain's security regime.

Cooper had been slow at answering questions, and was trying to gain sympathy by rubbing his ankle.

'That leg still bothering you?' Pennick to Cooper.

'Absolutely. I don't know anyone who was caught in a bear trap. The pain is terrible.'

Pennick folded his arms. Shaking his head in mock pity he sternly said, 'You can quit the mummy's boy stuff . . . It's in your best interests to talk straight. We haven't time to waste.'

'All right, boss,' he said, and made a defiant grin.

'You worked in the forensic department before joining SATA. Your valuable forensic knowledge was obviously given consideration in relation to the house search at Neville Court . . . You were the first to enter.'

'I can't remember.'

'At the time of entering, did you have in your possession Gland tubes containing the toxic uranic compound, Fluorohexane?'

Cooper stared, expressionless. He leaned back and said, 'You know I did.'

'Where did those tubes come from?'

'A drum that fell off a lorry.'

'Who found the drum?'

'You know who. SATA was sent in. The drum had to be found.'

'I repeat, who found the drum?'

'Meyers was given the job,' he replied after a defiant silence. 'The drum was carried down a swollen stream. The authorities were too dumb to work out what had happened.'

'But Meyers wasn't stupid, was he? He realised that a drum marked "Radioactive" might contain material that could be used to make a dirty bomb.'

Cooper's mouth tightened. He stayed silent. Ormond decided to take over.

'Last November, a website appeared which implicated the Amama with Perbury. This organisation was also used as a backdrop for disinformation, and as a means for inciting racial hatred and terrorism.'

'You have it in one. Well done.'

'Who was behind all of this?'

Cooper was smiling now. He placed his hands flat on the table. The smile fell from his face. He adopted a piss-take serious look. 'The DAC and McIver.'

'Yes. I gathered as much. They thought SATA might be dissolved, didn't they? And Tara Drake came along. What an unwelcome addition . . . What might she discover? . . . Your fears slowly turned into reality. Drake came close to lifting the lid off your treasonous plotting. Fortunately, for you, Kensai and Zidane's vile plan was discovered and you used them to eliminate Drake. You tried to murder Perry, too – the one man, the only man, she could trust.'

'You must be well informed . . . It's true – Perry and Drake knew too much . . . Well, what did you expect us to do?'

Ormond's face hardened. 'We don't condone murder, as well you know . . . Apart from Bryce and yourself, who else was involved in the Solihull raid?'

'McIver and Meyers. They befriended the Algerians.'

'And you prepared a bomb, carefully engineered so as not to kill the officers involved in the raid. Correct?'

Cooper nodded. 'Kensai and Zidane watched it go off from some derelict flats. McIver and Meyers were with them at the time.'

Henderson lowered his head and gave a sigh of disbelief. Cooper stared ahead expressionless, feeling no sign of remorse for what they had done. 'Our plan could have worked,' he said, his voice monotonous. 'Our dream was to save SATA and flush-out the enemy . . . SATA could have gone on forever.'

'You acted irresponsibly,' Pennick said, after a long silence. 'You added fuel to the terrorist cause. And now, because of your selfish, misguided ideals, the terrorist threat has become more serious.'

'So, we succeeded. We can all live in a safer country now.'

The mood in the monitor room was one of total shock. An SO13 officer silently entered and looked towards the Commissioner. 'They've found McIver's van in a lock-up, sir,' he said. 'There's evidence of explosive material having been stored in it. Past records show he was a dog-handler. He probably acquired the German Shepherd. We also have a message from the labs. Meyers requested Cryo-7. His reason for using it was to freeze some biological samples. The lab scientist who gave it to him didn't think the request was unusual. No doubt Meyers used it to freeze down the Flux.'

'Is that all?' Henderson asked.

'For the time being.'

The officer looked at the screen for a few seconds, wanting to know who was involved. Henderson sat down and buried his face in his hands.

Jason Bryce and Dash Cooper were duly charged with offences under the Terrorism Act, and with conspiracy to murder. Dennis Farron kept his silence. Andrea Peters resigned from her job. The thought of resignation had crossed Henderson's mind, too. He faced weeks of internal inquiry boards, headed by senior members of the security services. Their objective was to determine Henderson's level of involvement with the Perbury investigation. Had Henderson placed too much faith in his team? Should he be condemned for not questioning the irregularities in the execution of their duties?

Over two hundred miles away, Brooks had been subjected to the rigours of the Civil Nuclear Constabulary's intensive inquiries. In the end they conceded that his actions were justifiable. The weight lifted from his shoulders when he was vindicated of charges relating to malpractice. He was glad to return to work.

During his absence a pile of mail had built up. Somebody had kindly left it on his desk. His office was just the same, except for the letters. He pulled a face and slumped into his chair. Brooks hated sedentary work. He made coffee before thumbing the assortment of white and brown envelopes. One of them held particular interest. The handwriting was in capitals; the word 'Confidential' was underlined. He opened it and took out a DVD and a note from the foreman of Building 300, AGR canning plant. The note said: 'Inspector Brooks, this disc was found in Jack Samson's locker which has now been assigned to a new starter. Its content surprised me. In view of what happened to Samson, you may wish to watch it.' Brooks decided to give it a spin. He strolled to another room where a video/DVD player was kept. He switched the equipment on, looked at the disc and read the words, 'Knowledge is Power.' He repeated them again, a whisper this time, and recalled hearing those same words from Pez. He settled back and played it. At first the film was shaky. The hand-held camcorder was pointing at office windows. It focused on one window, then moved to the right and held firm.

Jack Samson had known where to look, and when. Brooks surmised, correctly, that he'd shot the film from the first floor of canning plant. Samson had spotted the action. His blackmailing scheme paid off . . . at least for a while.

Victor Brooks ejected the disc, rushed to his office and phoned Pez.

Laura tried to dissuade him from going to the Mushroom, but there was urgency in his voice. In the end, she drove him there and waited till he'd entered the building. She felt mild admiration for his dedication and, for the first time in many months, a longing to share her life with him again.

Spencer joined him in the incident room and told him how delighted he was with the recent development. He even suggested the best way forward, but his strategy was too far removed from Pez's plan of action. Shortly after he left, Harv appeared, carrying the profile that Pez was so interested in seeing.

'How are you doing, Harv?' Pez asked.

'Plodding along, as usual. I must say, you're looking more like your old self.'

Pez took the profile from him and quickly scanned the pages. 'I'm refreshing my memory,' he said. 'Let's see how accurate Colin Church was . . . "Samson was a threat that had to be eliminated . . . Murderer lives within ten to twenty miles of murder scene . . . Murderer fairly strong, above average intelligence . . . The murder is not terrorist-related and the writing on the feet is a false clue" . . . You know what? The profile is correct. What a genius!'

'You know something, don't you?' Harv said, excitement in his voice.

'I do. Samson was moved into the Flux lab as part of a plan to implicate him with the Perbury bombing. His work records were altered to give the impression he was working there before the bombing occurred. It was a clever move by a cunning, callous, power-driven egotist.'

'Pez, are you going to tell me what you know, or do I have to plead?'

Harv didn't have to plead with him. After Pez told him what Brooks had discovered he headed straight for his office to tell Mack the juicy news. Pez looked at his watch just as the phone rang. Brooks on the line.

'What news, Vic?'

'I've identified the girl. She still works here, so there was no problem tracing her. I'm certain she knows nothing about the murder of Samson, apart from what she's gleaned from the media.'

'Did you ask her about the Stringer painting?'

'Aye. She *was* the purchaser.'

'Excellent, my man. We'll make the arrest this afternoon.'

'Not possible. He's not on site until tomorrow, and I've got an idea . . .'

The following morning Pez rose early. Laura was only too pleased to help him dress and prepare breakfast. After he'd eaten he looked on Miranda who was sleeping soundly. He decided not to wake her.

At half past eight a car stopped outside the house. Harv was behind the wheel. Two uniformed constables occupied the back seat.

'I have to go now, Laura. I'll be home later today. Don't know when.'

'No kiss then?' she asked, before he opened the door. Laura was admiring him, thought he looked cool in his dark-blue suit, open-neck white shirt. He kissed her full on the lips, and departed.

Brooks was waiting for them at Seven Moons. He led them inside the police lodge and made sure they all signed the book. The reason for the visit was given as, 'On-going murder inquiry.' Without further delay he drove them to the lecture theatre, airing his plan along the way. When they arrived he led them up the stairs to the first floor. The two constables were directed to another room where they waited. Pez and Brooks entered the theatre. A few dozen people had already arrived, notably Geraint Marshall's attractive blonde secretary who was fiddling with the laptop and projector. She gave the two inspectors a lingering, frightened look. She knew something was amiss, and she wondered why Brooks had given her a replacement DVD for the one marked 'AP1000 – The Power of the Future.' He told her not to mention it to Marshall.

Brooks whispered to Pez, telling him to sit at the back of the room, on one of the end seats. Ten minutes later all the relevant managers had arrived. The attendance sheet was passed around for signing. Andrew Sharpe, the ASD manager, was seated on the front row, and behind him sat John Gregg. Gregg started fidgeting, and asked a colleague if he knew why Brooks was in attendance. It was assumed he was there for the same reason as everyone else.

When Marshall walked in the general chatter faded. He was wearing beige pants with razor-sharp creases. His dark-blue tie – with the yellow Seven Moons logo – stood out against an expensive crisp white shirt. He spoke briefly to his secretary, Susie Reynolds, and then addressed his audience.

'Good morning,' he began, with a restrained smile. 'For the next hour or so I'm going to talk about the new AP1000 nuclear plant. The AP1000 signals a better, more secure future for our country's energy supply . . .' He paused, his eyes fixed on Brooks. Under normal circumstances he would have nodded. His presence was unexpected. Marshall felt his confidence start to drain away. He had no option but to carry on. 'The ever increasing cost of fossil fuels will undoubtedly make the AP1000 a preferred producer of baseload electricity. The plant itself contains fewer pumps, less piping and valves. There are fewer items to install, fewer to maintain than in traditional plants. More importantly, AP1000 is safer than any nuclear facility ever built.'

He looked towards his secretary, and for the next twenty minutes she showed a series of slides showing the effects of global warming and its related causes. For each slide, Marshall added factual details. His concentration was weak and his memory started to falter. He felt relief when the slide session ended. The time had come to play the DVD. It was a welcome breathing space for him. Brooks sat upright, ready to make his move. Pez – who hadn't been spotted by Marshall – signalled his constables via his phone. They quickly proceeded to the theatre's entrance door and waited.

Susie Reynolds gave Brooks a worried glance, and passed the disc to her boss. 'Is this the right one?' he asked, concerned about the stick-on label.

'The original was damaged,' she said, showing a look of guilt. 'This one is the back-up copy. It should be all right.'

Marshall pressed the disc in place and moved away from the screen on the wall. The first image to appear was that of the main administration block, shaky and out of focus. Seconds later the camera was filming offices along the first floor. Marshall soon realized he had been duped when his previous secretary appeared on screen. He made a desperate dash towards the equipment. Brooks rushed at him and held him back. All eyes were on the screen. Susie's eyes opened wide in disbelief. The dark-haired secretary was now lying across a desk, arms outstretched. Her pleated blue skirt had been pushed to waist level, revealing black stockings and suspender straps biting into her succulent white thighs.

'Stop it!' Marshall cried, trying to free himself from Brooks powerful arms encircling his body. A wave of cries and gasps emanated from a totally confused and partly shocked audience. 'Susie! Turn that fucking machine off!' he yelled.

Pez walked swiftly to Brooks' aid. His officers stormed into the room. Marshall was on screen now, pounding into her from behind, enjoying every second of their hot-blooded, raunchy session. By now, most spectators were on their feet, wondering what the hell was going down. Pez switched the machine off. A heavily-panting Marshall was struggling no more. Pez waited a while for the noise to die down. He looked into Marshall's eyes and said, 'Geraint Marshall, I'm arresting you for the murder of Jack Samson.' He gave him a formal caution. The managing director shook his head in defiance. He was escorted off the premises.

Susie Reynolds broke down and sobbed uncontrollably.

EPILOGUE

Two months had elapsed since the arrest of Geraint Marshall. Brooks was staring into the Melt and casting his mind over the investigation. He cursed for not making inquiries with the foreman at canning plant. The fact that Jack Samson had two lockers wasn't unusual in itself. It all seemed simple enough, in hindsight: Samson being at the right place, right time. The reason for his use of a camcorder should have been fairly obvious. The spectacle of Marshall humping his not-so-pretty secretary provided the opportunity to make money. And make money he did. Marshall would have done anything to save his marriage and his future position at the new AP1000 nuclear plant in Norfolk. Brooks surmised that the demands made by Samson became too much. His greed was his downfall, and he had to be stopped. The missing Flux was the seed for Marshall's murderous plan.

A voice rose above the sound of flowing water. He turned and saw Pez waving at him. Brooks raised a clenched fist and went back to his table. Pez sat down opposite him.

'Good to see you, Pez. How's the arm?'

'It feels a lot better now without that bloody splint and sling.'

Brooks laughed a little. 'Not working, I see.'

'I'm on leave. Two weeks all to myself.'

'You lucky bugger. Let me buy you a drink. The wife's shopping in town. I've a couple of hours to spare.'

'A bit slow for Weaver's,' Pez remarked, when the ale finally arrived. His mind started wandering to a place not far away.

'Aye, but worth it in the end . . . You know, Pez, your inquiry could have ended a lot sooner if I had done my job properly. I mean, this business with the camcorder. Couple that with his overtime in the canning plant.'

'Well, we got him in the end . . . Maybe I should have involved the local paper in the Stringer inquiry. You realize your mistakes when you look back.'

'Do you think Pamela Wynn would have come forward?'

'Who knows?'

216

'H'm . . . Here's a question for you: why did Marshall not purchase the painting himself? Why ask his secretary to go into town and buy it?'

'Perhaps he was too busy. He could have given Samson the money to buy it. Anyway, It's not important now.'

'You're right . . . The trial starts next month. Do you have enough evidence to convict him?'

'The circumstantial evidence at our disposal is overwhelming. Abi Boudir will testify that he tried to bribe her into having an affair with Samson.'

'In order for him to turn the tables?'

'Guess so. We have the fingerprint evidence as well. Marshall's prints were found on the Citroën 6 and the Stringer painting. Pamela Wynn's prints also appear on the painting. There's the DVD evidence, and the fact that Marshall engineered a strategy which made it possible to transfer Samson into the Flux lab.'

'Sounds good. Anything else?'

'The white dog hair probably came off his clothing. The Marshalls once owned a white poodle . . . We'll get a conviction all right . . . His wife went ballistic when she was told about the affair. She even asked if we'd allow her to watch the DVD and see for herself. Stupid woman. We found a copy in Marshall's garage. Samson had complete control . . . *Knowledge is power.*'

Victor Brooks fell into silence. He gazed into the Melt for a while. 'Pity Drake had to die,' he said, and his eyes met Pez's.

He made no comment. After finishing his drink he stood up. Brooks noticed the forlorn look on his face. 'I'm going, Vic. See you at the trial.'

Brooks got up for a firm handshake. 'You take care now.'

'I will . . . Same to you.'

Market Place was bustling with town folk and visitors. An appetizing odour hung in the air, reminding Pez that Laura had asked him to buy a piece of steak for their evening meal. The steak can wait, he thought, worming his way through the shoppers until he reached the entrance to Bakers Alley.

A voice called from behind him. 'Inspector Perry. I haven't seen *you* for a while.'

'How the hell are you, Hazel?' Pez said, not pleased to see her.

'Just fine. I suppose you know the Red Coyote has been closed down?'

'Is that what you wanted to tell me?'

'This town will not tolerate filthy establishments.'

'Quite. I told you I'd bring it to an end, didn't I?'

She gave a look of suspicion. 'Hadrian's Bar is next on my list,' she said, with venom. 'Smoking is banned, I tell you.'

'Piss off!'

Hadrian's Bar was still the same dark, dingy, smoky place. Pez purchased a pint of Witch's Tit, took it to his usual seat and lit a cigarette. Fuckin' bitch, he thought. She'd stop pubs selling alcohol if she could.

Pez drank himself into a nice relaxed state of well being. He was on leave now, and this was his favourite haunt where nobody would bother him. He was happy once again. The jukebox kicked in. That'll do for me, he said to himself, recognizing the unmistakable intro to a Rolling Stones record.

Something made him look up.

'Can I join you?' she asked.

'Certainly,' he replied, wafting the smoke away.

She placed her drink on the table. Out came her cigarettes. She looked to be late-twenties and had large green eyes, long auburn hair. Her low-cut top revealed several inches of unashamed cleavage.

'Did you put this record on?' Pez asked.

'Yeah. Do you like it?'

'I love the Stones.'

She inhaled deeply and blew smoke above his spiky hair. 'Haven't I seen you before?'

'Dunno.'

She stared at him and said, 'I have . . . The Red Coyote. I was a dancer there.'

'I often used to go, but I don't remember seeing *you*.'

'I had blonde hair. Most of the girls dyed their hair.'

His eyes met hers, and for a second he was reminded of the woman whose memory would linger for years to come.

'My name is Jade. What's yours?'

'Call me, Pez.'

She fumbled inside her handbag, took out a small mirror and checked her appearance. She dropped it back inside and said, 'Can I buy you a drink?'

'You're very kind. I'll have a whisky, if that's all right.'

'Sure.'

She smiled at him and made her way to the bar. Pez admired her curves and pronounced calf muscles.

He thought about nights of forbidden passion.

Once over, he could have resisted the temptation.

If only . . .

END

Peter Hodgson